ROAD TO EMMAUS

SEAN CARLSON

Library and Archives Canada Cataloguing in Publication

Carlson, Sean

Road to Emmaus/Sean Carlson

ISBN 978-0-9952702-9-9

The Theodosian Press, Winnipeg

To my parents,

the communities of Domain and St. Margaret's,

and my daughters, Hunter and Chanel

CONTENTS

PROLOGUE
THE LAST APOSTLE

ISLE OF PATMOS, 96 A.D. - I recall the day I left my nets. The warm breeze of the sea was a calming reminder of the blessed simplicity of my vocation. How strange it was that Father never uttered a word as we clambered out of the boat. Nor did he ever question my intentions after that - never asked me why?

It is cold here. A good place to finish my days I suppose. The problem is I don't know how to die anymore. Death has swallowed all of us. All of us except me.

I am the last - an old sorcerer as the guards often call me. Leave it to Romans to condemn an "atheist."

Everyday I hear the villagers passing my cave, climbing up the hill to the temple of Diana. It is a very curious thing. I was a witness to the source of their longing not many years ago.

Yet here I am chained in this cold, damp prison, feet shackled as they trample over themselves running to worship on the hilltops. It is a sad thing to endure even as a prisoner.

Once a day for a blessed hour they let me walk along the sea cliffs, my feet in chains but my soul free. I miss the water. For most of the early years of my life it was all I knew. It was a simple life. One that made sense.

Then we left father's boat and nothing has ever been the same - sense and sensibilities lost and eventually found. The price of redemption is a wicked game.

He came by again yesterday. My visitors are rare but I've learned a writer needs his time and space and an island prison generously affords both. At my age I don't need much company.

Even in my late years and all the things we've been through our visits leave me in a state of transfixed awe and wonder.

I think of those precious days we were all together. The things we saw with our own eyes while the world slept! In three short years the foundations of time were rolled back and the universe exposed for what it was and the keeper of the flame revealed his face. And it was all there for the taking for those of us who dared to listen and ponder the mysteries. The veil of understanding - wafer thin, yet the darkness heavy.

Then I remember my own fateful slumber. I let him down terribly that night. Me, of all people!

"Could you not watch with me just a little while?"

Those words haunt me to this day...even all these years later.

We each had that feeling that night and the following days. But Cephas suffered most. There was no taming his spirit. So when he fell, he fell hard.

Still after all that, he held the keys to the kingdom and the prophetic promise: "Whatever is bound on earth will be bound in heaven!"

This link between Cephas and the coming centuries must never be broken. The hope of these few followers rests on the holy promise. The succession of leadership must continue despite the horrific cost.

Cephas and the pride of Tarsus have been dead thirty years.

Still the movement grows and the grandness and scale of the time passed is a deep reflection of its origin. All the prophecies were true.

But we're entering uncharted territory - again.

Our young bishops are terribly brave and utterly exposed. It is their fight now.

I'm tired.

My pen and scribe will soon rest. I must write Timothy and Clement.

We are old men now - the last of the old world. A new world, a new order is upon us.

I really never left that island. My glimpse of history revealed bound me to the rocks and sea cliffs of that space and time and lifted me above that empire's prison.

There are new empires now - battling for hegemony. This is perhaps the century I feared most.

Yet another old order has passed and given way to a new order that is the beginning - the birth pangs of my prison island revelations.

PART I

CHAPTER 1
SEVEN MILES

V.13 Now that same day two of them were going to a village called Emmaus, about seven miles from Jerusalem...

PALESTINE, 33 A.D. - The physician has long tried to convince me and secretly he may have succeeded. It may indeed be the greatest walk in history.

Carolus certainly agreed: "I can recall every detail of that day," he said. "I'd walked that road so many times before."

The midday sun was getting stronger and warming the dry Palestine countryside. The gentle breeze blowing inland from the sea ushered in the heat of the new season and the promise of a rich harvest.

Amidst the crowd of people headed west out of the city gates of Jerusalem, two men moved slowly in silence as the busyness of merchants, pack mules, livestock and their masters hurried by them seemingly oblivious to the chaos and turmoil of the last seventy-two hours.

Cleopas glanced back at the city's towering walls. It was nice to be leaving he thought.

"Those walls are a fortress of shame now," he said. "They cannot hide what happened. Word is spreading throughout Judaea."

Carolus shook his head dismissively: "Judaea? I met a trader yesterday from Capernaum. He asked me if I'd heard about it."

"Well if news has already reached Galilee," said Cleopas. "Then all of Palestine will soon know. All of those people Carolus... All those towns and villages he spoke in. What will they say now?"

Carolus shook his head again, "maybe we should've stayed with the others? But what's left to be done?" He squinted up at the sun directly overhead and pulled at the chord of his keffiyeh.

"I'll come back in a few days' time before the sabbath and see how the others are faring. The temple guards will be out for our blood next. At best, they'll be watching our every move. "I'm surprised they haven't arrested as many of us as they could find."

Cleopas hadn't thought of that. But now he was afraid - more so for the others than himself. Perhaps they should not have left the city?

He was heartbroken. It was a sadness stronger than the fear they all felt. It was a curdling sadness mixed with horror. He had seen Roman brutality many times before but this was very different.

He was completely innocent and the ignorance of the masses was staggering.

Even the prefect knew he was innocent. His own suspicions of the temple officials turned out to be true. Their supreme authority on all matters was rigidly defended in the name of a God shrouded in their own prideful image of understanding.

The crowded road was beginning to thin out as travelers and caravans splintered up headed cross country north into Samaria and others into Southern Judaea.

The two men walked on in silence, each lost in their own thoughts. The morning had been strange as well, Cleopas suddenly remembered. The body was missing. Perhaps not surprising - the soldiers may have had orders to reclaim the body and move it elsewhere to prevent any mischief.

But could the women be right? He could believe that the body was gone when they entered the tomb but their story was too strange. They claimed a vision saying he was alive. It made no sense. The trauma of the last few days was affecting everyone and who could blame them for wanting to believe it all really hadn't ended this way.

"What do you make of this morning?" Cleopas said.

Carolus sighed deeply. "Hard to fathom I suppose. I don't doubt the women's sincerity but they are grief-stricken. You know how Maggie felt about him. She can't accept his death. None of us can."

Cleopas shifted the small leather pack on his shoulder. It felt much heavier than it was. He looked up at the hot sun beating down from a cloudless sky. The road ahead of them shimmered from the heat in a haze of dust and sand.

"If I hadn't seen him die, I might have believed them," Cleopas said quietly. "But something did happen after that - that rumbling... the darkness? As if history itself was groaning in despair."

Carolus nodded. "A curfew will be imposed. Every council group will be demanding edicts to deal with the unfolding chaos. This was no ordinary execution."

The road wound its way down the ravine and narrowed through the pass and leveled off as it entered the Hinnom valley. Rocky outcrops dotted the landscape providing pockets of shade and vegetation along the roadside.

Cleopas and Carolus passed a caravan of traders coaxing their mules and camels up the pass headed east to Jerusalem and Jericho. The trade routes were getting busier by the day with the advent of the dry season.

Carolus stopped to remove a sandal, shook it out and tapped it on the rock he was leaning against. A few yards ahead Cleopas stopped to wait and set his small pack on the ground. He untied the pack and unwrapped a small bag of dried fish. He threw a second bag of dried fish to Carolus.

Carolus stretched leaning back against the rock and threw a sardine in his mouth. Only then did he realize he was hungry. He had hardly tasted the unleavened bread of passover Thursday evening in the wake of all the madness. He had barely eaten since then.

That bloody prefect, Carolus winced at the thought. He had played to the crowd as every Roman leader had before him. Romans were terrified of Hebrews. Always had been, like the Seleucid dynasty before them and the Ptolemaic Egyptians before them. They feared everything they did not understand, relying on the likes of Jupiter, Apollo and Diana to make sense of that strange Hebrew God - the one true living God of Abraham, Isaac and Jacob.

Surely this ancient truth had not ended the day before Sabbath? And surer still, he was who he said he was.

But he was dead.

A sudden grip of anguish seized Carolus. How could all this be?

History does not end abruptly when great promises and traditions are passed down and relied upon by generations?

Carolus realized at that moment the crushing weight that had been carried by this man. It had been too much - far too much to bear in the end. Carolus was suddenly angry at himself and the others. They had been a pitiful band of "hangers on" relying on one man to save them from a world of empires that would now stretch on through the coming ages.

They were a people enslaved to foreign powers and leaderless once again. Three years of promise extinguished in a thousand years of lies!

"Lost." Carolus said aloud. "Completely and utterly lost."

"Seems so," said Cleopas. He had been deep in his own insurmountable thoughts.

"Scattered like lost sheep." He threw his pack over his shoulder and continued walking.

Carolus caught up with him and they walked in silence for a few minutes.

"We are a scattered people," said Cleopas. "And even Rome is no match for the enemy lodged deep inside us. We have placed ourselves at the very fringes of a society within a people pushed to every historical boundary of time and place. How many years of wilderness and wandering can a people endure? Every Hebrew in Palestine needed him to liberate and unite Israel."

"It wasn't a political movement."

"But he was the rallying force of a nation!"

Carolus stopped, turned around and pointed back up the road towards Jerusalem. "And who crucified our king? Rome? It was us! The crowd was maniacal for his blood! A nation doesn't feed upon itself. It feeds on unity against a common enemy. No, we ceased to be a nation after the death of King Zedekiah."

"Zedekiah?" Cleopas was offended at this. "Have you forgotten all that has happened the last three years? The politics of Judaea and Israel are at the foundation of everything he taught and believed! The promise of nationhood to Abraham was the single greatest political movement in history. And it is a history that continued to define his teachings to this very day."

"True," said Carolus. "But in a very different way. His teachings made him an enemy of almost every synagogue in Palestine."

"Well his claims were too much for them. They were waiting for your kind of politics - a king who would reclaim and unite the kingdoms of Israel and Judaea."

"I'm not saying that Cleopas. Yes, our priests are largely blind to the truth. What I'm saying is his politics were not concerned as much with national resurrection as they were with the souls of its citizenry."

"Think of all the times we railed against Roman occupation. He lived it too, his whole life but never said much about it. I always had the feeling he was disinterested in it. Rome seemed to bore him. He accepted it as a fact of life. The priests and pharisees were his enemy. Even more so than Rome."

"Well," said Cleopas. "He may have felt differently as he was paraded to his execution."

That thought seemed to silence them again.

The road widened out a bit as it emptied into the valley basin. The rocky hillsides coloured with patches of scrub and grass cast their long shadows down to the valley's edge.

"I'm not sure he did," said Carolus.

"Did what?"

"I'm not sure he felt any different about the Romans even after he was handed over by the prefect."

"What makes you think that?"

Carolus kicked at a stone as he walked. "Expectations mostly. He was always saddened by their brutality but not necessarily disappointed. He expected little from Rome."

Cleopas grunted. "I'm amazed he escaped death as many times as he did.

Carolus nodded. "For someone who seemed to have little fear of death, it affected him greatly. His pain always ran deeper, cut sharper. He needed more time away from everyone. It's a shame he never got it."

"Cephas called him a loner once," said Cleopas with a chuckle. He shook his head sadly at the memory.

Carolus laughed out loud, surprising himself. "Cephas said that to his face?"

"No, to Thomas after he couldn't find him. Apparently a day after he had taught in Bethel to thousands."

Poor Cephas, thought Carolus shaking his head. He attached himself to his master and felt the pain of separation in a hauntingly acute way. Carolus had once been jealous of his devotion but like the others had come to respect the depth of relationship between them.

It struck Carolus at that moment. The bonds of apprenticeship had indeed belonged to Cephas. And now that too, was gone.

"The royal guards," said Cleopas. "Have they hauled you in lately?"

Carolus's thoughts were interrupted. "No, not for several weeks now but family has been questioned at synagogue."

"Have you spoken to the elders?"

He shook his head. "I don't want to bring more attention to myself or family members. They know I am a follower. My brothers are displeased with me at the best of times these days."

For several weeks palace guards under Herod's orders had been following Carolus and had twice arrested him and questioned him at length about his associations with other followers. They had also offered a bribe to report on certain members of the synagogue.

Carolus had skillfully talked his way through the interrogations but the palace guards threatened him with an accusation of insurrection should he not cooperate in future. He had suspected temple officials were keeping Herod well informed of potential troublemakers.

The Friday's horror had confirmed his suspicions but in ways previously unthinkable. Even the prefect was confused and visibly troubled by the charges. The sudden vitriolic hatred towards the accused Galilean was shocking.

Carolus had warned the others months ago when he had first been detained but it was certainly nothing new to them. They had all been harassed and threatened mostly by the pharisees and other temple officials at one time or another.

There was one incident that occurred over a year ago. The figure was chilling - so disturbing in fact that Carolus had questioned if what he saw even existed at all. It was a scene that unfolded in a flash.

That scene had flashed again on the hill at Friday's execution. The same figure - standing there in the middle of that angry convulsing mob.

Carolus had seen him last winter wearing the same tunic and long coat a few miles outside of Nazareth. It was dusk and raining lightly. Carolus was accompanying some of his relatives as they returned from a burial of a cousin.

Out of the corner of his eye, Carolus was startled to see a man standing by an outcrop of rock twenty yards or so off the roadside. The man was tall, younger but beyond that largely nondescript. When Carolus turned back for a closer look, the figure was gone - completely gone, causing Carolus to question if he had seen anything at all.

What haunted him for weeks later was that he knew he had seen that figure. Not only did he see him but that nondescript look of the man sent a chill through his insides. It was like trying to place a stranger in a crowd somehow connected in a dream one can't quite remember.

Then after forgetting all about it, Carolus had seen him again that Friday. But this time his face was clearly visible. The man was fair in appearance, younger and wearing the exact same clothes.

At first the man didn't even register with Carolus amidst the sheer tyranny and chaos of the moment. What caught Carolus's attention finally was the strange contrast of the man's expression to everyone around him. He was looking up, as they all were but with the most tranquil look on his face - arms behind his back, oblivious to the madness around him. It was a picture of dead calm.

Despite the intense heat of the desert road, this sent another cold shiver through Carolus as he recalled the scene. It was odd, he thought, that he had so quickly forgotten the image in the chaos of that awful afternoon.

An uneasiness was settling into Carolus's thoughts. It was more than the terror and turmoil of the last few days - something darker and stranger than current circumstances. It was a foreboding that bent the very spectrum of time itself, stretching history beyond the confines of the present days slowly unfolding and revealing a long protracted struggle.

Carolus's mind raced back to the tomb. The events of that early morning now struck him with the same pang of uneasiness. There was a danger lurking at the tomb but one that he could not fully explain or put his finger on.

The women should not have gone up there. It was dangerous on many levels. The tomb was being watched closely by the soldiers no doubt - though this was not particularly disturbing to Carolus. No, the danger was something more sinister. Perhaps it was just an aftermath or extension of the violence that lingered.

Perhaps that's what was most troubling with the women's story. The tomb was his resting place. The brutal end to this story needed to find a place of peace. Mercy for the dead.

But now the body was gone. Mercy herself had been revoked.

The two men passed a young family traveling in the same direction from Jerusalem. Cleopas nodded to the father leading two mules. On one, the mother held her newborn tightly, shielding the tiny bundle from the sun directly overhead. Another figure sat atop the other, wearing a long dark veil. A large wooden crate was strapped in place behind her.

"I suspect the city will see additional Roman garrisons in the coming days," said Cleopas. "It may be wise for you to stay in town for an extended time."

"I'm more concerned for the others right now." said Carolus. "We should send word to them of any threatening news. The temple in Jerusalem won't be safe for a while for any of us."

Cleopas glanced back at the young family. The mules walking side by side carried an almost grotesque look to it. The figure's slender back draped in her long veil towered over the woman and child on the mule beside her. The contrast was alarming in its disproportion. Cleopas turned and looked away.

He felt a wave of emptiness wash over him. It was a nauseating sense of loss.

There was also something else that Cleopas felt.

It involved the others perhaps?

No doubt, there was a clear and present danger in Jerusalem but that had more to do with the temple officials, palace guards and Roman eyes.

This was a different threat - an anguish that lingered alongside his sorrow and shock of the past few days. It was a cold fear.

It had everything to do with Carolus.

CHAPTER 2
MESSIANIC PROMISES

V.14 They were talking with each other about everything that had happened...

WASHINGTON DC, March 4, 1933 A.D. - *"President Hoover, Mr. Chief Justice, my friends... This is a day of national consecration and I am certain that my fellow Americans expect that on my induction into the Presidency I will address them with a candor and a decision which the present situation impels..."*

Raymond Moley had decided to stand in the crowd which fanned out from the east portico of the Capitol Building. Though he had been invited to sit in the viewing balcony with the other dignitaries he had wanted to see the president's face as he gave his inaugural address and hear it clearly as it was simultaneously broadcast to millions of Americans around the country.

"...Let me assert my firm belief that the only thing we have to fear is... fear itself! Nameless, unreasoning, unjustified terror which paralyzes needed efforts to convert retreat into advance."

Good, Raymond thought: Nice delivery - smooth, methodical - a balanced tone of fire and sincerity. He had basically memorized the speech in its entirety. It had taken him most of the week to write it.

Of course the president had reworked some of the main themes of the speech to focus on specific policy measures as he always did.

"...rulers of the exchange of mankind's goods have failed through their own stubbornness and their own incompetence, have admitted their failure and have abdicated. Practices of the unscrupulous money changers stand indicted in the court of public opinion, rejected by the hearts of men. The money changers have fled from their high seats in the temple of our civilization. We may now restore that temple to the ancient truths..."

Raymond smiled at that. He had argued with the president on some of the religiosity of the speech a few nights earlier. He thought some of the biblical imagery was a tad heavy and misplaced but the president would hear none of it.

"For goodness' sake Ray, what do you think this nation is built on? The Constitution does not rest on itself. It presupposes the laws and very nature of God. You disagree?"

"No, but I think we need to explain what we mean by 'ancient truths.' It's a bit vague don't you think?"

"What, you think I'm being pious? Old fashioned?"

"It could be construed that -"

"I'm referring to the value of people Ray. And the priority we place on their well-being. Goodness sakes! Do we have to spell everything out now in this day and age?"

"Yeah, we do. You're referring to social values."

"Fine, throw it in."

"Ok, done. Now what about this analogy to the money changers in the temple? What are you trying to say?"

"I'm saying I want the damn bankers to keep their hands out of the pockets of hard-working Americans."

"Well Mr. President" -

"Don't Mr. President me. If we want to call them 'money changers' we will. And frankly, that's what a lot of them are and it's created a dire mess."

"You're not worried about a backlash? Their campaign contributions?"

"Nope. They've ceased to be the 'hand that feeds us' - politically speaking and now quite literally. Everyone's wallet is empty. And they certainly did nothing for Hoover's campaign."

As most of the country predicted, the election was a landslide victory.

Roosevelt had criss-crossed America to sell his "New Deal" to a nation ravaged by a shrinking economy and deteriorating living conditions.

Despite the expected apoplectic nature of voters, they had cast their ballots largely in protest of the status quo. President Hoover's handling of the growing recession and the worsening state of America's working families had sealed his fate. He had even stopped referring to the endemic nature of bank panics, preferring to define bank closures as merely - a 'depression.'

The reference would stick.

Raymond found it hard to believe Roosevelt was now his president. The expectations already placed on this young administration would be staggering. It was only a year ago that Roosevelt had pried him away from his teaching job as a law professor at Columbia University. He had asked Ray to form an advisory team that would help propel him from New York governor to the White House. Ray recruited a solid team that became known as the president's 'Brains Trust' - a moniker they initially enjoyed and came to despise. Yet throughout the presidential campaign Raymond established himself as President Roosevelt's closest advisor.

He took his shots for it. A meeting with the president meant going through Raymond Moley who was often as blunt and direct as he was acutely sensitive in interactions with friends and foe. His intense gaze could be both intimidating and disarming, a trait he used wisely.

Rexford Tugwell held the car door open as the new president and first lady made their way through the crowd surrounded by security and a few of his aides and handlers. As one of Ray Moley's 'Brains Trust' recruits from Columbia University, Rex had eagerly accepted the offer to serve as an advisor to Roosevelt's campaign and policy development. His economics background placed him at the center of the storm in formulating a new set of policies that could pull the country out of unparalleled recession.

"Congratulations Mr. President!" Rex beamed as President Roosevelt and his wife, Eleanor climbed into the backseat.

"Why thank you Rex. Great the weather held out."

Raymond emerged from the crowd and caught sight of the vehicle. He smiled and pumped his fist. "Great delivery Mr. President!"

The President reached out the open air car and extended his hand to his prized speech writer and chief advisor. "A wonderful speech Ray. You wrote a magnificent page of history today. I'm so pleased."

Ray was moved by the affirmation. "Thank you Mr. President - an immense honour."

Just then James and Harry appeared at the far side of the car that was now engulfed by reporters, well-wishers and a few policemen. They were clearing the street for the motorcade and the presidential parade to the White House.

Raymond could tell James Farley was elated. In the months and weeks leading up to election day, the only person who had worked harder than James was the president himself.

As campaign manager and chief strategist, James had broken all the rules of a conventional election campaign - bolstering support from traditionally non-friendly states and allowing Roosevelt to boldly push his agenda unhindered.

It also helped that Harry Hopkins understood his role as special advisor to the new president. He was an administrative genius who quickly developed a loyal, hard-working staff and handled the bulwark of policy development, research and building a platform. The rest of it - organizing countless events and volunteers he left to James and his team. It was a system that had worked extraordinarily well.

"Super job Mr. President! Our agenda's perfectly set." James' face was flushed with pride. President Roosevelt grabbed his hand. "It was not possible without you Jim."

He leaned forward to shake Harry's hand. "Thank you Harry. Your guidance was invaluable."

"Thanks Mr. President. We all did our jobs and it paid off. Now the real work begins.

The president nodded affirmatively. "Yes it does Harry. By the way, congratulations, you're our new Federal Relief Administrator."

"Really? Do I have time to think about it?"

"No, sorry."

"Great. Then I accept. You in on this Jim?"

Jim shook his head.

"Of course he was," said the President. "He suggested it."

"You're a peach Jim."

A security agent approached the car. "All ready Mr. President? We should move out."

"Yes, let's go home." The president turned to the others. "I'll see you boys at the reception.

Jim and Raymond waved and were directed into one of the black cars lined alongside the curb. Raymond could see Harry and Rex clamber into a nearby car grinning and talking excitedly.

There would be massive expectations. It was the beginning of a wild and bumpy ride, Raymond mused.

They were headed for the White House.

President Roosevelt squeezed his First Lady's hand as the motorcade headed towards Pennsylvania Avenue. He had wanted a brief time with Eleanor so they could both soak in the moment quietly and enjoy it together side by side.

He slowly removed his gloves and laid them in his lap. The day had been sunny and relatively mild for early March but the sky was now overcast and chilly as the sun disappeared into the clouds of the late afternoon.

The president leaned back and closed his eyes briefly. He knew it would be one of the rare times he would be alone with his thoughts for the foreseeable future.

He turned to his wife. "Are we ready for this love?"

Eleanor smiled at her new president and took his hand in hers. "Of course we are dear. Have faith."

He smiled back.

Have faith, he thought. He wasn't sure he had it in him but he could battle and gut it out with the best of them. That he knew. If they could secure some early victories faith would come and the nation's confidence would grow because of it. They had to turn the tide of this depression. It was slowly bleeding the nation to death.

The package of reforms and programs had been studied and cross-examined by policy experts and economists from every region of the country.

Jim had met with hundreds of people representing a variety of state-level boards and commissions along with several advisory councils on agriculture, public infrastructure, taxation, social services such as healthcare, public housing, education and a host of others.

Their primary strategy was to find a common thread of identified problems in each of these sectors, review current policy and propose a new set of solutions. The challenge was the gaps and differences in policy from state to state were astounding. They had to find a palatable way to federally regulate a number of these publicly funded programs.

Roosevelt had been wary at first that the Republicans would pounce on any talk of eroding state powers. Hoover himself had railed against government waste and an increase of national programs he deemed unwanted and ineffective.

But Roosevelt had calculated wisely on the Achilles' heel of his opponent. Hoover was in denial as to the abject condition of the country and its working class. The economic downturn was unmatched in its devastation.

Hoover had chosen to align himself with the status quo hoping legislatures across the nation would over time customize and deliver a package of reforms unique to the strengths and regional diversity of each state.

It had not happened.

Most of the states were nearly broke. Governors were increasingly turning to Congress and the White House for more financial support.

The president checked his watch. It was half-past four. He had hoped to spend a couple hours before the evening's reception taking congratulatory phone calls and making several calls of his own to cabinet members. It would be imperative to come out of the gate swinging.

The first one hundred days were critical in charting a strong course for the nation's ambitious agenda. Ray Moley had figuratively beat this message into every member of the administration, no matter how junior their position. He had also reluctantly agreed, at the president's insistence, to serve as principal liaison with congressional leaders as New Deal legislation was passed.

Congress would have to pass most of the reform and recovery packages of his new deal. Roosevelt felt sure they could do this quickly with support in key areas of the country representing a variety of economic interests primarily in the banking and manufacturing sectors.

Prohibition would be ended. That was an easy sell though there were pockets of resistance amongst religious folk and institutions through the Midwest and New England states.

But the president knew he could cultivate and maintain popular support through a series of reform packages specifically designed to aid economic recovery in all parts of the country.

The National Recovery Administration and the Federal Emergency Relief Administration would effectively transfer federal dollars to the states for basic assistance programs to the poorest of the poor. Other programs were designed to reinvigorate different sectors of the economy in specific regions of the country.

The Civil Works Administration would target the nation's infrastructure deficit in its cities. The Agricultural Adjustment Act would assist the plight of farmers in the Midwest and Southern states.

The Tennessee Valley Authority would build necessary dams along the nation's most powerful rivers and ensure enough hydroelectricity for a country desperate for growth.

This new deal would need to be delivered with speed and precision within the first few months of office. There was precious little political capital and as such, mistakes or delays could paralyze Congress and cripple the White House.

President Roosevelt wanted to look forward to midterm elections in '34. If the new deal were to be successful they would need to win and build confidence early and often.

Political momentum could be an elusive animal - secure some early victories and they could ride them through the turbulent months ahead. But suffer a setback at the wrong time and it could snowball quickly into a crisis of confidence in a young administration still trying to find its way.

There was one phone call that worried the new president. He had to speak with his secretary of the treasury, a staunch conservative Democrat - William Woodin.

The first executive order of the president would be controversial - so much so that it was highly secretive, though it had been discussed by the previous administration. Only a few cabinet members were notified.

The U.S. Government was going to shut down the banks for a few days - a week if necessary. It was a confidence-saving measure and one Roosevelt felt Democrats could get away with politically.

A Southern Democrat far removed from the rancor of Wall Street might utter a few choice words and give him the benefit of the doubt.

Hoover's Republican Yankees north of the Mason-Dixon line had drafted similar legislation but in the end hadn't dared to touch the banks.

It was a well-calculated risk by Roosevelt and one he hoped would be remembered as a tipping point in ending the bank panics that plagued every part of the country.

The motorcade turned onto Pennsylvania Avenue. President Roosevelt felt a surge of pride as the White House grounds came into view.

"Home sweet home Eleanor."

His wife was too moved to answer.

A nation was waiting to be delivered. His hour was finally upon him.

Mother was there that morning with Maggie and Joanna. I've heard her recite the story so many times it's burned into my memory. As the years pass and the movement grows it's hard to believe.

She was actually there.

"The light was blinding," mother said. "I dropped the spices and they spilled all over the ground. An other-worldly fear is an astonishing experience. It is an instinctual, subservience and reverence to a far greater power," she said.

"The men were brilliant, dazzling - unapproachable and unfaceable. Even as they spoke, not one of us dared to look up. But their words were piercing and unforgettable..."

"Why do you look for the living among the dead?"

Mother said it became the answer to almost every question she had the rest of her life.

These words also comforted blessed Mary, his mother. We cared for her twenty years after all these things came to pass. They were not easy times for any of us.

Tarsus brought us fresh hope and a passport stamped for the ends of the earth.

And then there was Maggie.

Tarsus, though he would never admit it was scared of her and avoided her at all costs. In his defense, she could drive any man and mother to insanity. She was young, impudent, stubborn and dangerously impulsive.

I recall her fights with Cephas. They were worth any price of admission. It was a delightful spectacle for the rest of us. Those two were cut from the same cloth. And in so being, brought great love and boldness of faith to all - especially him.

Mother watched over Maggie, gave her no small number of lectures and secretly envied her joyful, adventurous spirit. She was born for the movement and found herself living it as it all began.

We were all young then. The wonder and excitement of those early days we thought would last forever... A juxtaposition of irony I suppose. We chose to ignore his prophetic warnings. We all avoided them like the plague.

So when Maggie and mother burst in on us that early morning and told us what had happened we didn't know what to think. Maggie was beside herself. Her mind was made up. No amount of calming her down to recount the facts made any difference.

And it sounded to us like complete nonsense. Mother kept repeating: "Don't you remember all he said?"

And Maggie's reaction to our confusion and shouting questions at her and mother was notably uncharacteristic.

She couldn't stop laughing or crying. She was in a state of euphoric joy that given the present circumstances was downright frightening.

Normally, Maggie would have been frustrated and indignant, like a child who claims to have seen a ghost and no one believes her.

But our reservations and doubt only seemed more endearing to Maggie. She laughed through tears that wouldn't stop and clasped our faces, kissing us and praising God!

In the moment, the fulfillment of all that had been promised seemed a lifetime away.

In retrospect, it was a wonderful scene.

CHAPTER 3
CAMELOT

V15. As they talked and discussed these things with each other, he came up and walked along with them...

The sun was no longer directly overhead but the few clouds provided little reprieve from the heat of the afternoon.

The two men had been on the road for over an hour still talking about the events of the past few days. They decided to rest their feet and found some shade by a cluster of fig trees near the roadside.

Cleopas took a long drink from his canteen and wiped his brow with his sleeve. "There was talk of a Roman detachment spotted marching north from Sychar."

"What on earth would they be doing up there?" Carolus asked. "Headed to Galilee perhaps?"

"Perhaps. Maybe they expect some rioting amongst his home clan? Unlikely though. Most Galileans hated him. I would venture that many of the temple priests made their way down to Golgotha."

"At least two, according to Nathaniel," said Carolus. "They were from Nain apparently."

"News certainly travels quickly."

Carolus pulled his knees up to his chest and stroked his beard. He could not get the reports from the women out of his mind.

"What is James and John's mother like?" He asked Cleopas.

"I don't know her well. I've heard she's very involved with the group, looks out for her sons. She's taken Maggie under her wing as well."

"Maggie," Carolus shook his head. "How can they both be so sure of themselves?"

"Carolus, it's Maggie. She believes what she wants to believe."

"Well it's dangerous to the movement right now. This confusion and hysteria are exactly what the temple priests and scribes want. If the body is missing -"

"It is. Cephas went there and confirmed. I'm sure the temple officials know exactly where the body is. They must have followed Joseph when he took the body down."

Cleopas gazed up the road at the horizon. "Nicodemus was with him too, I've heard."

"What?" Carolus was shocked. "The rabbi?"

"Yes. Many have thought him sympathetic to the movement."

Carolus was indignant. "Sympathetic? No pharisee has ever been sympathetic to anyone or any cause not bowing to his own protocols and ambitions."

Nicodemus! It was all starting to make sense now, thought Carolus. He had feigned his sympathies, fooled Joseph into locating the burial site and reported back to the temple.

"Cleopas, think about it. The rabbi used Joseph to find the site. The temple priests have taken the body. We all should have predicted this. How could we have been so foolish?"

Cleopas was silent. Perhaps Carolus was right - it was a rational probability. If it wasn't the temple priests then the prefect had secretly given orders to dispose of the body.

He suddenly felt sick for all of them.

Poor Maggie. She had been so sure of herself. At that moment the thought of ever setting foot in Jerusalem again made him nauseous with rage. The city of his forefathers had become a savage place - the ruthless fangs of a foreign occupier.

Then just as quickly, his rage lost its strength and dissipated into an emptiness that slowly seeped into every part of him.

He wasn't sure how long they sat by the roadside lost in their own thoughts.

Then he heard Carolus's voice: "We should get moving."

They got up and continued down the road.

ह

JERUSALEM, 33 A.D. - Usually he enjoyed Passover.

He loved the solemnity of its preparations and the richness of its traditions and history. It was a rare occasion to celebrate the privilege of being Jewish and the victorious remnants of a forgotten nation.

He especially enjoyed the children who, in preparation of the Passover were brought to synagogue and gathered at his feet to listen to the great stories of their bloodline.

Even the parents, grandparents and a good many of the temple priests and pharisees crowded around the children to hear the great teacher, Nicodemus grab hold of their hearts, eloquently recalling the stories of their predestined history under the living God of Abraham, Isaac and Jacob.

But yesterday had been different. Nicodemus, in order to keep up appearances had taught at synagogue and dutifully celebrated the Passover feast with family. All the while the smell of blood and aloe haunted his senses and he feared their lingering scent on his hands would betray his secret.

Late Friday afternoon he had witnessed a catastrophe.

He still could not fully explain it but the events of the execution - both before and after had only confirmed what he had been wrestling with for months. He had studied the prophecies in a new light. The irony was not lost on him. He had studied all his life and had become one of the leading experts in pharisaic law.

And one midnight visit had changed everything. Ten laws which had been crafted into six hundred and thirteen laws had now suddenly been reduced to one. One law - one man. The man was more than a prophet.

And now he was dead.

Nicodemus had approached Joseph. He was too afraid to ask the prefect for the body himself. Joseph had calmly agreed and the two had waited for the remnants of the crowd to disperse and approached the site under the cover of that wholly unforgettable shaming darkness.

He had never touched a dead body before - even though he had attended dozens of burials.

Joseph and he did not utter a single word the entire time. They worked in complete silence.

The body, in its lifelessness had been heavier than he expected and it took the two men considerable effort to bring the body down.

The nails...he recoiled at the memory.

He would never forget the nails.

They had laid the body down on the ground. It was only then that the magnitude of his suffering was visible. No man could suffer more in death.

As they knelt over each side of his body and prepared the linen strips in the perfume and spices, Nicodemus had suddenly noticed the tears of Joseph falling on the body forming rivers of blood.

It was only then that Nicodemus became aware of his own tears doing the same.

Once the linen strips were prepared they had gently wrapped the body. He remembered looking down at his own hands covered in blood and sweat and aloe. The smell of death mixed with the aloe and spices lingered alongside the cold sweat of the created order of humankind embalmed by hands that were ashamedly unworthy. Failing, trying hands that were suddenly much like his.

He looked closely at the fallen hands, bloodied and torn.

In that brief moment, there was something dangerous and powerful about them. Even in their lifelessness it seemed they were capable of holding the heaviness of things too great to comprehend.

Nicodemus turned off the narrow street and walked along the side of the temple. He headed for the back gate which led to a small private courtyard. At the back of the courtyard was a rear entry used by the priests and officials. He looked up at the stone facade of the temple. It was an inspiring and magnificent place of worship.

He entered the rear door and made his way down the narrow hallway.

Suddenly he felt a hand grab his shoulder.

"Where on earth have you been?" It was Gamaliel, his close friend and colleague. He was also one of the great pharisaic teachers in Judaea.

"Rabbi, I am well thank you. Was I expected earlier?" He was agitated by the question.

"The priests and scribes have called an emergency council meeting. As you know the city is in an uproar. Council is nervous."

"As they should be!"

"Quiet your voice," Gamaliel whispered, motioning with his hand. He led Nicodemus into a small prayer room off the hallway and drew the curtain behind them.

They spoke in hushed tones.

"Members of council are arriving now," said Gamaliel. Were you not sent for?"

"Possibly. I left early this morning to think and to pray for all of us."

Gamaliel sighed heavily. He was quiet for a moment. "Were you seen?"

"No, I don't think so. It was just Joseph and I."

"They will kill you Rabbi. They will kill us both."

"I have no doubt of that, my brother."

They stood silently for a moment. They could hear the voices of their colleagues in the inner chamber and the shuffling of feet on the stone floor of the hallway as others arrived.

Gamaliel put his finger to his lips and waited for the shuffling to pass the curtain.

"I warned them... I warned them," he shook his head sadly.

"We will need to be careful - very careful for the next few weeks, perhaps longer. It is best we not be seen talking publicly and assume our normal duties."

Nicodemus nodded. "Of course Rabbi."

He turned to leave. Gamaliel put his hand on his arm to stop him.

"He...he is dead?"

"He is."

"Yes, of course," said Gamaliel softly. "Thank you Rabbi. God be with you."

Nicodemus turned and headed towards the council chamber.

The busyness of the road was normal for the time of year with most people and caravans of traders headed the opposite way to Jerusalem.

Cleopas and Carolus had walked in silence for some time, each still trying to make sense of all the events that had passed since Friday.

Carolus was more sure by the minute that the chief priests had quietly raided the burial site overnight. They may have even had Roman assistance. The evidence of complicity had become increasingly clear since the arrest.

Cleopas interrupted his thoughts. "I worry about the safety of the synagogue. Where are we to worship now?"

"It will be dangerous for a short while," agreed Carolus. "But the priests and scribes will be looking to normalize things quickly. "They need the tithings of the faithful."

"I'll be very interested to hear further news from the group," said Cleopas. "What if the women did see something?"

This got them both stirred up again trying to determine what had happened. They discussed all they had heard between them from Friday afternoon to that morning. Still, there were few answers to be had.

Carolus was startled to see a man walking up beside them. He hadn't heard him walking behind them nor did he recognize him from the people they'd seen on the road that day.

"Greetings friends. If I may say so, it sounds like an interesting conversation?"

Carolus looked at Cleopas.

"May I walk with you? My name is Camelot."

CHAPTER 4
KRAKOW

V.16 But they were kept from recognizing him...

KRAKOW, POLAND, 1964 A.D. - It was a bitterly cold January morning. Józef shivered as he got out of bed and wrapped his house-coat around him tightly. He walked to the window and looked out over the frozen city. All of Poland was caught in a deep freeze as was most of Eastern Europe.

Outside, plumes of white smoke billowed from the chimney tops of snow covered buildings rising into the pale blue sky.

It was a cold sunny day. It was the kind of winter day Józef enjoyed most. The mild overcast days he found indecisive and melancholy. A day like today brought out in him a joy from the sun and a toughness from the cold that invigorated his senses giving him a familiar comfort.

Now in his early forties, Józef had lived almost twenty-six years in Krakow. He had left his hometown with his father and enrolled at the Jagiellonian University.

It had been the beginning of a bestial madness...

"You will come and visit me?" Józef was eighteen and more unsure of the future than at any time since his mother had died ten years earlier.

"I will visit you! Now hurry, you'll miss the train," Ginka scolded him.

Józef wasn't convinced.

Girls like Ginka didn't need to chase men across the country. She would have plenty of distractions in the form of suitors right here in Wadowice. She was beautiful. Her long black hair and big blue eyes had captured Józef's attention for as long as he could remember going back to their early school days.

Some of his friends had chided him for befriending a Jewish girl though he had been indifferent to these distinctions.

Even the football matches between Catholics and Jews, he had often played on the Jewish side.

"Come play goal for us!" Ginka would plead. And Józef would happily relent. He also took great pride in his goalkeeping skills and became known to his schoolmates as a gifted athlete and competitor.

Those early school years he recalled were about his friends, the football pitch and Ginka. He would stand at the top of his goal crease immersed in pure joy watching the match - his world playing out before him, directing his teammates while the shouts of encouragement from Ginka sang in his ears.

The playgrounds of one's youth are hallowed treasures, he had thought fondly years later. They are swallowed up to memories long before their time.

And now he was leaving.

He had watched her disappear on the train. She stood waving from the platform of the little station until she faded from his sight and his childhood. It was the last time he would ever see her.

Józef and his father settled into a small house in a modest neighbourhood in Krakow's west quarter.

The university was within walking distance and soon a new world opened up to Józef. It was a world of learning and study that his father made clear he pursue with the utmost devotion.

He had often wondered who his father was before his mother had died. He had a few precious memories of his mother but no specific memories of his mother and father together in a familial sense. They had strangely staked out separate poles in his mind's recollection.

There was a noble stability and strength in his father's character that had given Józef a happy childhood even amidst the death of his mother and his two siblings.

But there was also a quiet sadness in his father - a longing for a piece of himself that he knew could not be resurrected.

The move to Krakow had been good for them.

Father and son spent their suppers during the week talking about his work and Józef's studies. It was a new beginning for each of them on many levels and they secretly shared a sense of excitement as to what lay ahead.

Only once did his father betray his fears of the impending nightmare.

They were finishing up the supper dishes listening to the evening news on the big radio set in the hallway off the kitchen.

A shrieking voice filled the small house with a ranting vulgarity that Józef was becoming familiar with. Talk of Hitler's Germany was increasing at the university and the radio reports were broadcasting his proclamations of nationalist fury more frequently by the week it seemed.

Józef's language studies had to his delightful surprise, begun to shape his ear and gave him a new window of understanding of Europe's affairs. His rapidly improving German told him according to the radio segment of Hitler's rantings that a military buildup was underway on Germany's eastern frontier. Before he could hear the full report, father had marched to the hallway and snapped off the dial.

"I will not have that devil in my house," he said sternly. "Are we clear on that?"

Józef was startled at his father's reaction but nodded in agreement.

Little did they know how soon everything would change.

Life at the university gave Józef a creative energy that compounded his interests in the liberal arts. He had recently added French and Italian courses to his studies and found to his surprise that an introductory theatre course had uncovered his writing abilities.

His father had laughed when Józef had tried to hide a script for a play he was writing from his father's prying eyes at the kitchen table one evening after supper.

"Józef, stand tall behind your words! Whether spoken or written, they are an extension of you," he said.

It was an admirable cover. Józef knew his father would have been horrified if he had chosen a career as a playwright. Father respected the arts but was far too practical-minded to consent to "frivolous pursuits" on a full-time basis.

One of the interests father did wholly support was the compulsory military service in the university's Academic Legion. After all, father had been a military man.

Initially he was surprised to learn that military service was compulsory - especially within a university program. However the Academic Legion was a longstanding institution dating back to the Great War and had a dedicated record of service.

The Legion Sierzant was a heavyset Polish nationalist who had fought in the great war with the First Army Division. He was observant, demanding, and pushed his fresh recruits especially hard.

Sierzant Lenz understood the difficult balance between academia and the military. He taught the importance of fundamental discipline through the concepts of order and due diligence.

This could be applied to any vocation within the military or in civilian life he was quick to remind people.

At his initial assessment Józef grudgingly took a liking to the sierzant. Lenz was much more perceptive than he let on. In the physical examinations he noticed Józef's agility and coordination.

"You move like a goalkeeper," he correctly observed.

Lenz also noted Józef's language studies and spoke to him in Spanish and French giving him a brief lecture on the role of linguistics in forming a national identity.

There would be other more unwelcome lectures by the Sierzant but this was a lecture Józef took to heart.

One morning in late November, two months into basic training, Józef arrived at the tiny barracks on campus to find an army issued Karabinek rifle hanging inside his locker. Each of the new recruits had received one.

One of the instructors, a Starszy Kapral ordered them to bring their weapon into the classroom. He spent the next two hours teaching them how to strip down the Polish bolt action short rifle and reassemble it.

Józef had enjoyed this exercise. He carefully disassembled the headstock and removed the firing pin as he'd been shown. He learned to clean the barrel and the action and align the front sight in relation to the target distance.

It was precise work and reminded Józef of working on farms in Wadowice. He liked the feel of the machine oil in his hands and the intricacies of the metal components of the barrel and trigger mechanism all fitted perfectly together.

Józef ran his hand along the woodgrain of the headstock. He held the rifle up and peered through the front sight. The wood headstock against his cheek gave off a warm counterbalance to the cold touch of the bayonet mast and trigger mechanism.

It was a rather intoxicating delight.

"Gun down please!" The instructor motioned to Józef. "You'll get a chance to fire it on the range once we've completed the ammunition loading and safety training this afternoon."

By lunchtime Józef had an intimate understanding of his weapon and could expertly strip down and reassemble it in minutes. He had felt quite pleased with himself.

Finally out on the range the eager recruits received their target and station numbers and Sierzant Lenz appeared in front of them about thirty yards from the firing line.

"Soldiers! In a few minutes you will receive your ammunition. You will be instructed step by step how to load your rifle and how to discharge your rifle safely and accurately. Now, all of you - point your weapon at me."

The young recruits had looked at each other tentatively.

"Do it!" The sierzant yelled. They raised their rifles and steadied their feet.

"Now, pull the trigger," he said calmly.

The click of the unloaded rifles could be heard as the recruits pulled back on the trigger.

"Feels a little different shooting at a man instead of a rabbit doesn't it?" He said. "Then see if your brain can tell your finger what to do. Not all of you are soldiers. But all of you must learn to be fighting men. The day is coming when you will learn more about yourselves than you ever wished to know. Starszy Kapral! Get these men their bullets."

Several minutes later Józef received his ammunition. It was fed from a double box magazine and held five rounds. He reached for the magazine feeling its weight in his hand. Suddenly he felt nervous and unsure.

He barely heard the loading and safety instructions. He did hear the sierzant threaten to shoot anyone himself who didn't keep their rifle pointed down or straight ahead at the target.

Something had dampened his enthusiasm. Józef fumbled with the ammunition as he loaded his rifle. The loaded chamber felt like a weight of lead as he struggled to bring the rifle up to the target.

His hands were suddenly not his own.

The sierzant was watching him as he brought the barrel down and re-steadied himself.

"Fire!" Lenz yelled now standing directly behind him.

Józef brought the rifle up again. He turned off the safety and curled his index finger around the trigger. He felt the cold metal pull back ever so slightly. Still he couldn't do it.

"Fire!" Lenz was right in his ear now.

Józef didn't move.

"Dammit boy, you fire your rifle! That is an order!"

Józef set his feet apart to steady himself again and brought the rifle up a third time. By now the range had gone quiet as the other recruits stared at him and the comandante who stood inches away from Józef.

It was futile and Józef knew it. He lowered the rifle and laid it on the ground in front of him.

He braced for the screaming. It never came.

"Soldiers, who told you to break?" Yelled the sierzant. "Resume firing!"

Józef turned and faced the sierzant and stood at attention amidst the crack of gunfire. To his surprise he wore an expression of indifference on his face.

"Son, you are not a soldier. A man who chooses to fight without a rifle must choose his battles wisely."

He leaned in to Józef. "Learn to be a fighting man. You may have to battle harder than the most ardent soldier. Now, if you won't fire your rifle you will be responsible for the cleaning and maintenance of every service rifle issued here. You will also remain in active service. Dismissed!"

❧

The Germans came in '39.

The Nazi scourge swallowed Poland whole. It would devour much of the rest of Europe with lightning speed.

The blitzkrieg was for real.

Even the German Chancellor himself was surprised at its severity and efficiency.

Józef would never forget the sound of the jackboots on the pavement the day the Nazis marched into Krakow. It was a deafening sound of terrifying precision that filled the whole city with fear.

One of the first things they did was shut down Jagiellonian University.

Sierzant Lenz didn't even have time to address the Legion soldiers before his arrest. He along with the Starszy Kapral and two recent graduates of the Academic Legion were driven to the edge of the city and shot.

They were buried in a nearby ditch. It would be six years before their bodies were exhumed and given a proper burial.

"Learn how to be a fighting man..." The sierzant's words to Józef became real that day.

Everyone's fight for mere survival quickly became a daily battle. Every able-bodied man in Krakow was put to work.

Józef was eventually sent to labour in the limestone quarry. It was difficult work and the twelve to fourteen hour days - six days a week took its toll, especially on the older men.

Józef's father had been an officer in the Polish Republic. He had a distinguished service record and did his best in retirement to serve his fallen country now in the death jaws of German imperialism.

Most of all he worried about his son labouring in the quarry. He also worried about the constant threat of deportation to Germany. Its factories were maniacally churning out machines of war and cheap labour was always in demand. Many of Krakow's neighbourhoods were routinely inspected for able-bodied workers.

Many evenings Józef would arrive home late. His father remained a steady guiding hand and was a spiritual mentor through the dark days of Nazi occupation.

Even the ability to study and attend classes at the university seemed a faraway dream. The back of Krakow had been broken.

Every street corner was hostage to the occupation. German soldiers were everywhere. The battle early on became psychological warfare and the Nazis used their dominance and visibility on the streets to indoctrinate its new citizens of the Third Reich.

Fascism would reign for a thousand years they were told. Its political and military machinery was unrivalled anywhere in the world. Leaflets flooded the streets depicting Stalin as the devil and the words: *Poland has been saved from the great demon of communism!*

News spread as to the worsening conditions in Warsaw and the growing restrictions being placed on its Jewish population.

Józef wondered how his Jewish friends back in Wadowice were faring? Surely the black hand of fascism had not reached his hometown?

He would later learn many people had been killed and a great many more starved to death.

Death had also come close to taking Józef on two separate occasions. He barely survived being hit by a tram. The doctors managed to drain the blood around his brain and stabilize his fractured skull. It was a long and slow recovery. He began to think in new directions.

Several months after returning to work in the quarry Józef was hit again. This time by a truck. He suffered a terrible shoulder injury that would bother him the rest of his life.

Then two years after the occupation the unthinkable happened. Józef's father died suddenly of a heart attack.

It was an awful blow for the twenty year old. All of his immediate family members were dead and his country was in ruins.

Years later Józef would single out the death of his father as a watershed moment in the development of his life.

His father had given him a liberal education within a traditionally conservative moral view.

The brutality of the Nazis and the hardships Józef endured shaped his worldviews and the importance of community in combating this brutality and hardship.

One night after visiting his father's graveside, Józef had slipped onto the grounds of the Archbishop's Palace and quietly knocked on the huge oak door. He had been wrestling with his demons ever since that day on the firing range with Sierzant Lenz barking at him.

Now it was time to face the truth about himself. It was a truth he had been fighting for some time.

He wanted to join the priesthood.

While the war ravaged Europe a battle had been raging inside Józef. Why had he refused to fire his weapon that day?

Such foolishness.

Here his beloved Poland was being slaughtered and its closest allies were being systematically overrun and torn apart by the fascist wolves. Even Britain was doomed to destruction.

Was it not history's hour for honourable fighting men to take up arms?

If ever there was a time it was surely now.

But Józef was tormented. His father, a military officer would have expected him to fight. A Polish soldier could die honourably defending the principles of the nation. And with the growing Nazi atrocities even the principles of humanity itself were inarguably at stake.

This was obvious to Józef. The real question was: How could one fight most effectively against the injustices of a ravenous imperialism?

Perhaps Sierzant Lenz was right all along Józef had thought?

He would have to learn how to fight.

One did not necessarily have to be a soldier to be a fighting man. Most Poles were fighting daily, each for their own lives and for each other.

The quarry and chemical factory where Józef worked was his own daily battle. He had hoped that would keep him from deportation to Germany as this was everyone's worst fear.

Still, there had to be a better way to fight. He had joined an underground movement to help those most at risk from the Germans. It was courageous work yet the restlessness grew within him.

He had exhausted all his options. And now he had optioned away all his excuses. Once he had asked to join the priesthood the gauntlet of excuses had been tossed.

It felt right. Like a soldier who could perform his duties well with good conscience.

Józef knew he was called to be a priest.

Soon after he joined the clandestine seminary and threw himself into his course. He would engage in a greater battle and fight for the lives and souls of the oppressed and the conquered.

Over the next two years beginning in '42, Józef had met daily with Cardinal Rospond who served as his academic advisor at the seminary.

Officially the seminary did not exist. The Nazis allowed the longtime Archbishop, Adam Stefan Sapieha, to continue his duties in overseeing the Catholic Church in Krakow but they operated under a shadow of intimidation and explicit warnings.

The Gestapo and certain members of the Schutzstaffel became avid church-goers making sure priests and their bishops understood they were being watched and their words notated and filed. Many of the priests joked their sermons had never been listened to so attentively. Any incriminating references to the war and the occupation were swiftly dealt with.

They did not discriminate.

It had been explained very clearly to Archbishop Sapieha by an overzealous SS officer:

"It's a very simple equation Your Eminence - one dead priest shot in the public square sends a message equivalent to the execution of fifty men. Govern your responsibilities accordingly. Your Fuhrer will be counting on it. After all, war will not last much longer and this is just the beginning. Heil Hitler!" The officer had extended his arm and snapped to attention.

The archbishop merely nodded. "I will be sure to mention your calculations to your superior, Mr. Kuntzel. He attended service at the Cathedral last Sunday."

Cardinal Rospond had delighted in telling Józef and his fellow students in class one evening that Kuntzel had offered a hasty apology. The young officer was apparently quickly reassigned to Berlin.

Józef had learned much about the enemy during his time in seminary. Covert tactics were far more tasteful in bullying the church into submission. A good Nazi cleaned the dirt from under his fingernails. It was better to diet on the cold calculations of a swift occupation than be seen feasting on the bloody frenzy of full-out warfare.

The blitzkrieg had given Germany a civilized conquest - its naked thirst for domination camouflaged in a maniacal order and calm amidst its own fury.

One gold watch...one pair of spectacles...one black leather hand-bag...all neatly and meticulously recorded and filed.

One must feed on one's own contrived sensibilities while engaged in the unspeakable. Maybe that was their secret, thought Józef. And perhaps that was why he couldn't fire his own rifle that day on the range.

Cardinal Rospond worked tirelessly in the palace of the Archbishop as the unofficial Vice-Chancellor of the underground seminary. Classes were held every evening in the basements of various churches and at two safe houses that were apartment flats near the downtown district.

Special meetings and study sessions were held at the palace usually in the early morning or at the main Cathedral after the Sunday morning mass.

Course curricula were hidden away, kept under lock and key. Class schedules and locations were written on a small blackboard at both of the safe houses. Students were strictly forbidden from writing this information down and were drilled in committing all schedule and location information to memory.

Textbooks could not leave their assigned location and students learned to carry their notes and lessons hidden in the linings of coats, brief-cases and handbags. It was terribly risky but few options remained.

By Christmas of '43, Józef had managed to rebuild a daily routine in the wake of his father's death. His uncle, a younger brother to his father had taken Józef into his own home a few blocks away from where he and his father had lived. It had been a welcome arrangement.

Work continued at the quarry and the chemical factory for Józef and he carefully but diligently kept up his studies at seminary.

The Polish underground grew at an alarming rate and many of these groups were so intertwined that the infiltration of Nazi informants into one group often threatened several others.

There were underground political parties, clandestine militia groups, saboteurs, escape organizations, arms dealers, mercenaries and bounty hunters - both Polish and German. And in the midst of it all was an underground seminary that was becoming dangerously full.

Józef had been introduced by one of the clergy instructors to Stefan Welsk and Victor Smyl in the spring of '44. They were in his ethics class at the north safe house.

As three of the more senior students, the young men were assigned as duty officers to "tutor" a block of newly enrolled students. A block consisted of twenty-five students. Each block was assigned to three duty officers who would instruct and strictly enforce the seminary's code of conduct and safety operations.

Any carelessness of lapses of judgement were grounds for expulsion. The risks were simply too great. But even in the face of constant danger Józef and his classmates thrived. They were often hungry and exhausted from life under their Nazi oppressors. Yet there grew a stoic exhilaration in the resistance.

Initially, Józef had not thought of his studies as "resistance." He only wanted to survive and fulfill his vocation.

Stefan and Victor began to change his mind. It had all started that summer.

Buoyed by the uprisings in Warsaw that were brutally countered by the Nazis, smaller pockets of revolt were gathering strength in the poorest districts of Krakow. Neighbourhood gangs of youth and men of all ages with nothing left to lose smelled an opportunity as stories of German losses became increasingly apparent.

The underground was boiling to the surface.

"Father Rospond is opening a third safe house," said Victor one evening at supper in the Cathedral basement.

"What? Why?" Stefan was surprised.

"There are too many students here and at most of the bigger church-es. Some priests and bishops are starting to complain."

"That's absurd," said Stefan. "It's a risk we all have to take. The safe houses now are far more dangerous than the churches."

Józef had nodded in agreement. "There were fifteen in class at the south," he said referring to one of the two safe houses.

"The north is even smaller," said Stefan. "Why take the risk?"

Victor reached over and stabbed at one of the boiled potatoes with his fork. "It's a question of space," he said. "All of those vacant flats on the east side are just sitting there unpatrolled and out of the way."

"Wouldn't that draw more attention?" Said Stefan. "All these young people congregating in the middle of nowhere?"

"Some of the houses nearby are still occupied. The duty officers will arrange careful arrival times. As long as they travel in pairs they won't attract attention."

"Besides," said Victor: "The goons are getting lazy. They know it's over and just want to go home. It won't be long now."

"Well let's hope you're right," said Stefan. "We need every bishop and priest on side. Resistance is only as brave as its collective willpower. Let's hope it all doesn't blow up."

The boom came.

They came for Cardinal Rospond the following week. He was walking down the street headed to his rectory. As he turned the corner three SS officers were waiting.

One of the officers struck him over the head with his pistol. They threw him into a waiting car and sped off into the night.

An elderly woman had witnessed the attack from across the street and had sent word to the Archbishop's Palace.

The news spread quickly throughout the seminary. Both safe houses were immediately shut down and all classes were suspended.

The archbishop made several calls to local and high-ranking Nazi officials but despite his efforts no acknowledgement of the arrest was made. Cardinal Rospond had simply disappeared.

Victor had run into the basement of St. Paul's Church and found Józef and Stefan sorting through boxes of writing materials and supplies.

"Father Rospond has been arrested!"

Józef froze and immediately felt sick.

Stefan gasped. "When?"

"Last night," said Victor. "A witness reported it but the goons have denied everything."

"They know the seminary is operating," Stefan said in a daze.

"Hard to say. Everything was shut down within minutes by the palace," said Victor.

"He'll be interrogated!" groaned Stefan. "We're finished."

"See you tomorrow," said Victor vacantly. He disappeared into the hallway.

It wasn't until three weeks later that Józef had learned the truth. Victor was a brownshirt informant for the Nazis.

Two days after Cardinal Rospond's arrest the Gestapo and SS struck en masse

with a fury.

On August 6th of '44, forever after known as Poland's Black Sunday, eight thousand men and boys were arrested in Krakow in response to the uprising. Many were sent to prison camps or deported to Germany to work in factories. Others languished in local jails or labour camps.

Many were taken out of the city and executed by death squads.

Few were released.

Stefan had been one of the eight thousand arrested that day.

Four days later while being marched out of the city to be loaded onto a train to Dachau prison camp with hundreds of others, Stefan saw him.

Victor was one of many Brownshirts loading men like cattle onto the train cars.

He never saw Stefan nor did Stefan unlock his rigid gaze on his seminary friend until he was pushed into the cramped darkness of the boxcar.

Anyone who claims to be in the light but hates his brother is still in the darkness... he had vividly remembered thinking in the suffocating heat of that rail journey to hell.

Józef had managed to elude arrest and hid in his uncle's basement. Later he snuck back to the Archbishop's palace where he lived for the next six months.

So much had changed in twenty years, thought Józef as he leaned on the window sill. The city was covered in a blanket of fresh snow that had fallen overnight and now the morning sun shone over it and sparkled like a sea of diamonds across the white landscape.

It had all turned out as the convoluted events of life often do. Stefan had survived Dachau and returned briefly to Poland after the war. He was ordained as a priest in '46 and moved to America.

He served in a small church in New Hampshire for fourteen years before losing his life in an automobile accident.

Victor not surprisingly, had been killed by a gang of Polish youth as Germans fled the city in '45, one year after Black Sunday.

Many Sundays had passed since then. But through each one of them Józef had served their succession with a spirit of gratitude and purpose.

He had survived.

And now he was to step into his next succession of days to serve an even greater purpose in the face of new uncertainties.

General Secretary Joseph Stalin was closing a clenched Soviet fist around Eastern Europe.

And today, this Sunday - Józef would be installed as the new Archbishop of Krakow.

Old Lenz was right. He had learned to be a fighting man. But his toughest battle was just beginning.

CHAPTER 5
THE GREAT EMANCIPATOR

V.17 He asked them, "What are you discussing as you walk along?"

ATLANTA, GEORGIA, MARCH, 1933 A.D. - Frances Perkins was in a hurry. She didn't want to keep Senator Russell waiting. They needed his vote.

The three days since the inauguration had been an absolute firestorm of activity.

President Roosevelt had kept his promise, one he had secretly made to her months before and appointed her to his cabinet as Secretary of Labor.

Frances Perkins became the first woman ever named to a U.S. cabinet position. She was deserving of the challenge having received a variety of academic and political appointments and served on numerous boards and task forces.

But the magnitude of responsibility and the immediate call for action placed her at the epicentre of the nation's affairs.

All over the country the banks were in crisis.

In a growing number of states the public's confidence in the banking system was unravelling quickly. People were withdrawing money and draining their accounts to keep their money safe.

This run on the banks was crippling the country's financial institutions and exacerbating the effects of the depression. Something had to be done.

So yesterday the President had announced a "bank holiday" which simultaneously shut down every bank in the country until it decided which banks could reopen and which banks would be permanently closed.

It also temporarily stopped the run on the banks and kept precious cash deposits in the banks' vaults.

Now many state legislators and members of congress were in an uproar while the mood in most cities was surprisingly calm - resigned to the frustration and apathy of the times. Many state governors and Federal Reserve Bank officials accused the administration of dangerously abusing its powers in a collective brand of socialist totalitarianism.

President Roosevelt calmly stood his ground.

He had dispatched members of his cabinet to key regions throughout the country to quell the storms of discontent.

Secretary Perkins looked at her watch in the backseat as the car headed up Peachtree Street. She was meeting Georgia Senator, Richard Russell Jr., a conservative Democrat who was deeply suspicious of the young administration steeped in Roosevelt's Yankee roots.

The declaration of a bank holiday only confirmed the senator's suspicions.

The President had dispatched Secretary Perkins and Secretary of the Treasury, William Woodin to meet with Senator Russell and lobby for his support in congress.

It would not be an easy assignment. To make matters worse, Senator

Russell, former governor himself, had craftily organized a luncheon at his old digs, the governor's mansion.

Georgia Governor Eugene Talmadge, his successor, had wanted to discuss some of the finer points of any future bank legislation, she was told by Senator Russell. It was the perfect ambush played out in their own backyard.

The press would have a field day.

Secretary Woodin had caught an earlier train to Atlanta the day before and had met with several nervous and petulant bankers who, while relieved mass withdrawals had been ended by the bank holiday, remained wary and largely skeptical of the administration's plans.

William was to meet her at the governor's mansion for lunch followed by a meet and greet with some prominent business leaders and bank officials.

They had talked through a discourse strategy that morning over the phone:

"Frances, you just remind them that it's their workers and Southern families that are being put first by protecting their hard-earned assets and cash deposits. It's just a temporary measure to stop the bank runs."

"Well then, we need to give them a clear timeline. If it's a week, call it. If it's two, tell them outright," she said. "If they sense any ambiguity or hesitancy on how long banks remain closed we'll lose them before we get back to Washington and Russell's "no" vote in congress will be echoed by every senator and congressman in the south."

"Ok," said William. "I know the president wants at least a week and doesn't want to get pigeonholed on timelines. Let's say a week to ten days."

Frances had shaken her head over the phone. "Don't say ten days. Say a week and a half. Use the phrase: ten days and the press will have us on a countdown to the apocalypse."

William laughed. "Copy that."

The car turned off the road and headed up the hillside drive that led to the governor's mansion. It was located in the Prado on three acres of beautiful parkland.

As they approached the large granite house Frances was startled to see several head of cattle and a few goats grazing near the front lawn of the mansion. Apparently the governor had added raising livestock to his growing list of responsibilities.

A good icebreaker anyways, she thought.

Conversation would be difficult. Not only was she a northern Democrat defending Washington's interests, she was also a woman.

She was curious to see how they would respond to her.

She wondered if Secretary Woodin was already there and silently admonished herself for hoping that he was.

She didn't need any help. This was what she had signed up for. They needed Congress to act and this was the real battlefield. Senator Russell's vote would be won here and then he would do the rest of her Southern lobbying for her.

Any indecisiveness she allowed Russell to bring to Washington would be a vote killer. Once the emerging conservative coalition between Southern Democrats and Republicans smelled blood on the Congressional floor any "undecideds" or fence sitters would be easy prey.

Congress needed to pass this bill. The economy and the country were on the verge of collapse.

As the car came to a stop Governor Talmadge and Senator Russell appeared from the mansion.

The Governor was dressed in a grey pin-striped suit. He wore round, black-rimmed glasses that gave him a congenial but slightly stoic look. His full head of hair and healthy stature added a youthfulness to his appearance.

He strode briskly to the vehicle and opened her car door.

"Secretary Perkins! Welcome to Georgia."

His rich Southern drawl and friendly demeanor quickly put Frances at ease though she knew better than to soften her guard. The first five minutes would be crucial in setting the right tone.

"How was your trip down?"

"It was lovely Governor. Georgia is absolutely beautiful!"

"So glad you enjoyed it. Secretary, meet Senator Russell."

"Pleased to meet you ma'am!" The senator smiled warmly.

"Very nice to meet you Senator. It was kind of you to accept our visit."

"Our pleasure ma'am. We have a lot to discuss."

"Indeed we do. However I must insist you call me Frances. It's nice to leave the stiffness of Washington for awhile and enjoy some Southern charm."

Governor Talmadge laughed. "We'll do our best. As long as we're still on a first name basis why don't we leave the politics for later?"

Frances nodded her approval.

She was anxious to get down to business but understood how the game was played. Politics was a slow dance when courting rival interests.

If she could score well on a few Southern dance floors she could score big on the congressional floor in a few days' time. She quickly decided to reschedule her overnight train to Virginia if necessary.

"Secretary Woodin is arriving right behind you Frances," said the Governor. "Richard will show you around and there's some refreshments waiting on the back veranda. I'll join you both with Secretary Woodin once he arrives."

"Thank you Governor. Your hospitality is appreciated."

She was not about to call him, "Eugene" just yet nor did the governor offer to correct her.

There was a lot of ice to break. Often it seemed seventy years' worth ever since the Union had declared war on the Confederacy.

The Southern notion of a meddling North was never far from the surface of any conversation between the two. Frances knew she would have to tread carefully.

"Shall we?" Senator Russell offered his arm and motioned to a path that led around the house. "And do call me Richard."

Frances smiled and took the senator's arm.

The path led behind the stately home and emptied onto an acre or so of perfectly manicured lawn that ran down to several large groves of pine trees. The colourful undergrowth was filled in with painted buck-eye, sweet azalea, Georgia basil and other trees and bushes that Frances couldn't identify. Several lush magnolia trees towered over the property.

"Goodness, this is beautiful," said Frances. "What kind of tree is that?" She pointed at a huge tree a few yards away with a sprawling canopy of narrow leaves that hung down.

"That's a black walnut. Pretty isn't it? A lot of it is harvested for veneers and furniture. If you come back in a couple months you can see everything in full bloom. It's breathtaking," said Richard proudly.

"I believe it," said Frances staring up at the maze of branches and greenery. "It's amazing what grows down here. So I can count on your invitation Senator for a second visit?"

The senator chuckled as he led Frances across the lawn towards the veranda.

"Anytime Frances, and remember - it's Richard."

"Yes, sorry Richard. I stand corrected."

The warm gentle breeze was a pleasant reprieve from the March gusts she was used to.

"I was going to ask the Governor about the cows and goats out front. Do they belong to him?"

The senator rolled his eyes and rubbed his forehead in mock embarrassment.

"Unfortunately Frances, they do. Why he chooses to graze them on the grounds of the Governor's mansion is the subject of endless rumours and speculation. Some say he likes to poke fun at the establishment under the guise of "keeping his hands dirty." But I've been around enough to know he rarely goes near them. The truth is he grazes them here to send a simple message - I do what I want. I'm the governor."

"And people don't object?"

"Down here Southern charm operates under a guiding principle: Keep your nose clean and mindful of your own business. Then all is well."

"I get that," said Frances sensing a turn in the conversation.

"You may Frances. But I don't believe the President does. Charm is a fickle thing," the senator cautioned. "It presents an illusion of understanding before perpetrating its will against the other side. A Southern man will charm you with hospitality before picking a fight. A Yankee will promise you the world before picking your pocket. You tell me which is worse?"

"Well Richard, two things stand out in your somewhat biased illustration." She subtly tightened her grip on his arm to draw him into her attention.

"First of all, you speak of a guiding principle of Southern charm - specifically, being mindful of your own business which is overt code to Washington: Stay out of my affairs."

"True," said the senator.

She smiled and continued: "But Washington is responsible to Georgia to provide good economic policy to ensure the state can indeed run its own affairs. Look Richard, neither I nor the president expect to win your blanket approval of the federal government in good times or in bad. And I certainly don't want to debate the merits of federal and state powers."

She glanced at the senator, pleased to see she still had his attention.

"This is about Georgia pulling through this depression."

"Just Georgia?" Said the senator with a smirk.

"No, of course not. But I need your help Richard."

"You need my vote."

"I need more than that. I need your support and influence to get every Southern vote possible."

"You overestimate my influence, Frances."

She stopped and faced the senator. "Not at all senator. You're respected on both sides in the House and in the Senate. People follow your lead."

They walked for a few moments in silence until they arrived at the veranda. The senator held out his arm, widely motioning her up the steps and to a waiting table that had been prepared.

"Please have a seat and make yourself comfortable."

"How lovely. Thank you Richard."

They both sat down. There were two other chairs at the table presumably for the Governor and Secretary Woodin.

Frances looked out over the lush green lawn and trees where they had walked. The open air veranda was quite large and extended out from the house. The flat roof provided plenty of shade from the hot sun that was peeking over the magnolias.

An elderly Negro woman appeared from a nearby patio door.

"Welcome ma'am. Some iced tea?"

Frances smiled. "Thank you very much."

"Now how's mah favourite Senatah?"

"Doing well Anna. You keepin' that Governor in line?"

"Always Senatah," she laughed.

She poured him a glass of sweet tea and set the pitcher and a plate of cookies on the table.

"Something to tide you over until lunch."

Frances smiled at Anna who disappeared back inside.

"So what was your second point?"

Frances took a sip of iced tea trying to recall - "Oh yes," she remembered putting her glass down. "You spoke of a Southern man and a Yankee."

"Yes," said the senator. "You feel that language to be antiquated perhaps?"

Frances wasn't taking that bait, not in this conversation.

"No, I think those divisions are in some ways just as strong today as they were during the civil war in some pockets of the country. Once a rebel, always a rebel to the extent that the South feels they're always up against the establishment."

"It's a powerful sentiment," agreed the senator. And Washington sets the tone," he added.

"Exactly!" Frances brought her hand down on the table harder than she'd intended.

"Richard, Washington is changing. Hoover's America is gone. And with it potentially now the last vestiges of the status quo."

"Well that may be a bit of a stretch, Frances."

She ignored him and continued: "Now is the time to seize the New Deal reforms and recovery the president is offering."

"Why?"

"The South has never had a greater stake in shaping the policy and growth in this country than it does right now. We're all basically starting from scratch when it comes to economic reform."

"Well you know how I feel about government planned economies. But good riddance to Hoover I'll give you that," said the senator raising his glass.

"But all that campaign talk of a new deal for America is actually pretty hard to stomach quite frankly. The president talks about the 'forgotten man' but forgets where that man lives. He lives in the south."

Frances bit her tongue but said nothing.

"The south is the poorest region in the country. Incomes are half of what they are in the north. All of this new deal spending will go to political swing states up east and out west. A southern democrat is taken for granted by this administration. How about addressing the raw deal most of the country has been getting from Washington for well over a hundred years? Acknowledge that and the dire mess it's caused and then we can talk about reforms and a better deal."

"But that's my point Richard. The president has acknowledged it through the proposal and promise of mass reform. That's why I'm here as the president's emissary to acknowledge the past and push forward together. We need your help and all the Southern help we can muster to fix this mess. "New York, Michigan, Illinois - they all have their own brand of policy reforms they're already screaming for."

"God help us," Richard deadpanned. "I've read some of Senator Lewis's proposed reforms - straight from Lincoln's playbook."

"Then work with me Senator, This is a ground floor invitation straight from the president."

Senator Russell was quiet for several seconds.

"It'll be given careful consideration. I know time is critical. I'll be up in Washington for the ninth. Don't you worry about that."

"Good," said Frances. "Every vote counts."

"Are you two hard at the politics already?" Governor Talmadge walked onto the veranda with Secretary Woodin.

"Nah, Frances and I were just warming things up a little," said the senator giving her a wink.

"Nice of you to show up William. I was beginning to think you'd left me here to do the heavy lifting," Frances joked.

William chuckled. "Never crossed my mind!"

"Welcome Secretary Woodin. I'm Richard Russell," he said standing to shake his hand.

"Thanks Senator Russell. Call me William."

The governor and Secretary Woodin sat down at the table. Anna came out with two glasses and a set a big bowl of watermelon and sliced peaches on the table.

"Sweet tea sir?"

"Yes, thank you."

Anna filled their glasses and returned inside.

"So how well do you know each other?" Asked the governor looking at Frances and William.

"Not too well I'm afraid," said Frances.

"Yes," said William. "The cabinet hasn't formally met yet. It's been a baptism of fire that's for sure. Frances and I met a few times during the campaign in New Jersey and Kansas City."

"Well, I don't envy your positions," said the governor. "Especially with what the president has planned. He's got guts. I give him that. Any idea when banks will reopen?"

Frances glanced at William.

"A week - a week and a half," said William.

"Are you prepared to give a statement as Secretary of the Treasury over lunch confirming these timelines?

"Of course."

"Well Georgians will be pleased to hear it," said the governor. "My only concern is this: "What if the bank runs just continue where they've left off? Surely you just can't shut the banks down again?"

"Sure they can, it's Washington's playground," said Richard sarcastically.

"No, no!" Frances interjected. "The president has proposed safeguards in place."

She quickly nodded to William, who taking her cue turned to the senator. "Reserve banks will back all reopened banks deemed viable by government examiners."

"You really expect the Federal Reserve pariahs to lend freely to the banks?" Said the governor.

"Exactly," echoed Richard.

William held up his hand to continue. "If bank customers make a run on their deposits the president will guarantee reserve banks protection from their losses. By indemnifying the reserve banks, all federal reserve banks have nothing to fear from loaning money. They'll cooperate gentlemen," said William confidently.

And this indemnification will be enacted through an executive order?" Said Richard.

"No, the president will ask Congress to pass it."

"What else will be tied up in this bill?" Asked the governor suspiciously.

Frances could tell William was getting annoyed though he was a grizzled political veteran.

"Everything in the bill will be limited to the banking crisis," said Frances. "This issue is too important to be muddled with anything else - even labor reform."

That drew a laugh from the table.

"God help us all!" Said Richard. "So the president didn't send us his labor secretary to spring any additional surprises?"

"Not this time," said Frances with a wink.

"She's here to make sure I get back to Washington," joked William.

Governor Talmadge chuckled. "Who's ready for lunch?"

They all headed inside. Frances was sorry to leave the charm of the veranda.

The luncheon didn't go well.

It was a members-only country club affair. Frances and William were outsiders and made to feel the part. They were purposefully seated early at the large empty table that formed a u-shape along three sides of the cramped dining room.

As the two cabinet members sat alone sipping their drinks a loud, boisterous crowd of Southern businessmen and state politicians stood in the center of the room talking and laughing, their backs mostly turned to their northern guests.

"Well Frances, I can see tomorrow's headlines: Washington snubbed by Georgians…"

"We're on our own William. Let's mingle."

The two got up and headed to opposite ends of the room. Suddenly a voice boomed: "Ladies and gentlemen, the Honourable Eugene Talmadge - Governor of Georgia!"

Governor Talmadge entered the room shaking hands and slapping backs amidst clapping and cheering. He finally took his seat at the head of the table alongside Senator Russell and several members of the state cabinet. Frances and William were seated inconspicuously near the end of the table at the far end of the room.

"Do you see any Congress members here?" Frances asked William as the applause died down and people took their seats.

"Not a single one as far as I can tell."

"Unbelievable. This whole visit was a waste of time," said Frances.

William shrugged. "This is Russell's way of sending a message - killing two birds with one stone."

"What do you mean?"

"The senator is making it clear to us and to his friends where his allegiances lie. We'll never win in Georgia" -

"But the vote's in Washington," finished Frances.

"Exactly. As long as Georgians know their senator is holding his nose while casting his "yes" vote in congress, most people will forgive him. If he planned to oppose us he would've told us straight out earlier. Anyway, I think the bill is a given. It's the only viable option left. Hoover should've pulled the trigger on this legislation when he had the chance."

The meal was served and a delicious plate of pan-fried chicken, mashed potatoes, cornbread and mustard greens was placed in front of her. Despite the sweet aroma teasing her tastebuds Frances was worried.

"What about the rest of the Southern vote? We need it."

"In my experience Frances, this will be well-rehearsed and choreographed by Russell and a few key Southern congress members in a matter of hours. Their loose coalition of conservatives is gaining some traction on both sides of the House and they'll want to stay unified to carry some weight on the Capitol..."

William carried on but Frances didn't hear him.

She had given in to her senses. "This food is amazing," she said with a mouthful of cornbread.

"The whiskey is even better," said William studying his glass.

Only a handful of people bothered to talk to either of them at lunch and the meet and greet after was swift and uneventful.

A reporter asked Frances how she was "enjoying politics" and a few benign questions about her role as labor secretary.

William, Secretary of the Treasury during the nation's worst economic disaster was asked if he knew of any potential investors by a local textile manufacturer.

Other than a few polite handshakes - that was it.

The senator had kept his after-dinner remarks congenial and focused on Georgian families. He had introduced the treasury and labor secretaries and thanked them for their visit. But there was nothing beyond that. There was no mention of bank panics, closures or proposed solutions.

William had waited for an invitation to give his statement regarding bank reopenings and timelines but strangely it never came.

On these matters Senator Russell had made it clear to Washington's emissaries: they would be discussed in private and would not be publicly debated in Georgia or anywhere south of the Mason-Dixon Line if he could help it. He wanted it all kept under the table.

Frances feeling disheartened chatted amicably with a junior partner from a local law firm and a female reporter with the Atlanta Constitution.

She felt a hand on her shoulder.

"Sorry Frances. I have to catch my train." It was William.

Frances excused herself from her conversation shaking their hands and thanking them for coming.

"Sorry to interrupt. You still planning to visit Virginia on the way back?" Asked William.

"I am. Don't worry about me. With any luck I'm right behind you."

Secretary Woodin waved and headed for the door. The governor was waiting for him and escorted him outside to his car.

"So how did you enjoy the afternoon?"

Frances turned around. It was Senator Russell.

"I enjoyed it very much senator. The food was delicious."

She hoped he'd noticed the formalities were back on. Frances suddenly felt tired and ready to leave. She had done all she could and hoped William's assessment was right.

The senator smiled and offered his arm. Frances took it grudgingly.

"Thank you for coming secretary. I know you've had a long day. There's a car waiting to take you back to the hotel."

"To the hotel now?" Frances feigned disappointment. "I could've just jumped in with Secretary Woodin. I thought you were taking me for another walk?"

Senator Russell laughed. "It would be my pleasure."

They headed out through the patio door onto the veranda and down the steps leading to the green expanse of lawn.

Frances instantly felt better.

The smell of fresh grass and hanging foliage filled her with a new sense of relief and some hope. She had done her job the best she could. There was satisfaction in that.

They spent the next half hour walking the beautiful grounds talking about where they'd grown up and the families that had raised them.

They headed up to the drive where Governor Talmadge was playing the gracious host, seeing off the last of his guests. He smiled and waved when he saw them.

"I thought I saw you two sneak out back. I'm sorry I couldn't join you."

"Thank you governor for a lovely day. It was very kind of you to have us."

"You're welcome here anytime Madame Secretary. Your visit was a breath of fresh air. I'm used to hosting ornery old men like this one." He pointed at the senator who rolled his eyes at Frances.

Frances laughed. "I'm glad to hear it governor. Some don't know how to take me."

He stifled a grin. "Ah, a few hens are good for the coop."

She bit her tongue and decided to play along. "Only if they find the right rooster."

Governor Talmadge laughed. "Well sir?" He said turning to Senator Russell.

"Cockadoodledoo," said the senator forcing a smile. "You've got my vote for now and I'll lobby the others. But let me make our position crystal clear - "The president gets our votes on the floor this time. Then you can throw a few eggs in our basket."

The smile was gone.

"You can count on it," said Frances.

"Oh we will be," said Governor Talmadge with a stone-faced expression. "We will be."

And there it was, thought Frances.

The day's polite repartee had been replaced with an icy undertone.

"Goodbye Secretary Perkins," said the governor as he held the car door open for her. "Safe travels home."

The two men watched the car head down the hill.

"So, what do you think?" The senator asked, still staring down the drive.

"As long as she's mindful of her place and guards her ambitions I see no need for concern."

"And if she doesn't?"

"Leave that to me. No Lincoln-lover Yankee will dictate terms to me. Not in Washington and certainly not here."

❧

CAPITOL HILL, WASHINGTON D.C., MARCH 9, 1933 A.D. - The gavel came down and echoed throughout the House.

"Order please! We will have order in this House!"

It was pandemonium in the chamber and the Speaker of the House could not quell the madness.

The chamber was packed as it was a special joint session of congress. Both members of the House of Representatives and the Senate were charging in every direction of the chamber to confront adversaries, demand answers and exchange threats - angrily shouting their reprisals and displeasure.

To add to the confusion there were almost one hundred new Democrats in the House largely unfamiliar with processes and protocols caught in a good-old fashioned "free-for-all." The speaker had his hands full.

One figure sat quietly without expression as the chaos unfurled around her.

First Lady, Eleanor Roosevelt was determined to carry on the demure tone of the president. She remained seated, hands folded in her lap - a picture of unflappable, reserved modesty.

As a special guest in the House she seemed to take no offense at the current proceedings or lack thereof.

The relentless smack of the gavel eventually wore down the wild antics of the House though it took another twenty minutes for the worst of the shouting to subside.

Finally the most ardent combatants returned to their seats amidst a few remaining shouts of scorn and fierce rebuttal which threatened to spark the furor all over again.

"The Honourable Representative from Alabama has the floor!" The Speaker of the House shouted and held up both hands for quiet.

"Where are the copies of the bill?" A voice demanded again.

"We cannot vote blindly!" Shouted another.

"Produce it to the House!"

The speaker hammered his gavel several more times for order.

"The Honourable Representative from Alabama has the floor! Order please!"

Henry Steagall stood once again to address the House.

"My esteemed colleagues, never before and certainly not since the dark days of the Civil War have we been asked to fashion so urgently a timely response to so grave a national emergency. Such sweeping measures are not, I can assure every member of this House - a reckless act of partisanship but a calculated necessary response to this nation's banking crisis."

Congressman Steagall glanced at his reluctant audience. The disruptive murmurs of disapproval could still be heard throughout the chamber.

"As Chairman of the House Banking Committee, I have in my hand a draft law previously prepared by the Treasury of President Hoover's administration."

He held up a single piece of paper wrapped around a newspaper that substituted for the draft bill. He raised it high above his head for several seconds for all of the House to see.

The chamber went quiet.

Satisfied, he slowly reached for his glasses inside his breast pocket, surveyed his now captive audience and continued: "This critical piece of legislation is imperative in its immediate enactment and should have been introduced to this House previously by its own authors who for reasons unknown, chose not to act."

This drew a volley of scattered outbursts from both sides of the House.

The member from Alabama ignored them.

"Let there be no question of the necessitous nature demanded of this legislation. As evidenced by this administration's introduction of a Republican-authored draft law, bipartisanship must be demanded from the consciousness of every member and senator in this chamber."

More rumblings rippled through congress.

"The Emergency Banking Relief Act enacted by this Seventy-third United States Congress will effectively and immediately stabilize the nation's banking system by ensuring one hundred percent deposit insurance to restore the American people's confidence in the banking sector."

He adjusted his glasses and looked out over the chamber.

"Federal Reserve Banks will be allowed to supply unlimited currency to reopened banks with proven assets. As time is of the essence, I will again with the understanding of the House, attempt to read aloud the draft law before it is put to the floor. Again, I regret that there was not sufficient time to provide copies. It is my under-standing that copies will be made available to the senate for their deliberation,"

This brought a new wave of loud objections but Congressman Steagall gave no time for the discord to swell. He held up the proposed bill and began to read...

Several rows up Secretary Perkins was keeping a close eye on Senator Russell who was seated on the far side of the chamber. She had hoped to speak with him before the session began but could not spot him in the congested quarters. Eventually she had given up, content to engage in the endless introductions with new congress members eager to meet their fellow colleagues.

As the bill was read, Frances studied Senator Russell's expression. He was poker-faced while exhibiting a hint of boredom.

If Secretary Woodin was right it was a good sign. Senator Russell would keep his "yes" vote secret to the last possible moment and then release his consent with a feigned ill-humour and resignation in the whole sordid affair.

After the bill was read the expected storms of debate never materialized.

A few Republicans took the floor to decry the president's regulatory measures only to be derided by House members from California and Minnesota who promptly reminded the House the proposed legislation was drafted by their own Hoover administration.

The speaker stepped forward. "All in favour?"

"Aye!" The affirming response was deafening.

It was unanimous. Frances could scarcely believe it.

In a mere thirty-eight minutes the bill had been passed in the House.

Now it was headed to the senate. Surely all senses would prevail and the legislation would be signed into law by the president in a day or two? She thought.

She was wrong.

The senate convened later that afternoon to debate the bill. By seven that evening the bill passed by a vote of 73 - 7.

Eight hours and fifteen minutes after the legislation had been introduced to congress, President Roosevelt signed the bill into law.

At no time in history had legislation been passed so quickly.

Four days later the banks were reopened and all across the country people stood in long lines to redeposit their money into local banks that had only days previously, been stashed under mattresses and buried in backyards.

The run on the banks had been stopped. The crisis was over.

One evening later that week Frances was strolling the Capitol grounds as she often did. As she walked by the newly renovated Botanic Garden a respected senator passed her on the walkway.

"Good evening," he said, tipping his hat.

"Good evening Senator."

He stopped and turned to face her - his expression grave. "Secretary Perkins, while I commend the president's increasing of the money supply to end the bank panics, this administration's economics are deeply concerning."

His voice lowered to a hushed tone. "Much of the proposed legislation is extremely dangerous."

"How so?" Asked Frances. She was slightly unnerved by this unexpected encounter.

Your 'brains trust' friends have convinced the president that Keynes's theories will work."

"The economist?"

"Yes. He's in love with Keynes' argument: the government can stimulate the economy by burying bottles of money in abandoned coal mines and let private enterprise contrive ways to dig them up."

"Hardly the best illustration of his theories," said Frances dismissively.

The senator shook his head. "It's a heck of a gamble. Massive government spending of borrowed money doesn't guarantee jobs - only unbalanced budgets and mounting deficits."

"Temporary measures that are necessary to help millions of Americans," said Frances with a hint of defiance. "This new deal is addressing our present dangers."

"Oh? You'd stake our collective existence on this certainty?" His eyes locked onto her. "These policies pull at the financial threads of a monetary system that threatens to unravel the delicate balance of a global economy." He tipped his hat and walked away.

Frances felt an unsettling pulling at her insides. She believed she was right but knew his fear wasn't wrong. He had struck a politically sensitive nerve. The government was betting with a new set of dice on a high stakes gamble that reached round the world.

UNNAMED BALTIC SEAPORT - "Come in Colonel, please have a seat. It is good of you to come."

"I was told you could help us."

"Indeed I can. I am a most trusted companion - invaluable and readily available."

"You can secure our shipments and locations?"

We are already hidden in lonely caches waiting to be unleashed. We are everywhere the price has been paid - in the currency of your choosing."

"I see."

"May I inquire as to the nature of your request? I needn't know specifics. Discretion is guaranteed."

"It is a paramilitary force - a youth wing."

"Ah, a most powerful concoction."

"It is."

"You and I can do business Colonel - exclusively if you wish? I have several agents at the ready. Our extensive network holds a monopoly on market forces.

The man extended a long bony hand. "It is very nice to meet you. My name is Kalashnikov."

"A drink perhaps?"

"No thank you."

"I have heard much about you Colonel Basbug. So, you are also the de facto leader of the Grey Wolves. The great eurosceptic. I am of a similar mind. You are to be congratulated!"

"The nation state must be protected."

"It must, and at all costs Colonel."

"We require your services in Dagestan and Chechnya."

"That can be arranged."

"And the terms?"

"They will be sent to you through the regular channels."

"Fine then."

"My offer is a standing one of course. You need not decide anything now."

"Most considerate sir."

"Colonel, I am always willing to avail myself at a moment's notice. My services will prove invaluable. I'm sure our paths will cross again."

CHAPTER 6
AVTOMAT KALASHNIKOVA

V.18 "Are you only a visitor to Jerusalem and do not know the things that have happened there in these days?"

BALTIC SEA, 1983 A.D. - A seventeenth-century poet once called me the "artful destroyer" - a rather harsh sentiment but one I can stomach.

These post-reformationists are quite astonishing in their gall.

They pine for things beyond their grasp and backfill the chasm of their pitiful shortcomings with a blind acknowledgement of everything they can never be.

How much better off they were when that book of lies was closed to the masses.

If only they knew how powerful they could become.

Instead these same dregs who scheme for crumbs and cobble together a shameful existence, guilefully enthrall each other in their newfound profundity - unabashedly discussing the priesthood of Melchizedek as if they are suddenly privy to all understanding!

These fools forget they hold an acquired taste for the fruit of knowledge.

There is no turning back now.

The age of enlightenment is infinite if you understand where to sharpen your focus. And still I'm constantly amazed at the naivety of the world.

The medievalists were somewhat confounding; the modernists more easily confused; the post-modernists - an absolute delight!

Still, there are far too many dregs who could be princes and far too many playgrounds waiting to be transformed into kingdoms.

The blight of this world's existence is its own short-sightedness...

The shame of defeat has lost its sting. There is much work to be done.

But even in defeat, an emerging governing politik has finally crossed the threshold of new possibilities.

Leave Europe's reconstruction to the eternally distracted. There are new battles to be fought.

A deep thirst has indeed been quenched in the bloodlands of central Europe. The taste of death has become as sweet as honey to those who see beyond the blood-soaked battlefields.

A greater glory is within reach. The next wave is just beginning.

And this time, I am introducing myself to the poorest of the world. The ordered open fields are yesterday's battlegrounds.

There is a better way to kill.

We will soon be armed by the thousands - strapped on the backs of every dreg.

Forget the bloodied fields of Europe and the corpse-filled deserts of North Africa. Bring forth the isolated corners of the earth's oppressed.

The euphony of battle will be heard in the remote jungles of the forgotten and in the city squares of the nobles.

I am now the weapon of choice.

The revolutionary's iron cross - a trusted liberator and creator of a global economy of annihilation.

Finally! My legions can see the finish line.

We almost had him in '81.

I have stood on that stone tablet in St. Peter's Square. The resting place of the succession lies marked for a future glory - the end of his race and the beginning of mine.

What a glorious century it has been!

The consuming power of ideology has swept my emissaries into action on many exciting fronts. Who would have thought the human mind to be so utterly capable?

Nationalism has become the emissary of the pure and has sown its seed in the fertile grounds of this scorched earth. Now it is time for the labourers to reap what has always been rightfully theirs. We will no longer tolerate our own dilution at the scabbed hands of foreign interests.

We have laboured for generations in the purity of our ancestors... Why should we not covet what belongs to us? And to us alone!

We will be our own caretakers of justice. The days of paying taxes to a meddling master are over.

Caesar is long dead.

Now, allow me to make some introductions. Gentlemen, please do come down and join us. It is chilly on deck. Welcome gentlemen. Please sit anywhere you wish. Hot drinks will be served shortly with vodka and brandy.

Now my young recruit, listen closely!

Together we have sung to thousands. Do not pass judgement or confuse disdain with envy. You are one of us. Remember my offer?

Time has encapsulated us as peers in this tiny space. You are a part of this history.

Now, please Colonel.

"Thank you Kalashnikov. Young man, my name is Colonel Basbug.

One of the great things about a revolutionary is they are of no fixed address and are highly transient. They are disciplined and bide their time patiently often appearing out of nowhere to lay their claim. They are vigilant in their preparations.

You understand the essential nature of loyalty in this movement do you not?"

"I do sir."

"There is no refusal of duty. Your commanding superiors and fellow brothers depend on the subordination of its members to execute their assignments with the Grey Wolves to perfection. There is no room for error. We are all still paying the price for the mess at St. Peter's square. The panic and indecisiveness of a single member has cost us dearly. The matter has been dealt with. Consider yourself his replacement"

"Understood sir."

"Very good. Your next assignment will be Chechnya. When we return to port you will pack your things and await further instructions. Do not leave your flat."

"Yes sir."

"Thank you Kalashnikov."

Wonderful Colonel!

My generals are also extremely well-versed in my distribution and their methods of extracting truth most effectively. Remember, everything is purposed to further the cause.

The mobilization of peasantry is not an easy task. They are singular-minded in their work and must be courted intelligently.

I myself am rooted in peasantry. I certainly laud their simple ethics but the lack of ambition can be astonishing. In the end, they all must make a basic choice to join a greater calling or, like my old friend Sayyid enjoyed saying - submit to having their teeth broken.

Effective words of the inviolable, no doubt.

The wise ones remember - I am the blood in their veins. Without me, they are as weak as infants.

Now here are two young lieutenants who can speak to that. They are successful recruits serving General Sar.

Lieutenant Kim?

"Thank you Sir. My young recruit, as you prepare to join the field, allow us to inform you of our successful mission in southeast Asia. We, and now you, are personal safeguards of a much greater reality on the battlefield. We secured the gun crates buried beneath the jungle floor and returned them to the base."

Yes, well done gentlemen. It is always good to be found. We were all distributed a week later and launched a successful counter-offensive.

I sang to thousands that day.

General Sar understood me implicitly.

These two lieutenants who stand before you were decorated accordingly for their find and two divisions pushed into the coveted highlands."

Now before we adjourn these formalities my young recruit do you have any questions?

"Only one Sir. I apologize for the confusion as I am new to the organization and do not know of many of these past events. But who are you?"

Ah, a logical question and one I can answer directly.

I am the manifestation of ideology. I am the ultimate call to arms. I am the most trusted companion of the revolutionary.

My full name is Avtomat Kalashnikova - conceived in Moscow in 1946 and born a year later as AK-47."

"That is your code name or a nickname?"

Haha! Delightful! Yes, yes - my code name of course, or nickname, whichever you prefer.

You will meet the others in due time. General Ugarte and Chairman Gonzalo have employed my services loyally and in return I have given them great victories in the south.

General Zia continues to prepare my agenda in Pakistan and Taliban-controlled areas of Afghanistan.

Now, do not question your assignments. Simply execute them and Colonel Basbug will elevate your rank accordingly. You are a young man in a new world order. Take advantage of the opportunities afforded you.

"Yes sir."

Forever keep this in mind: The state is power. You will be ridiculed as an ultra-nationalist, a thug, a heretic. Pay no heed to these petty insults. A strong nationalist ideology breeds a contemporary society where everyone has a role in their proper place.

The current battle for position is a price we must pay for that order.

There are very real threats to this order that we must always be willing to confront. The ancient threats continue to pose significant dangers to the established order of this world.

"Ancient threats Sir?"

Son, remember this - inflate the pride of the masses and they will carry me to any end you set before them.

How I wish my dear friend Sayyid was here to offer his counsel on these matters.

"Who is Sayyid, sir?"

Who is Sayyid? Good heavens boy!

His revolution brought down the Shah and two thousand five hundred years of Persian monarchy rule.

"A man will come from Qom and he will summon people to the right path."

Almost twelve hundred years later in 1978 his face appeared in the full moon - witnessed by millions! It was a sign of the promised one's return. And return he did, triumphantly to his people.

The revolution was upon them. The enemy's head crushed underfoot.

Our Persian monarchy has been around two thousand years and *our* Shah resides by the square of St. Peter's.

We will do the same.

CHAPTER 7
NIGHT IS FOR THE POETS AND THE MADMEN

V.19 "What things?" he asked.

SANTIAGO, CHILE, 1973 A.D. - "I will ask you one last time amigo! Do you like the mountains or the bush?"

The helicopter swung sharply over the city and headed west into the black night.

"No, no, no! Please compadre! I have a family - all young children, compadre. Please! I am begging you."

"You should've thought of that before shooting your mouth off on the streets."

"I support the General, compadre. No problems! No problems with Ugarte! Please, compadre!"

"Yeah we've heard more confessions than the pope this week amigo."

The lights of the city disappeared underneath them as the towering dark silhouettes ahead seemed to swallow the sky. He brought the chopper up higher as they approached the mountains.

"The Andes it is," muttered the pilot.

An awful scream jolted him from his seat.

He quickly glanced behind him. "Carlos!" The prisoner was covered in blood, his hands bound behind his back. "Enough! You're making a mess back there!

He turned to his co-pilot. "Get back there and settle him down. Keep him quiet."

"Aye Captain."

The pilot rubbed his eyes. This was a bad business.

It was their seventh midnight run in as many days. Everyone was the same pleading chaos.

"Captain! Here, have a drink - calm the nerves a -"

"Carlos, we're on duty. What are you thinking?"

"Trying not to Captain."

He was quiet for a moment. "Give me that." He took the flask and took a quick sip. Then a longer one. The liquor flashed in his throat and instantly warmed his insides.

"Takes the edge off quick, eh Captain?"

"Yeah, until we open the doors."

"You find a place to hover and we'll take care of him."

"Just get em out quick. I don't wanna hear that - that stuff at the end."

"Ok Captain."

Carlos staggered as the chopper veered slightly left and made his way to the back.

"Hey Franco, you put him to sleep?"

"He's preparing himself."

The man opened his swollen eyes. He looked up at Carlos, a resigned look on his battered face. "No mas."

"Relax amigo. We're almost there. "Here, have a drink,"

The man shook his head.

"Ok guys, get him ready! Approaching drop off."

"Grab the hood. Get it on him."

Carlos grabbed the canvas bag hanging on the hook above them and tried to slip it over the man's head. He thrashed his head violently kicking madly with his legs.

Franco kneeling on one knee beside the terrified man drove his fist into the man's ribs.

"Stop it! It's over. You're as good as dead."

The frantic prisoner felt nothing, fighting for his life with every ounce of strength he had left in him. He screamed for all he was worth - "Murderers! Murderers! Your caravana de la muerte! You will all die with Ugarte!"

"Would you shut him up!" The captain wiped his forehead and dipped the nose of the chopper down to get into position. The sudden maneuver sent Franco sprawling over the still screaming prisoner. The man sunk his teeth into Franco's shoulder and bit into him like a terrified animal.

Franco screamed in pain.

"What the?" The pilot looked back. "Carlos! Help him!"

Carlos regained his balance and grabbed the man's head with one hand and shoved the canvas bag over his head with the other. He drew the drawstring tight, threw him back to the floor and collapsed beside Franco.

"You alright?"

Franco grimaced. "No."

"Look at that. Bit right through your stripes"

"Get him on his feet. Captain! We're ready. Settle her down!" He motioned Carlos to open the door. "Wait until we're in place."

The chopper moved into position and hovered over the darkness.

"Ready!" The captain turned back and gave the thumbs up.

Carlos opened the door and the cool air rushed in.

"Help me get him to his feet!" They grabbed the man from each side and hauled him up. They steadied themselves as they hauled him to the open door two thousand feet above ground.

Suddenly the man twitched and let out an ear-piercing scream. He kicked his legs furiously and then lunged to one side causing Carlos to lose his balance and fall towards the open door.

"Help!" Carlos yelled.

"Get up! I can't hold him! He's crazy!" Franco jerked the prisoner back from the door who was frantically trying to push Carlos out with him. Carlos caught the corner of the door with his foot and braced himself back to his feet. The man threw his head at Carlos again catching him in the face with one of the straps on the canvas bag.

"Get him outa here!" The captain screamed.

Franco drove his knee up into the man's stomach. The man doubled over and went limp, the wind knocked out of him.

"Padre, Padre," he whispered.

"Ready! Now!"

He felt hands at his back and the cool night air rushed into him.

Carlos and Franco thrust the man out of the helicopter and watched him disappear into the darkness below.

"Adios amigo." Carlos wiped the blood dripping from his forehead.

"Let's get outa here." Franco yelled as he closed the door.

"Roger that," the Captain muttered.

The chopper swung around, climbed up into the night sky and headed back towards the city.

❧

The Santiago Metropolitan Cathedral shone like a jewel in the night in the city centre across from the Plaza De Armas.

It was spectacular. Built during the latter half of the eighteenth century it stood as a monument to the holy protectorate of the Catholic faith having outlasted the devastation of earthquakes, revolutions, coup d'états and the ill-competing promises of its military and political rulers.

The front facade of the stone cathedral was wonderfully lit with its two adorned steeples rising as illuminated shrines into the dark heavens. In between the columned steeples standing on its own prominent archway a towering statue of Jesus Christ watched over the cathedral's entrance, his left arm pointing to the way of the Father. Below, three archways invited Chileans to its massive wood doors leading inside.

A black Bentley pulled up in front of the cathedral and stopped. After flicking its headlights two armed policemen appeared and stood at the grand entrance beside the centre doors. It was well past midnight and the street and plaza were deserted.

Two men exited the vehicle. One of them opened the rear door. A tall figure emerged and walked with the two men to the entrance. The centre door opened and the men entered. The door closed quickly behind them leaving the two policemen at their post.

Inside the narthex a young priest welcomed them with hushed whispers and shook the tall figure's hand.

"Please, this way sir." He motioned the tall figure to follow him while the other two men remained behind.

The priest led his guest into the nave down the centre aisle way of the cathedral. The nave was dimly lit but its incredible beauty washed over them from every vantage. The tall figure stopped briefly, looking up and to each side and then up again, gazing intently at the detailed imagery carved and painted into the elaborate vaulted ceiling that towered overhead drawing them forward. The long aisle way stretched the entire length of the nave, its path leading like a pilgrimage to the awaiting beautifully lit sanctuary shining its brilliance in the distance. The priest turned and waited patiently for the man, then continued walking.

Up ahead a robed figure appeared in front of the altar which shone softly like a brilliant white diamond at the end of the nave.

As the priest and his guest approached the sanctuary the robed figure descended the few steps into the nave and walked towards them, his hands folded in front of him.

The priest nodded to the robed figure, bowed to the altar and walked swiftly through a side door off the nave.

"General Ugarte, welcome. How kind of you to pay us this visit."

"Thank you Archbishop for the privilege. I know the hour is late."

The two men shook hands. "Please, have a seat." Archbishop Raúl Silva Henriquez motioned to one of the wooden pews that filled the nave. "Now, what can we do for you General?"

The general stretched his legs trying to get comfortable in his cramped wooden seat. "Archbishop, you are aware of the transition challenges of this new government?"

"To a degree."

"The previous leadership has left us in a difficult position. Its ideologies have scattered Chileans and divided the country. The unpredictable nature of many of these former movements are proving to be quite contentious. I know the Catholic church has also shared in these difficulties."

He paused, waiting for the archbishop to respond.

"Yes, it is true the church's place in the life of Chilean society has come under much scrutiny in recent years. But General, your government is barely a year old. Your reforms will take time."

He smiled warmly, taking time to gauge the motives of his visitor.

"I humbly encourage you to remain patient and allow your policies to take root. Sow with patience and all of Chile will rejoice in the harvest of these new beginnings."

"That is wise counsel and I thank you for it Archbishop. But how do we sow our policies and reforms in the midst of such turbulence? We are struggling with Marxist and communist disruptions in our workforce, in the universities, even in our judiciary. The fire is burning beyond our means to control it without it consuming the values and morals of the people."

"Speak to me of these fires, General."

"The fires of unlawfulness and disorder are threatening Chilean society - every aspect of it - what is taught in our schools and universities, how our workforce is structured, how our laws are applied under the current constitution - even the laws of the church are being attacked and undermined by the incessant plotting of neoliberalism. Surely this concerns you Archbishop?"

"Indeed it does. But our response must be in accordance with the very laws and principles of a just God who wishes peace and security for all Chileans. Patience General is your greatest ally in achieving the law and order you seek."

"Of course." General Ugarte shifted uncomfortably in the pew. "Perhaps that is a fundamental difference between the church and the state Archbishop. The church has all the time in eternity. The state has only the short time it can remain in power. You understand the nature of our respective politics I am sure."

"Yes, I am sympathetic to your position, General. Your presidency however - goodness me, forgive my impertinence. Shall I be referring to you in the excellence of your presidency?"

"Certainly not." In your holy presence I prefer informality. He smiled quickly. "You are my superior, Archbishop."

The archbishop nodded courteously. "As I was saying, our tenures though structured differently need not change our methods of governance."

"The church's governance has historically ruled unquestioned and beyond reproach, has it not?" There was some condescension in the general's tone.

"Yes, that is true. But I would argue that our approach, of which my authority has been complicit, has created as much unrest as it has given."

"Surely you are not convicting yourself Archbishop?"

The archbishop was silent for a moment. "Yes, yes I am General. We are all convicted under God.

General Ugarte sighed. "Yes, I suppose we are."

"But we do not stay convicted. The archbishop motioned to the altar. "The blood of forgiveness has already been shed."

"The blood... yes, the blood. I'd almost forgotten," said the general.

"Please, allow me to hear your confession and then partake of the eucharist before you leave.

General Ugarte nodded and breathed deeply. The two men bowed their heads and the president's confession was heard. The whispered exchanges softly echoed into the beautiful archway above them.

Finally Archbishop Henriquez rose from their pew and led the general to the altar where the bread and the cup were waiting.

"Let us pray..."

The archbishop finished the prayer and presided over the elements offering the bread to his parishioner. "Quia corpus Christi fractum."

"Amen." The general took the bread kneeling before the altar.

The archbishop laid his hand on the general's head and offered a prayer for his presidency, the new government and the people of Chile.

After the blessing General Ugarte rose to his feet. He crossed himself and bowed low facing the altar.

The archbishop put his hand on the general's back motioning him back down the nave leading to the front doors in the narthex.

"It was very good of you to come General."

"My sincere gratitude and thanks to you Archbishop for your counsel and understanding."

"I hope I was able to offer some words of wisdom. These conversations I realize are always unfinished. Please General, do not hesitate to contact me or visit us here at any time, at any hour."

"Thank you Archbishop. That is most appreciated."

The archbishop hesitated… "General, I feel compelled to urge you. I have heard through certain channels of an - an Operation Condor?" He shifted his feet nervously.

"Yes. What've you heard?" General Ugarte flashed an icy glare and then recovered himself. "The rumour mill is churning all sorts of propaganda, Archbishop."

"Yes, I'm sure it is. These… these deaths," he cleared his throat. "These so-called death caravans. They are -"

The general cut him off. "I can assure you they are greatly exaggerated. Remember, we are dealing with cold-blooded terrorists. Enemies of the state. Enemies of this church, Archbishop."

He glanced at the waiting Bentley. "We will not place you in a compromising position, that I can assure you. However law and order will be restored. I know many of your bishops have been very supportive of these initiatives. I'm sure they are comforted in knowing that their archbishop stands behind them." General Ugarte raised his eyebrows at the archbishop.

"My bishops understand their duties very well General. We can both rest well in the truth of this fact." The general stared at him for several seconds. "Excellent," he smiled. "We shall keep in close touch then." He offered his hand.

"Good night Archbishop."

"Good night General."

He watched as the car drove away into the night.

It was a scene he had witnessed before. It was burned into his memory, his senses, his very being.

He stood in a grove of palm trees across from the Cathedral. He glanced at the time. Even the hour was the same. It was now well past midnight. He saw them enter the cathedral and decided to wait.

It was easier before, he thought. That blissful ignorance of time and events was indeed a blessed veil.

This was a heavier existence having to return to endure these long sufferings played out on the dim minds of the unknowing. Now he felt caught between two worlds aching for the duality of their respective promises - those received and those unfulfilled. 'No one can see the kingdom'... he recalled the words. He had crossed the threshold of understanding.

A warm breeze gently rustled through the trees. One night, he thought - framed for all eternity. 'How can this be?' His own words flooded back to him.

The center door of the cathedral opened and the archbishop and General Ugarte walked out slowly together. They spoke briefly, shook hands and the general got into the back of his waiting car.

Young disciples forever trapped in the coliseums of Rome, he thought. He had seen it all from the very beginning

Some days it seemed the apostolic succession would be devoured by the flames of empire. This was one of those days. A victory for the lions of Emperor Trajan.

Alone in the grove of palms, Nicodemus watched with the archbishop as the general drove away.

PART II

CHAPTER 8
THE KILLING OF CAMELOT

V.20 The chief priests and our rulers handed him over to be sentenced to death,
and they crucified him.

Cleopas caught Carolus's nervous glance and stepped forward. "It's nice to meet you brother," he said, extending his hand. "I'm Cleopas and this is my friend, Carolus."

"Carolus nodded and shook the stranger's hand. "Camelot, you say?"

He smiled. "I am."

"We're headed as far as Emmaus. You're welcome to walk with us if you wish. You mentioned you're from afar?" asked Carolus.

Camelot nodded.

The three men continued walking. "You asked of what things we were discussing," said Cleopas. "We will tell you all about this man."

"He was a prophet," said Carolus.

"Yes, chosen by God," added Cleopas. "We saw so many things..."

Carolus listened as his friend recalled the stories and the signs. His mind drifted in and out of the conversation as his own recollections found him. It was odd how second-nature many of the accounts had become and their powerful hold on many throughout Palestine.

The few clouds that had provided occasional reprieve from the sun's glare had disappeared leaving an endless expanse of blue sky stretching out as far as one could see.

Carolus glanced at Camelot who was listening quietly to Cleopas. It was hard to believe the entire world did not know of this catastrophe given the events that had followed the execution.

"He was handed over to the prefect who wanted nothing to do with the whole sordid affair," said Cleopas. "But the chief priests and the people demanded his life."

It's true," said Carolus. "The fury of the crowd was almost incomprehensible. The prefect tried to negotiate his release but the screaming mob would have none of it. He was beaten and flogged. Then finally led away to his execution."

"It all happened so fast," said Cleopas.

The shock had not left them, thought Carolus. It lingered and stung in the way only a sudden death can. He remembered his father's death several years earlier.

Carolus came home one day to the sound of his mother sobbing and his uncle standing over her whispering comforts to her in vain. They were absorbed into his uncle's family.

Now here, I must tell you. There was another encounter at Capernaum that had greatly affected Carolus some twenty years later.

Carolus had followed him along with many of the others to the synagogue in Capernaum where the condemned man had preached. His message that day had not been well received...

"This is the bread which came down out of heaven... he that eats of this bread shall live forever."

Many of us, including myself, I must admit were uneasy about the words he spoke. Some were very disturbed. "This is a hard saying," they said. "Who can hear it?"

He asked us: *"Does this cause you to stumble?"*

And truthfully, how could it not? Even the most faithful of us wanted him to stop in the synagogue. It was simply too much to comprehend. It was dangerously provocative.

"It is the spirit that gives life." he had said. *"For this cause have I said unto you, that no man can come unto me, except it be given unto him of the Father."*

Well, this was the breaking point for many of them and they left him, never to return. But a few did stay.

Carolus was one of them.

Then he looked over at us, the twelve and said: *"Would you also go away?"*

And here again, Cephas answered the call. He said, "Lord, to whom shall we go?"

Cephas had a knack for calling out the obvious and in so doing, threw himself and the rest of us into waters too deep to understand, yet too glorious not to immerse ourselves in fully, even to the point of dying.

I have argued with the physician - that was the day of our baptism, in a manner of speaking. The powers of heaven and hell and our place in it all became real to our group of followers that day in Capernaum.

That day was our collective point of no return. And he plainly asked us if we wanted out - if we'd had enough.

We were miles from home; had given up everything. He had taken us to the cliff's edge.

And now he wanted to take us further. My nets, father's boat - were gone forever.

☙

AMBASSADOR HOTEL, LOS ANGELES, 1968 A.D. - "On to Chicago and let's win there!"

The New York senator waved to the excited throng of campaign supporters crowded into the ballroom and left the podium.

How many times do we have to go over this?

Go... Go... C'mon, move!

"Bobby, this way. There's been a change of plans. The press want a statement." William, his security agent turned to clear a path through the crowd.

"Congratulations Senator!" He turned to shake more hands and headed towards the back exit. He soon lost sight of William as the exuberant crowd closed around him.

Get into position.

"Senator, follow me." The head host grabbed his wrist.

"Lead the way Karl. "I'm right behind you." The senator did his best to keep up despite the endless handshakes and words from well-wishers.

Wait... wait. Not yet.

They entered the kitchen area and headed down a hallway. "Congratulations sir!"

Now.

Shots rang out.

I was there but I must confess, I didn't kill him - not directly anyways. It was the work of a lesser colleague - Iver Johnson. His handler was a bit-player without a cause. Give a fool a gun and he thinks he's immortal.

We stood in the kitchen by the icemaker waiting together. Then he made his rush. There are revolutionaries, soldiers and patsies. This dreg's hands were shaking so badly he could barely hold him.

For a brief while I thought it was another missed opportunity like the mess at St. Peter's square thirteen years later. But out of every scene of chaos, an endgame does emerge. It must be recognized, seized upon and executed to perfection.

There is a misconception that I prefer to work in chaos - that I relish the mayhem of the moment. This is not true.

Take a look at history. Patience is not just a virtue of the saints. It is a discipline of those who have learned the secret to longevity in a world that despises its own existence.

If you hold up the mirror long enough, people will begin to see whatever you want them to. They will see themselves in every opportunity.

And I will become their perfect reflection.

RATANAKIRI PROVINCE, CAMBODIA, 1968 A.D. -   The narrow red-dirt road wound its way through the thick jungle. A convoy of six Chinese-made military trucks, coated in red mud slowly snaked deeper into the bush. The seasonal rains had refused to let up and were making for a miserable December.

Lieutenant Kim had been recruited by the Khmer Rouge two years earlier when the Worker's Party, soon to be the Communist Party of Kampuchea had moved its headquarters to Ratanakiri. He, like hundreds of other indigenous Khmer Loeu of the region had gladly accepted the invitation as their hatred for Prince Sihanouk and the central government grew in the face of recent attacks.

He had risen quickly through the ranks, humbly accepting his promotions and widening responsibilities. His duties now aligned himself with the top brass of the Khmer Rouge. Their influence was growing throughout the country as they worked to consolidate a strategic alliance along the Ho Chi Minh trail with the National Liberation Front in south Vietnam and the northern Vietnamese army. These were exciting times.

The lead truck bounced around a deeply-rutted curve in the road which then straightened out and led to a small clearing that was fenced off with barbed wire. The convoy rolled to a stop, the cacophony of their idling engines echoed their arrival. A young boy in military fatigues smartly saluted Lieutenant Kim who was seated in the truck's passenger seat and opened a crude bamboo gate. The trucks pulled into the clearing which led into the military compound. They passed a few small bamboo huts and came to a stop in front of a larger bamboo storehouse with a thatched roof.

Lieutenant Kim jumped down from the truck and adjusted his red-checkered scarf. "You three," he said, pointing to some soldiers perched on the back of one of the trucks. "Get the men organized and start unloading as I instructed."

"Yes, sir," they barked in unison.

"And check the manifest again. I want every brick, every sack of rice, every weapon accounted for and submitted as registered inventory. Got it?"

"Yes sir," they barked again.

"Lieutenant." An administrative aide stopped in front of him and saluted. "General Sar is waiting for you."

Lieutenant Kim nodded and headed to the main offices housed in a modest single story bamboo structure sitting on stilts in the middle of the compound. Like every other building on the compound it had a thatched roof to help conceal it from aerial reconnaissance and attacks.

He adjusted his cap and scarf as he jogged up several wooden steps onto the covered porch of the building and cleaned his boots on the edge of the wooden step as best he could. Then he opened the door and entered a small reception area. The smell of cigarettes filled the building as the smoke wafted over the walls through the open ceiling and up into the exposed rafters of the thatched roof.

"Good morning Lieutenant. The general will see you now."

He marched past the uniformed secretary sitting at her rickety wooden desk and continued down a short hallway. He turned left at the end and knocked on the door.

"Yes, come in."

Lieutenant Kim opened the door and entered the large office. It was sparsely decorated with wooden floors and bamboo walls covered with dust and grime. On one of the walls a large red flag with the hammer and sickle in its centre hung precariously from two small nails.

The general sat at a big wooden desk leaning back in his chair. Three of his top advisors sat on small wooden chairs across from him.

Lieutenant Kim saluted the general and nodded at the military men who stood and nodded their greetings to him. He recognized two of them as General Sar's closest advisors but did not know the other man.

"The supplies arrived safely and are all accounted for?"

"Everything arrived safely General. We quickly checked the manifest as we loaded and I have my men confirming the manifest as we speak. It looks like it's all accounted for."

"Excellent. Let me know if there are any irregularities."

"Yes, General."

"One of the advisors whom the lieutenant recognized turned to him. "Any trouble on the river?"

"No sir, we went in and came out clean. No sign of the enemy."

"The river?" asked the man seated closest to Lieutenant Kim who was still standing.

"The Sesan River, sir. It flows down across the border southwest into Ratanakiri. It's one of our main supply lines. The North Vietnamese army either floats them down river and we intercept them or we receive them at predetermined crossing points - always on our border side."

General Sar intervened. "Lieutenant Kim, I would like you to meet Mr. Kalashnikov."

"Kalashnikov? Yes, pardon me sir. The name... it is very good to meet you." He was youthful in appearance with piercing dark eyes and wore a military uniform that Lieutenant Kim had not seen before.

"Mr. Kalashnikov is an important strategic partner - a foreign interceptor of the necessities of war, shall we say."

"That is very interesting, sir," said Lieutenant Kim. He was still confused.

Kalashnikov smiled. "I deal primarily in the supply of logistics and weaponry."

"Ah, I see," said the lieutenant. We just collected a shipment of AK's early this morning from the river."

"And you have this man to thank for it," said General Sar.

Lieutenant Kim offered his hand to the man, surprised. "That's wonderful sir."

He guessed that this man was involved in covert planning and espionage with either the Khmer Rouge or a related organization. He decided not to ask any details. Unwelcome questions could be lethal.

General Sar motioned Lieutenant Kim to a nearby wooden chair.

"As you know," said the general. "Our supply lines are being ambushed at many access points and our Vietnamese allies can only provide so many airdrops. You are all well aware of this."

Something was coming, thought Lieutenant Kim. General Sar rarely held meetings with military subordinates that weren't deeply tied into his inner circle. He trusted no one. But this Kalashnikov, he clearly trusted.

The General stood and leaned forward on his desk. "Gentlemen, it is time to take Phnom Penh."

Lieutenant Kim was shocked. He didn't dare look at the others.

"We have the guerrilla forces necessary and will continue to aggressively recruit the peasantry into a new army - the Kampuchean Revolutionary Army." He glanced at the three men seated in front of him and then over at Lieutenant Kim.

"The time to strike is now. We will mobilize to encircle the capital and slowly close the noose around the enemy. Our Vietnamese allies will help us."

"But General," one of his advisors said, shifting in his seat, "the Americans are pouring their troops into Vietnam. Hanoi and the Viet Cong have their hands full as it is."

"They will help us," said the general.

"Will it be enough?" The second advisor spoke up. "The bombing raids are destroying all of Vietnam. It's inevitable American bombers will target us next. It's just a matter of time."

General Sar held up his hands and shrugged. "Perhaps, but we're a secondary target. They won't fight a protracted war on two fronts. Hanoi is already giving them a taste of hell and the Viet Cong will fight to the last man."

Lieutenant Kim leaned forward in his chair. "Why now General? What do you see?" He hoped General Sar would be flattered by the second question and in so doing be more forthcoming in answering the first.

General Sar smiled widely and sat down at his desk. "What do I see..."

Lieutenant Kim knew he was going to get his answer.

"I see an opportunity to strike. There are changing political winds to engage. Revolution is as much about the execution of timing as it is its own ideology. I've invited Mr. Kalashnikov here to brief us further."

"Thank you general." Kalashnikov rose to his feet. Lieutenant, you asked: 'Why now?' I will tell you exactly why the time is upon us."

He glanced out the small window behind the desk. "A well-executed revolution must be timed perfectly. A patient sword is its own precision, is it not?"

No one dared answer him.

"Revolution must only be waged under favourable conditions."

He tapped his boot on the floor and crossed his arms. No one moved. Even General Sar seemed on edge with this strange man in the room.

"It has been a devastating year for the American aggressors. Do you know why?"

"They're losing thousands of troops in Vietnam," one of the advisors said.

"Yes, but that's been going on for a few years now," said Kalashnikov. "Anyone else?"

There was silence.

"General?"

General Sar took a long drag on his cigarette. "Gentlemen, what Mr. Kalashnikov is trying to say is that the emperor has no clothes. America has played out its string. Now is the time to take advantage of their preoccupation with Hanoi and seize control of this country. That means securing the capital city."

"Precisely General."

"The emperor has no clothes? What do you mean by this?" said Lieutenant Kim.

"It has run out of gas and revealed its true identity," said General Sar. "Ideology fuels action. But thin out a collective ideology and it becomes fractured, loses its potency and is eventually revealed for what it is. Many American civilians oppose the war and that movement has cost them a great deal of political capital. Now is the time to crush our enemy in the cities while the American imperialists are looking elsewhere."

"Well said." Kalashnikov walked over to the desk and stood beside the general. "You may not be aware of the domestic situation in America at the moment. It is a fractured state. There are mass demonstrations protesting the war."

"Why would they protest?" asked one of the advisors.

"They are weary of death, my friend."

"Weary of death? Then why escalate war against NLF forces? Soldiers are expected to die."

Kalashnikov laughed loudly, surprising the others. "Yes, yes indeed they are. However, forget the war for a moment." Kalashnikov smoothed the red-checkered scarf he wore over his shoulder. "There are others who have been killed in recent months. A senator in Los Angeles and a preacher in Memphis - saviours to many though hated by others."

Lieutenant Kim was growing impatient. "I'm not sure we follow you sir."

"No, I reckon you don't Lieutenant." His eyes locked on him with an icy stare forcing the lieutenant to look down at his boots. He wouldn't speak again unless spoken to.

"Camelot is dead," said Kalashnikov.

"Camelot?" said one of the advisors confused.

"I have explained the revolutionary significance of this to General Sar. Now I will explain it to you. As I said previously, revolution must only be waged under favourable conditions."

Lieutenant Kim noticed the rain had finally stopped and the sun was poking through the clouds. A ray of light shone through the window and found the stack of papers on the general's desk.

"This American senator was running for president when he was assassinated. He was from a powerful family. His brother was removed from the presidency himself by an assassin's bullet only five years ago."

Kalashnikov surveyed the room. "Their reign was referred to as 'Camelot' meaning - one brief shining moment. It galvanized a nation with a foolish hope, one I have seen before and one, like all others previous, was never realized. Their shining moment has passed them by. Camelot is officially dead."

"And now the conditions are ripe for action," Lieutenant Kim offered cautiously.

Kalashnikov nodded. "A new president has been elected and takes office next month. President Nixon's Republicans will chase a new agenda. Former President Roosevelt's New Deal programs are essentially dead. A nation in transition is vulnerable. Conditions are favourable." He paused for a moment.

"Gentlemen, understand you are a small but integral part of a long protracted struggle. One that has been going on for some time and extends far beyond national borders. Now, I must leave you. General Sar will brief you on the details of the operation."

The general and the others scrambled to their feet and saluted their guest who was already halfway down the hall. General Sar sat down at his desk. "Dismissed. You will be briefed in due time."

He waved them out the door.

Lieutenant Kim was confused and angry as he walked down the steps. In due time? What were they waiting for? Something didn't make sense. A protracted struggle extending beyond national borders? They were being left in the dark for the time being.

General Sar ground his cigarette into the ashtray on his desk. Kalashnikov had briefed him on his plans before the others had arrived. That was wise of course. Those dregs could not be expected to understand the gravity of such actions. He himself was more than a little shocked at the magnitude of the assignment. Others he had never met were involved too.

And for how long had this battle been raging?

He leaned back in his chair. Kalashnikov had taken them this far. He would finish what they'd started. Now he understood all of these battles were intertwined somehow. But Kalashnikov's explanation and orders were beyond his comprehension...

"General, I'm talking about bringing down empires."

"And how do we do this?"

"We knock out its prevailing authority."

"You mean Sihanouk?"

"Think bigger than the kingdom of Cambodia, general, much bigger."

General Sar had shaken his head. "You speak of things I do not understand."

"Yes, I do. You will understand in time General. But I have chosen you among a few privileged. You will follow me and carry out my orders as if they are your own."

The general nodded slowly.

Kalashnikov stood over the desk opposite him. "Now, just listen... the prevailing authority at St. Peter's square holds a precarious dominion over its empires in the west - specifically Western Europe and the Americas."

St. Peter's square? he thought. Was he speaking of Rome?

"History of which we are a part does not operate on a linear timeline. Time cycles itself over and over. Time and as such, opportunity can be recaptured."

He was lost.

"Everyone waits for that one brief shining moment to capture and hold onto. That pinnacle of our existence we hope will last forever. It never does. Surely, you can relate General?"

"Perhaps. Such moments are elusive."

"They are. But it is true power when you capture the allure of its search. The masses will chase this idea of 'Camelot' to the ends of the earth."

"You propose to hide this moment - this truth?"

"I propose to become it, General."

"To become truth?"

"Precisely. I am the masses' one brief shining moment of truth that can always be captured and recaptured."

"For what purpose?"

"For the chase General, and to serve our purposes. I am a recruiter for revolution of mind and soul which I have set in motion here, and around the world. We will continue to recruit them unwittingly by the thousands. They will chase the ambitions and the fears we set before them and overtake the succession begun by Cephas. St. Peter's square will be my footstool."

"Footstool? What use am I in all this? I am only a field general sir."

"Nonsense. That is dangerous talk General. Your power will be consolidated on the backs of your people and you will lead them to build your great society."

"Yes - yes sir."

"Use your double mindedness carefully General Sar. I lurk in the seams of the double-minded always availing my assistance for those seeking clarity. But in the end, allegiances must be decisive."

"Double mindedness sir?"

"Yes. Take the reluctant sentence of the prefect for example - an old acquaintance and one of your predecessors. I handed Camelot over to the prefect bound and beaten, ready to die. Finally, a man worth killing. And then he tried to wash his hands of the whole damned thing. In the end, condemned to two hells."

General Sar stood up in the empty room. He gazed through the metal bars of the small window. Then he lit a cigarette, grabbed the stack of papers on his desk and walked out the door.

CHAPTER 9
ONE BRIEF SHINING MOMENT

V.21 But we had hoped he was the one...

CAMELOT, SOUTH WALES, 516 A.D. - The castle could be seen from across the river nestled on the hillside in the heart of the kingdom. It gleamed in the morning sun rising above the thick green forest that surrounded it.

The sound of galloping hooves could be heard on the cobblestone road that led to the castle's open drawbridge.

"My men are beginning to arrive. We should head back soon."

"Oh, a while longer, Arthur. Row us to the bend and back."

He smiled down at her and kissed the top of her head. "As you wish darling." He leaned back on the oars and the small wooden boat rippled the water as they glided upriver. The morning was beautifully calm. The grassy riverbanks and arching trees reflected their canopy perfectly on the clear water.

Guenevere leaned her head back on her husband's chest and breathed deeply. This was how she had imagined things from the beginning. The kingdom was safe for the moment. A fragile peace was in place with the Saxons and the last embers of Rome were turning to ash. The fires of war had abated.

"Do you think this will last, love?"

"What's that, Guen?"

"This feeling of peace. It's real isn't it?"

"Of course it is. This is the time of our true reign."

"Our true reign?" Guenevere looked up at her husband.

"Yes love, finally an age where violence is not strength and compassion is not weakness."

He let go an oar and put his hand on her cheek.

"The triumphs of battle can now shine their glory on the kingdom and its people. And you are the people's queen, my Guenevere." King Arthur reached for the oar and continued rowing.

"There will always be more battles to fight Arthur. The Saxons will eventually grow restless and the ghosts of Rome persist still."

"Our knights will continue to serve the kingdom faithfully. We will shed the bonds of empire."

"Can you Arthur? Some say you fight for a world that does not exist. You have served Rome loyally but these are your people now. Rome is dead."

A white crane swooped down ahead of them and splashed across the water gliding to the far bank. It plunged its head into the water and shook out its feathers.

Guenevere looked up at King Arthur. "You are both British and Roman." She reached up behind her and pressed her hand to the side of his face. "Can you finally take us home my king?"

"Yes, my queen. I will take us home."

He swung the boat around and rowed back towards the castle.

છે.

HYANNIS PORT, CAPE COD, 1962 A.D. - "Hey Ken, How are ya?"
He tossed him the football forcing Ken to make a one-handed grab as
he juggled the cans of beer in his other hand. "I'm good Bobby."

"Jack's out back. You eat yet?"

"No, us regular folk work weekends. Whaddya got?"

"Well I don't know." He stuck his head inside the screen door. "Hey
Beth! Can you fix something up for Ken and bring it out back?"

"OK, Bobby," a voice inside answered.

"Thanks."

"Beer?" Ken held out his arm still holding the football in the other.

"Yeah." Bobby grabbed a can, cracked it open and took a quick
swallow.

"So what did you hear from the defense department?" asked Ken as
they walked around the house to the backyard overlooking the cape.

"Aw Ken, you know the drill. It's a bureaucratic nightmare."

"Tell Jack to get rid of the dead weight. We're riding high these days
Bobby. Let's use the capital."

"You know Jack. He wants to save it up. Use it for the next crisis."

"Had enough of those Bobby." He spotted the president sitting on the
porch tucked into the back of the house that looked out over the
ocean. He was reading a book.

"Jack, heads up!" He stepped forward and threw the football across
the yard. Jack looked up startled, threw the book on his chair as he
got to his feet and brought the ball into his chest on the lawn a few
feet away. He pointed at them with the ball, grinning.

"I've still got the hands Ken," he said as they reached the porch. "It's my back that kept me out of pro ball."

"Right," said Ken. He shook the president's hand. "How ya keeping Jack?"

"I'm great Ken," he said smiling. "How are you?"

"Couldn't be better. Even got some work done today."

"What? You're making us look bad. Take the rest of the day off."

"Thanks boss." Ken threw himself into one of the wicker chairs across from the president while Bobby stood leaning back against the white siding of the house, the football back in his hands.

"Beer?" Ken held up a can.

"I've got, thanks," said Jack reaching down and taking a sip from a green bottle.

"You get a chance to read the intel briefing today?" asked Ken.

"Yeah, nothing new - troop movements in Laos; Sihanouk in Cambodia has some concerns about a growing political rival - a General Saloth Sar. You know who's getting away on us is Duvalier in Haiti. He's turning into a nightmare."

"Then let's bring in their ambassador. You know who it is Bobby?"

"Uh... Mars - Louis Mars. His father served in government for years."

"Ok," said Ken. "I'll set up a meeting at the embassy. No need hauling him into your office."

"Why do I have to meet with him?" Bobby leaned forward from the wall. "What's this got to do with the attorney general? Have him meet with Ambassador Thurston. He'll see him, and he knows what's going on over there."

"Thurston's gone isn't he?" said Jack.

"Yeah," said Ken. "No one's officially commissioned right now.

"Well, who bloody well cares who goes Ken. Find Thurston and tell him to meet with him anyways or someone else in the Latin American bureau. I've got better things to do tan scold an ambassador."

"What are you scared of?" asked Ken. Jack grinned and took another swig of beer.

"I'm not scared Ken. I've dealt with bigger morons than Duvalier. I've got half the mafia families in the country after me. I can't be putting out every fire that comes up."

"Fine," shrugged Ken. "We'll get a junior hack to take care of it."

"Keep us informed," said Bobby. "We don't want this Papa Doc stuff messing with our Cuba plans. The geography is sensitive to every recon plane or vessel we put out there."

"And Khrushchev is watching," added Jack.

"I'll find someone," said Ken.

"I know a guy in the state department. I'll get him to meet with Mars," said Bobby.

"You know a guy?" Ken raised his hands, amused. "What, you're not naming names?"

"Don't worry about it," said Bobby stifling a smirk. "I'll take care of it."

"So, you'll take care of it now?"

"Yeah, relax. It's done."

Ken looked at Jack. "Your brother's a piece a work."

The president smiled. "I think Duvalier's going to be sore at us for awhile but it shouldn't hurt us. He hates Castro as much as we do. But we had to stop the aid. It's just been lining his pockets."

Bobby leaned back against the wall and tossed the football to Jack. "The biggest tactical mistake we made in Haiti was sending in the

Marines to train his henchman." He shook his head. Have you read about those guys?"

"The Macoute," said Ken.

"The Tonton Macoute," corrected Jack. "The gunny sack men."

"The what?" said Ken.

"Gunny sack," repeated Jack. "Apparently there's a Haitian fairytale about a man who runs around collecting kids in a gunny sack. Good bedtime reading."

"Sounds disturbing."

"Well, the pictures sure are. They wear straw hats, denim shirts and carry machetes and AK47's."

"Sounds more like the hired hands on Lyndon's ranch," said Bobby. They all laughed.

"Keep the press away from that one, Bobby," Ken said, still laughing. "Lyndon would never forgive us and Texas would be lost forever. Jack chuckled and finished his beer.

"Have a real beer," said Ken tossing a can to the president.

"Why not," said Jack. "A simple man, simple tastes."

"That's why you hired me."

Jack smiled. "So Appointments Secretary, who's up Monday?"

Ken had been a long time friend of the two brothers. They trusted him. As special assistant and appointments secretary, he was responsible for organizing the president's time and was the gatekeeper to the White House. Whoever wanted to meet with the president had to go through him.

"Nothing pressing. A couple meetings with congressmen from Oklahoma in follow up to your speech last month at Rice University. Great speech by the way."

"Thanks."

"Then a meet and greet with a member of the Roosevelt family. Mrs. Roosevelt is not well."

"I've heard that - a shame," said Jack.

Bobby crumpled his can and tossed it to the floor. He motioned for Ken to toss him another. "You should mention in your meeting with the family member that our civil rights agenda is an extension of many New Deal programs and is carrying on the spirit of President Roosevelt's vision and ideals."

"Good thought Bobby," said Jack nodding his head. "Ken, can you have a message sent from my office to Mrs. Roosevelt and the family echoing those thoughts? It's important that be conveyed."

"I'll have that ready for your meeting Monday chief," Ken said.

"That's great. Thanks."

The screen door opened and a middle-aged woman appeared carrying a tray of food and a jug of lemonade. "Here Ken, I fried you up a steak and there's a baked potato and some veggies. Keep these guys away from your dinner.

"Thanks Beth, looks delicious."

Bobby came over and smelled the tray. "Wow Beth, you outdid yourself again and wasted it on the company," he laughed.

"You get your nose out of Ken's supper. He probably hasn't eaten all day the way you guys work him."

"Aw c'mon," chuckled Bobby. "You hearin' this Jack?"

Ah, O'Donnell's tough. That's why we hired him."

"You boys finish that lemonade now," said Beth pointing to the pitcher on the wicker table. "That's enough beer for one afternoon. You guys are running the country, remember?"

"Thanks Beth. Don't tell Mom we each had two beers," said Bobby.

"Tell Dad we each had six and we're still running the country," Jack said chuckling. "He'd love that."

Beth laughed. "Yeah, he sure would." She disappeared inside.

"Have you given any further thought to Rome?" asked Ken looking at Jack and then over at Bobby.

"You mean the Vatican?" said Jack.

"Yeah, the Vatican. You're the first Catholic U.S. President. You need _"

"Ah Ken, I hate that label, you know that."

"I know you do but it doesn't change the facts. You need to go."

"He's right," said Bobby. "You need to go. They're a powerful ally and deserve your tacit support. Plus, we could use a backdoor channel to Pope Paul. They quietly have to hold the line against East Germany and the Soviet bloc in ways we barely recognize. They dwell in the eye of the storm. Who's to say they couldn't use our help from time to time."

"How do you think the press would frame it?" Said Jack. "I don't want to get bogged down in a religious standoff with the evangelicals. It'd be like campaigning with Lyndon all over again."

Bobby was pacing, with a hand on his chin. "Well, we frame it for them. We say the president's been invited to meet the new pope to discuss mutual issues of peace and global affairs. I can get in touch with our Vatican contacts and procure an invitation. I don't think it will be that hard."

"Ok," said Jack. "But it has to look like the invitation came from them."

"Easily done I think," answered Bobby. "Eisenhower met Pope John only three years ago so there's precedent here Jack."

"I don't know Bobby. It's a big risk and for what really?"

Ken shook his finger, deep in thought. He looked like he was trying to remember something.

"Get it out Ken. Whaddya got?" said Bobby impatiently.

Ken stood up and walked to the edge of the porch floor where it met the perfectly manicured lawn. "Ike's visit with Pope John. His pontificate was a strategic one -"

"Pontificate?" Bobby interrupted. "Whose?"

"The pope's," said Ken incredulously. "Presidents have mandates, popes have pontificates."

"Yeah, yeah, I get it," said Bobby. "Make your point." Jack smiled. "Yeah, let's hear it."

"Ok," Ken turned and faced them. "Pope John had an interesting two-part mandate. He wanted to open the windows of the church and provide an outreach to the world. Nothing new, they've been doing that for centuries going back to the first apostles."

"Well, the Reformation and most Protestants would argue its success but continue," Bobby interjected.

"Right. More importantly, Pope John wanted to take things further and open the *doors* of the church to establish and maintain relations with all nations of the world to foster peace and goodwill."

Jack pulled himself out of his chair. "They want a seat at the foreign relations table."

"That's right," said Ken. The biggest difference being - with the Vatican, no relations are 'foreign'. Even the Soviets and their godless satellites in Eastern Europe and Cuba, Asia, South America, wherever communism threatens - the church has been there first."

"And look at the Catholic and Orthodox faiths the world over. They permeate the deepest and darkest corners of political oppression and evil," added Bobby.

"What about *this* pope?" said Jack. He shares the same view? This open door policy of the Vatican still stands?"

Ken feigned disgust. "You mean the most powerful man on earth doesn't know the policies of his own global church?"

"Very funny Ken," said Jack. He chuckled. "No one ever accused me of being a good Catholic."

Bobby spoke up - "Pope Paul's mandate - his pontificate mirrors his predecessor in terms of carrying out the reforms of the second Vatican Council. I read it in a magazine at church but wasn't aware of the details of these reforms. I say we take advantage of it."

"Ok, let's quietly start making plans," said Jack.

Ken nodded. "Bobby and I will work out the details."

"When would I go?" asked the president looking out at the cape.

"Let's do it next summer," said Bobby. "Gives us the better part of a year to plan."

"Perfect," said Jack nodding his head. "We can make some progress on civil rights, Vietnam and this new NASA program. And re-election is only two years away."

"One week at a time boss," said Ken.

The president turned to the two men. "So really, why do they call the president the most powerful man in the world? Am I really more powerful than the pope?"

Ken and Bobby looked at each other. For once, his most trusted advisors didn't have an answer.

§&

AYACUCHO, PERUVIAN ANDES, 1962 A.D. - The beautiful buildings on the small campus of San Cristóbal of Huamanga University dated back to the seventeenth century when it had served as a catholic seminary. The Peruvian government, wanting to educate the local population, had reopened the campus as a university only three years earlier.

Nestled quietly in the Andes mountains in the city of Ayacucho, the region had long shed its bloody past as the last battleground for independence against the Spanish. Simon Bolivar had renamed the city Ayacucho, meaning *death corner* as a reminder to the lives that had been lost to the cause of freedom.

In the almost three hundred years since, the region's native population was largely unchanged. They were an impoverished hard working people tending their meagre farms in an isolated and forgotten region of the country.

Efrain Morote always looked busy scurrying about the campus with a load of books in one hand and a tattered briefcase in the other. As the new rector of San Cristobal University he had an agenda and was prepared to go to any lengths to see it established. He was both intelligent and inexhaustible. He also came from a wealthy family that had afforded him the opportunity to pursue an academic career purely on his own terms and interests.

This morning he had a meeting with his latest recruit - a philosophy professor who was proving to be an interesting character and promising asset. The rector hurried up the stairs to his office.

"Professor Guzman is waiting for you sir," said a young man seated at a small wooden table. "I already showed him in."

The rector nodded as he walked by and opened his office door.

"Professor, pardon my delay. Thank you for stopping by."

"My pleasure Mr. Morote. No pardon is necessary. It is very good to meet with you." The two men shook hands.

"Fine, fine Professor. So how have you been settling in these last couple months?" He carefully hung his hat on the coat stand in the corner and sat down at his desk.

"Very well sir, thank you. My fellow colleagues have been quite accommodating and many of the students are keen to learn."

"I'm glad you perceive such things. I have been very surprised by, shall we say the enthusiasm and vigour to which many of our young minds are willing to aspire."

"Yes, the energy of youth is a powerful commodity, Mr. Morote. With the proper guidance and direction they have much to offer this country."

"Well as you are probably aware Professor, I've asked you in today, to discuss the paper you submitted last month. It is a rather astonishing document." He eyed his professor carefully. "You do realize your aims and tactics are both dangerous and treasonous to the current national government of Peru, do you not?"

"Of course I do. My dear Rector, I would not place you in such a compromising position if I did not think you would be sympathetic to this cause."

"Well you're making an extraordinary assumption my dear Professor. This government does not make distinctions between sympathies and complicity. You are aware of the position you've placed yourself in? Not to mention this institution?"

"Yes, yes. That is why I came to you first."

The rector took off his glasses and studied the strange man seated across from his desk. "So to be clear professor, no one else has seen this paper - this manifesto?"

"No sir. You are the first."

"I see." The rector removed his glasses again and rubbed the bridge of his nose. He was momentarily lost in his thoughts. Where did this strange fellow develop such a brazen self-confidence? It bordered on delusional. He was an unsettling character.

"And Mr. Morote, it is not a manifesto as much as -"

"Pardon?" The rector looked up, his thoughts interrupted.

"The manifesto sir. It's not a manifesto as much as it is a directorate."

"A directorate?"

"Yes, that's correct sir."

Mr. Morote stood up and retrieved a key from his briefcase. He returned to the desk and opened the bottom drawer. "Ah yes, here it is," he said, taking out the professor's paper. "A 'Revolutionary Directorate' - you prefer Mao to Stalin." He smiled faintly.

"Yes, I do sir. The document is a very rough draft. It may take years before it can be properly ratified by its members. I imagine it will be redrafted several times over."

The man smiled a mysterious smile. Sometimes Efrain couldn't tell if this small, quirky man was looking at him or right through him.

"Professor Guzman, you have developed an idea, a set of principles and directives that are quite intriguing."

The man's expression did not change.

Efrain was exceedingly more sure of himself. Yes, this man would do the heavy lifting without blinking an eye but could never be fully trusted. He would serve as the rudder and let the professor man the throttle. In the end there would be no stopping him anyways.

He continued. "Professor, there is already some appeal as you yourself know for such a doctrine. A true communist state serving all can only arise through armed struggle followed by a series of carefully orchestrated political reforms."

"Yes, Mr. Morote. We have a nation of soldiers waiting to fight. The rural peasantry will constitute our base. Let Lima sleep for now. We will awaken the world in due time."

"That is precisely what I want to talk to you about."

"What about precisely?" Asked the professor.

"Timing."

"You need not worry sir. We will be patient in our plans moving forward. This organization will take three to five years to get off the ground."

"That is wise. Spend the necessary time cultivating your base. And do it quietly. Stay out of the cities."

The rector got up from behind his desk and stood at the window looking out over the campus. Beyond its small cluster of buildings and pathways the expanse of mountainous terrain swallowed them up on all sides.

"We are hidden here," said the rector. We shall use that to our advantage. Did you know that Ayacucho is known as the 'city of churches'?"

"I was not aware of that, sir."

"Yes, there are thirty-three churches here. One for every year of his life."

"Aha, how interesting." The professor sensed his rector had studied his paper more than he had let on. He waited for him to continue.

"Much can be accomplished Professor in a very short time. The body of work laid out by the early church exploded out of a mere three years of teaching." The rector turned away from the window and faced the strange professor who remained slouched forward in his chair, legs crossed.

"You need followers to ignite your movement. I will help you with this."

Professr Guzman nodded his head and pursed his lips to suppress a smile. "I am very much obliged, Mr. Morote. What do you have in mind?"

The rector walked across to the chalkboard that hung on the wall in one corner of the small office. He drew four boxes, two on top of the other. Then he carefully wrote above the upper left box - PROLE-TARIAN WORKERS.

"These of course are your wage earners; the workers of the nation who are the backbone of the movement." He wrote on the board as he talked. "Yes?" He glanced at the professor.

"Most definitely sir."

He wrote in the second box. "Here we have the PEASANTRY. These are your farmers."

The rector removed his glasses and pointed with them at the second box he had drawn. "The success of the movement depends upon the cultivation of this quadrant of society. The farms are the source of your ammunition to sustain the movement and spread its fire. These are your soldiers."

"You are suggesting they are our initial target?" The professor asked, still slouched forward in his chair.

"An armed struggle requires soldiers. They are the active weaponry for the movement. Without them, you don't get out of Ayacucho."

The professor nodded. He was finding it increasingly hard to suppress his excitement. He had made a calculated gamble and taken a consider-able risk. How far would the rector support him, he wondered?

"Next we have?"

The professor glanced up at the chalkboard and suddenly realized the rector was asking him a question.

"Surely Professor you know where I'm going with all this? The theory is not mine." He smiled wryly.

The professor couldn't contain himself any longer and sprang lightly from his chair. He was about to grab a piece of chalk from the ledge of the chalkboard but stopped himself.

He was the rector's student for now and would play the part compliantly.

"The petty bourgeoisie," he said.

"Correct," said the rector. He wrote in the lower left box - PETTY BOURGEOISIE. The small -"

"Mao's new democracy," the professor interrupted. "Pardon me sir."

"Yes, correct. Your friend, Mao's new democracy. The bloc of four classes nicely frames a plan of action and parallels your paper's thesis. Agreed?"

"Agreed."

"Now as I was saying, these small business owners and merchants will follow the first two classes perhaps reluctantly at first. They must be courted wisely."

"Well with this new president's tax policies and a roll back of social programs, small business should play favourably to our agenda," said the professor.

"That clown Godoy won't stay in power long," muttered the rector. "Soon a new junta will be offering more empty promises and small business owners will bite. It will take the workers and peasants to persuade them over time to join the movement."

The professor cocked his head. He wasn't sure he agreed with this assessment but chose not to pursue it. "Mr. Morote, what are your ideas about the last box?"

"Ah, our capitalist dilemma," he sighed as he wrote - CAPITALISTS in the lower right box. All private ownership and their profits must be confiscated and nationalized for the good of the whole."

"Not an easy task, Mr. Morote. Hence the need for armed struggle and revolution. There can be no gradual or peaceful transition. The capitalist forces will not allow it."

"No, they will not," said the rector. He pointed to the chalkboard again. "You must unite these three boxes against the tyranny of the fourth." He rapped his chalk on the word - CAPITALIST.

"You reject a market-based economy?" asked the professor.

"It is necessary but must be kept in the national interest. It must be governed under the dictatorship of the proletariat. I personally support import substitution. We need more local industry to increase domestic production. But ultimately, the working class must control all political power."

He pointed a long finger at the professor.

"Your roadmap for revolution must adhere to this model to be successful." The rector placed his chalk down, brushed off his hands and returned to his desk.

The professor smiled faintly and returned to his chair. "So, those are your conditions of support?"

"Those are my conditions." The rector nodded affirmatively.

"And your motives for supporting this agenda?"

"A fair question, Professor. I am tired and Peru is tired of these kangaroo courts that have governed indiscriminately for far too long. Military juntas have proven a multifarious lie. They are rarely corporate nor are they intelligent or principled."

"I am appreciative of your support, Mr. Morote." He leaned forward in his chair. "What support can you offer?"

The rector peered back at him over his glasses. "Professor, we can provide diversity in discussion, unity in action. You have heard this rallying cry before? Yes?"

"I have."

"Then welcome to your new headquarters. San Cristobal University is well-positioned to become a growing hub of communist thinkers and planners."

"And the students?" Asked the professor. "We can be open in our agenda?"

"Yes, recruit them. But teach them first. Prepare them for battle. They are sponges that will soak in the movement we develop within them. Ignite their senses, comrade."

The professor stood up and thrust his hand across the desk. "Yes comrade. We will ignite their senses and unleash the revolutionary power of the people to transform Peru and Latin America into the fourth sword of communism that will slay the imperialist dragons."

"The fourth sword?" asked the rector as he shook the professor's hand.

"Mr. Morote, apart from my teaching duties here I will be operating under a pseudonym to stay out of the public eye."

"Oh? A wise decision perhaps." He paused to think. "Yes, most prudent given the circumstances."

The professor leaned forward, a crooked smile appeared. "Our followers will come to know me as Chairman Gonzalo - leader of the Shining Path revolutionary movement. We will be sir, after Marx, Lenin, and Mao, the fourth sword of communism."

The rector tried to suppress his alarm. The professor's narcissism was both shocking and comical, he noted to himself. The man was a dangerous combination of ambition and naivety. His actions beyond the campus would officially be of his own doing. He released the professor's tenacious grip on his hand.

"I wish you success Chairman in this new organization, Shining Path. As your rector, I am always here to offer guidance and assistance. We have limited resources but will avail to you what can be offered moving forward.

"Thank you sir."

"Remember Chairman, stay out of the cities. Cultivate your base patiently among the farmers and workers. Geography is presently our best asset and defender."

Chairman Gonzalo nodded and opened the office door to leave. "Today begins our collective march, Mr. Morote. Someday we will mark this moment as Peru's shining counterpoint to the chains of its history."

He quickly closed the door behind him.

֍

THE WHITE HOUSE, WASHINGTON D.C., JUNE 1933 A.D. - "Forget about what the New York Times thinks. Rex, listen to me - if they want to coin my team, the 'brains trust' let'em. I've heard worse believe me - so have you." President Roosevelt held the telephone receiver in one hand and shuffled through a stack of papers on his desk with the other.

 He nodded as he listened.

"I realize that but to everyone else you're Assistant Secretary Tugwell and fair game like the rest of us. Give the *Times* the story, Rex. We're closing in on a hundred days in office and look what we've done - we've ended the bank crisis, passed dozens of laws, and it's only just begun. Get it out there."

The president nodded again, and walked over to the table near his desk as he listened. On the table was one of his model ships he liked to keep on display. He adjusted one of the sails on the USS Constitution.

"Yes, I'm listening, Rex, go on." He rolled his eyes. Secretary Tugwell was a strong advisor but like some of his other 'brain trust' advisors they sometimes thought they were lecturing back at Columbia University instead of briefing their commander-in-chief.

"So you'll speak with him, Rex?" He walked slowly to the windows behind his desk and pulled the drapes back to check the weather. It was clearing up. That was good, he thought. He had a meeting after lunch scheduled in the rose garden.

"Ok, good. Mention your work with Hugh Bennett on the Soil Conservation Service. Talk about it at length if you can. I want the whole midwest to hear what we're planning to do for farmers." He paused. "Yes, focus on the erosion issue and how we plan to battle the dust storms."

The president leaned against his desk and checked his watch. "Okay, I've gotta run. I will," he nodded impatiently. "I'll let the others know today. We're meeting at two.

He nodded quickly. "You as well, Rex. Thank you." He hung up the phone. Good, he thought. Tugwell was on the march and on target. Half the battle with his advisors he was discovering was keeping them focused on the tasks at hand while making them feel their ideas were being regularly incorporated into the administration's objectives.

In the distance he could hear the jackhammering had started again. He chuckled to himself. With all that had gone on in the last three and a half months, he and his staff had decided it would be a good time to start some major renovations on what was now being referred to as the West Wing of the White House. More executive offices were being added and he had decided to move the oval office to the southeast corner across from the rose garden.

The new location of the Oval Office would give him what he often missed - his privacy. At the moment, his office was in the center of it all and he was often in full view of the West Wing staff. A perfect microcosm of his position. The new office would allow him to slip comfortably back and forth from the West Wing to the main White House.

Eleanor had suggested it. Sometimes he secretly wished she sat in on some of his meetings to swiftly administer a good dose of common sense when needed.

They had both spoken at length, usually at the end of a long day neither thought would ever end, about how little time was available in the daylight hours to get things done. Time was a most precious commodity. And eight years was the blink of an eye. To waste a moment of it seemed absolutely criminal.

He looked at the set of plans lying on his desk and remembered he had wanted to speak to the architect about some scheduled White House events and how they would affect construction. I'll do that over lunch, he thought.

Something was bothering him about his conversation with Secretary Tugwell but he wasn't sure what it was. There was a missing piece, a doubting perhaps. Or maybe it was just settling into a new working relationship? The administration was young. And look at all they had accomplished. He quickly forgot about it.

President Roosevelt carefully picked up a section of the papers on his desk, placed them into a folder and headed out of the West Wing for lunch

He stopped just outside his office. There's no time, he thought. He wanted to get a handle on his briefing notes before his two o'clock meeting.

"Missy, can you have lunch brought to my office?"

"Of course, dear." She smiled at the president from behind her meticulously organized desk. Missy was the president's private secretary and had worked for him in New York, both at his Wall Street firm and in the Governor's office. They were close confidantes.

"Remember your doctor's appointment at four today," she said.

"Oh my, I forgot about that. Can we reschedule?" The president sighed.

She waved a finger at him. "I told you yesterday. Don't worry, he'll see you in your office."

"Okay thanks, Missy. If I'm late offer him a coffee or something. The day's running away from me already."

"Not a problem," she said. "He knows who you are."

He grunted and walked back into the Oval Office.

At five minutes to two, President Roosevelt was still buried in his briefing notes and a half dozen reports and summaries were strewn across his desk.

The phone rang.

"What is it Missy?"

"It's almost two. Mr. Moley and Mr. Hopkins are here and Mr. Farley may be a few minutes late."

"Oh god grief. I'd lost track of time buried in these papers. I'll be - "

"Sorry, Mr. Farley just arrived," said Missy.

"I'll be right there. Send them into the Rose Garden."

The president hung up the phone and collected his papers, carefully placing them in his folder in their proper order. It would be good to see the three of them, he thought. They hadn't had a chance to all meet together since the inauguration.

He slowly rose up out of his chair, collected the thick folder under his arm and headed to the rose garden to see his friends.

"Mr. President, great to see you!" said Harry.

"You're looking well Mr. President," boomed Jim. The burly Irishman shook his hand firmly.

"Thanks, Jim. It looks as if the duties of National Committee Chairman and Postmaster General are still serving you well."

Jim smiled. "No complaints, boss."

President Roosevelt turned to Harry, who was turning out to be an invaluable advisor.

"Hello Harry. Great to see you too. It's been awhile."

"Well, scheduling visits with the Oval Office isn't easy," he laughed.

"I know, I know," said the president shaking his head. "Sometimes Eleanor's amazed to see me at the end of the day."

Raymond Moley stepped forward and extended his hand.

"Hi Ray," the president shook his hand warmly.

Two staff members placed a carafe of coffee and a platter of fruit and pastries on the glass table situated on the lawn near a row of perfectly manicured green hedges.

"Help yourselves gentlemen," said the president motioning to the table. The four men settled into the folding wooden chairs around the table.

"I have just over an hour," said the president, opening his folder. You all received an agenda and accompanying documents?"

Jim patted the folder in front of him and Raymond and Harry nodded.

"Now I spoke with Secretary Tugwell on the phone earlier and he sends his regards."

"How's old Rex doing?" asked Jim.

"He's fine," said the president taking a sip of coffee. "However, he's concerned with some pushback from the *New York Times* on our economic policies."

"What's the big deal?" asked Jim.

"I don't know, you tell me? Rex was all uptight about being labelled a 'brains trust' member again."

Raymond waved his hand dismissively. "That was probably Kieran from the *Times* digging for a story again. Tell Rex to relax and give that Abercrombie the good news. There's plenty enough to go round for Pete's sake."

"That's what I told him Ray. Rex can't be getting a bee in his bonnet every time a reporter wants to throw a bit of dirt on his shoes. Something's eating at him."

"Well, he's not untouchable anymore," said Harry, winking at the president.

"You mean he's not at Columbia anymore," the president chuckled.

"Anyways, Rex did want me to tell you guys any dirt the Times throws our way didn't come from his interview."

"Aye, he's not here so we'll blame him anyways ahead of time," Jim said with a grin.

"Yeah, don't miss a meeting," laughed Harry. "There's always room under the bus for one more bureaucrat."

"On that note Harry, let's start with you." President Roosevelt pulled a section of papers from the top of his folder marked *Federal Emergency Relief Administration*.

"Thanks chief," said Harry.

The president leaned back in his chair, lit a cigarette and held the papers in front of him. "These preliminary FERA numbers look good Harry. Take us through it."

"Well Mr. President, in this initial quarter we're already ahead of projections forecasted to our year end."

"You guys didn't waste time," Jim said, taking a puff on his cigar.

"Nope. Now we've correlated these first quarter numbers by state and then by a variety of different cross-sections of the national population."

"Yes, I reviewed them last night," said the president shuffling through his papers revealing a series of colour-coded graphs. "Very interesting."

"It's a telling story both from our financial indicators and a political perspective we can monitor as we approach midterms," said Harry. "Of the allocated $500 million to date, we should have most or all of that dispersed by the beginning of the third quarter."

Raymond let out a whistle. "That's a lot of sawbucks on the backs of the taxpayer being shot out of a cannon."

The president looked surprised. "What's the problem Ray? You were one of the central architects of these programs."

"I know. It's just the optics of a lot of money being invested at once. I can see why Hoover was nervous introducing FERA last year."

"Paralyzed is more like it," snapped the president. "We were elected to take action. This program was specifically designed to take effective action immediately. I'd say we'd better be nervous about it. FERA cannot be allowed to fail. It's the backbone of the new deal we're offering America."

He motioned Harry to continue.

"Remember, this is direct aid being given to the states," Harry said, turning to Raymond. "Our primary goal here is to alleviate household unemployment through the creation of more unskilled jobs in state and local government."

Raymond nodded. "Right out of your playbook."

"How many jobs are we talking?" asked Jim.

"We want to put upwards of thirty million people to work."

Harry dropped a page on the grass and picked it up with an aggravated grunt. "Now, the breakdown of our job sectors, performance-wise is trending well even though it's early."

"Any surprises?" Asked the president.

"Well the workers and adult education programs are rapidly increasing their enrollment throughout the country and the professional programs are strongest in the urban centres which is to be expected."

Jim snickered. "I ran into Senator Russell from Georgia last week on the Hill. You should've heard his comments about public support of the arts for professionals."

President Roosevelt waved his arm in disgust. "Don't even want to hear it Jim. Anyways, Secretary Perkins has that senator eating out of her hand. Frances takes no prisoners when it comes to constructing strategic alliances."

"She's sharp," said Harry. "Send her down south regularly, chief. We need her lobbying for our construction sector of FERA. Here's the surprise - our construction projects are being received coolly by many states."

"I saw that. Why?" asked the president.

"State officials are afraid of the 'make work projects' label. Some are questioning the value of them."

"Well, do they want our help or not?" President Roosevelt slapped his hand on the table.

"They do," said Harry emphatically. "They're putting the money into projects but the construction sector has been a little slower out of the gate than expected with the exception of California, Texas and the northeast. But it'll compound in growth quickly as state and county planners get their act together and move forward with the tendering."

"Where are we struggling most?" Asked the president.

"Kentucky, Indiana, pockets of the midwest and most of the deep south."

"No surprise there," sighed the president.

Raymond interrupted. "Remember the timing of these implementations is key. We need to be in perfect coordination in the administration of public works and industrial recovery provisions. These projects need to happen fast to have an impact. The timing now is critical. Codification of industry can follow at a distance."

"Exactly, keep regulatory procedures in the cart behind the horse for now," said the president buried in his papers. Something else had caught his eye. "These numbers for consumer goods production look really good." Ray winced. He'd lost the president's attention.

"That's the biggest surprise," said Harry. He shuffled his papers and dropped a few on the ground again. He bent down to pick them up and a small gust blew them into the hedge behind them. "Aww, come on," he said annoyingly.

"That's classified information Harry," said the president grinning at the others as Harry made a dash for the hedge to recapture his papers.

"Check the hedge while you're there Harry," said Jim. "Hoover may have stashed a dossier on the Russians in there."

The three men laughed as Harry shook some leaves off his suit and sat down again, papers in hand. "Very funny guys." He laughed. "Where were we?"

"Consumer goods," said Raymond, chuckling.

"Right. The production of consumer and household goods is scaling well across the country. Canned food for one and textiles are performing really well." Harry paused. "Here's the thing -"

"The private sector," President Roosevelt cut in.

"Yep. They're not happy," said Harry.

"And who can blame them?" Raymond added.

"I suppose. Your thoughts Jim?" said the president turning to his post-master general.

"It's an awfully dangerous precedent. We can't be subsidizing production that's competing against the private sector. Ray's right. The private sector won't stand for it."

"So you're saying we axe it?" Asked the president.

"Phase it out as quickly as possible. Obviously it serves a purpose right now. But once the country gets its footing again and markets start responding we've gotta shut down government subsidized production."

"I agree," said Harry. "A shortage and necessity for these goods keep demand high for now but we need to step out of the way once private manufacturers find their stride again."

"Okay," said the president. "Then let's gear up for shutting this sector down in eighteen to twenty-four months. We can use its success for midterms with the added promise of phasing it out to silence the wolves. Anything else?"

"That's it for me, boss."

"Good. Thank you Harry." President Roosevelt refilled his coffee. "Anyone?" He motioned with the carafe.

"Sure, thanks," said Harry.

"I'll stick with the pastries." said Jim, grabbing his third. "Good thing I don't live here. I'd eat myself into oblivion."

"Eleanor runs a tight ship," said the president. "Some days I've tried." He refilled Raymond's cup and set the carafe down on the table.

"Now Ray, can you prepare a couple press releases highlighting the progress of FERA?"

"You bet. We should also focus some details on the south to invigorate our base."

"A southern Democrat won't stray far," said Roosevelt.

"Be careful Mr. President, they may break rank sooner than you think. They're desperate. How many of them know their incomes are 60% less than their northern neighbours?"

The president conceded a nod. "Let's keep the consumer goods production numbers out of the mix for now. We don't need to draw attention to potentially unfair competition practices."

"I'll focus on worker education and construction sectors," said Ray. "It'll be on your desk tomorrow morning."

"Thanks Raymond. We should also work on a speech for radio broadcast sometime in the next couple weeks to commemorate our first one hundred days in office."

Ray nodded. "Let's work on an outline over the next few days and I'll get to work on it."

"Sounds good."

President Roosevelt brought out a single page from his folder and placed it in front of him. At the top in small letters was typed: 'Normalizing Relations With the Holy See'.

The president removed his glasses and looked carefully at the three men seated around the glass table. Overhead a pair of purple finches surveyed the green expanse of the rose garden, circled its perimeter and gently descended into one of the nearby hedges.

"The last item on our agenda is a sensitive one and I ask that you treat it as such. At this point in time it's strictly confidential. Understood?"

The three men nodded.

"I've asked Jim to look into the question of re-establishing formal relations with the Holy See."

"The Vatican?" asked Raymond.

"Yes, in a manner of speaking. Jim, can you take us through it?"

"Thank you Mr. President." He reached inside a separate folder and placed a thin bound document on the table in front of him.

"Now gentlemen, first my disclaimer. As you all know I'm an Irish Catholic. So my personal bias in this matter I wear on my heart and sleeve." He waited for a good-natured dig but the table remained quiet.

"I'm also not here to debate the political jurisdiction of God upon the earth."

"Good to hear Jim," said Harry. "I've got a midnight plane to catch." Raymond looked down stifling a grin while the president cleared his throat and took a sip of coffee.

"Yeah, I get it," said Jim. "Several weeks ago the president asked me to look into the process of restoring diplomatic relations with the Bishop of Rome - Pope Pius XI and his ecclesiastical jurisdiction of the Holy See."

Raymond looked confused. "Forgive my ignorance here, but I thought we already had formal relations with the Vatican?"

"Surprisingly not since 1867. We did have formal relations with the Vatican going right back to George Washington."

"What happened?"

"Interesting story. In the aftermath of Lincoln's assassination a Catholic woman, Mary Surratt was hanged as an accomplice to Wilkes Booth. Her son, John was also accused. He fled to Italy and was given sanctuary by the Roman Catholic Church."

"Really?" said Harry. "And this terminated relations?"

"It was a contributing factor. Further anti-Catholic sentiment was fueled by alleged restrictions on Protestant worship in Rome around that time."

Harry shook his head. "I had no idea. So what's in place now?"

"For the past sixty odd years we've had a personal envoy appointed by the president to the Holy See."

"Has it been effective?" asked Raymond.

"Not really. Relations are purely symbolic. Periodic visits to Rome; an audience or dinner with a cardinal or on rare occasions with the Bishop of Rome himself."

"You mean the pope?"

"Correct," said Jim. "So there's a bit of the history." He turned the page of the bound document in front of him. The president and I have spoken briefly on why we think normalizing relations could be timely and how we might go about doing this."

The president nodded emphatically. "Take us into the meat of this Jim," he said, rapping his finger on the table.

Jim raised the document in his hand. "The ecclesiastical jurisdiction of the Holy See - of the Vatican has historically been and remains an extremely complex and powerful body in its scope and reach of authority."

Raymond cringed and shook his head slightly.

"Hear me out Ray. I know what you're thinking: The power of the Holy See isn't on the same scale as the political and military power of nation states. I'm not arguing that. I'm arguing the sphere of its influence can be far-reaching, blurring the geopolitical lines of jurisdiction."

"I'm not sure I follow you, Jim," said Raymond.

"The ecclesiastical jurisdiction of the Bishop of Rome does not begin or end in the Vatican. Its leadership and authority permeate every corner of the world as it governs the global Catholic church. It may be persecuted, oppressed and condemned in many countries but its national or regional influence remains."

"Are we looking here to circumnavigate our own isolationist sentiment?" asked Harry.

"Yes, for the time being," said the president eyeing Raymond.

Raymond caught the president's stare and decided to bite his tongue for the moment.

Jim, sensing some tension continued. "We need some strategic partners in the centre of the world. We need to improve our foreign relations to expand our own jurisdiction and influence to gain a stronger foothold in Europe."

"Do we?" Raymond objected. His isolationist stance was no secret to anyone who knew him.

"Look Ray, there are two sides to this. First, Europe is turning into a powder keg. Nationalism in Germany and Italy have made heros of Hitler and Mussolini."

"What concern is that to us? At this point," Ray added, knowing he had hit a nerve at the table.

Jim bit his bottom lip and breathed in. "Fascism is on the rise gentlemen in the heart of the civilized world. With the changing landscape in central Europe threatened not only by communism to the east but now these fascist regimes we need to quietly align ourselves with the highest moral authority on earth."

"The Southern Baptist Convention?" asked Harry.

The table was quiet for a second. Then it broke out in laughter. The four men laughed heartily and didn't stop. The tension was broken.

"That's terrible Harry," the president scolded, still laughing. "Some of my closest friends are Southern Baptists."

"Did they vote for you?" asked Raymond.

"Of course not," laughed the president. "Carry on, Jim."

"Okay." Jim was glad for the change in temperature around the table. "With apologies to the SBC, we'd like to tighten relations with the Vatican to show our solidarity with their ecclesiastical jurisdiction and also to gain a quiet inside perspective into the situation and pulse of central Europe."

"You mentioned there were two sides to this," said Raymond.

"Yes. The other side is perceptions here at home."

"Aha, now you're talking," said Raymond. "We need to keep pushing our agenda forward."

"That's right. We need to be showing clear consistent leadership at home and whether we like it or not, abroad."

"Some tricky maneuvering in this current geopolitical climate," said Harry shaking his head.

"It is," agreed Jim. "We're seen abroad as a growing imperialist giant by our enemies. At the same time isolationist sentiment here is at an all-time high and our proposed neutrality laws do little to change that perception from our global allies."

"So we're looking for some strategic moral high ground to anchor into without sustaining serious backlash at home or abroad," said Raymond.

"I think that's accurate," said Jim looking at the president. "With our decision to skip the London Economic Conference this summer we've already been accused of practicing economic nationalism and -"

"That's ridiculous," scoffed Harry.

Jim shrugged. "And our establishing of formal ties with the Soviet Union later this year is certain to ruffle some feathers," he added.

He closed the bound document in front of him. "In summation gentlemen, what this document outlines is our desire to re-establish diplomatic relations with the Holy See so that we can always find ourselves abroad in any part of the world. We choose to willfully engage a jurisdiction that unlike us and unlike any other nation state is not bound by the geography and politics of this world."

President Roosevelt leaned forward and folded his hands on the table. "Gentlemen, this mighty nation of ours is cut to shreds everyday by both ends of the sword by friend and foe alike, by its citizens who dwell under its protections and by foreigners who will never set foot on American soil. Still, we remain."

The table was silent.

"The Holy See is the mercy seat - the seat of grace on which God himself did appear. From this episcopal throne governs the apostolic succession. It remains today and reaches back through the ages, through the Gospels to Saint Peter himself, who along with St. Paul traveled to Rome and appointed the first successor, Linus who became the Bishop of Rome around the time the blood of these first apostles was spilled."

He glanced around the table.

"Seventeen hundred years later, many of this nation's beliefs and attitudes were gleaned from these events and truths. These are now our own adopted rules of engagement. And we cannot be tossed about on the seas of dissent aimlessly appeasing our enemies for the sake of a false peace that compromises these truths."

President Roosevelt looked up at the sun that cast its warm brilliance in the gray blue sky. "We will not neglect nor bleed away the guiding principles of this nation."

He threw some pastry crumbs to an eavesdropping wren. "That blood has already been shed."

As Ray followed the others out of the rose garden another set of guiding principles tore at his mind: *To every thing there is a season, and a time to every purpose...* But the president had set his course.

LINCOLN MEMORIAL, WASHINGTON D.C., August 28, 1963 A.D. - The crowds continued to swell, filling the grounds of the National Mall in front of the Lincoln Memorial and stretching down both sides of the reflecting pool. Behind the crowds in the eastern sky the Washington Monument reached up into the heavens towering over the quarter of a million people demonstrating in the March on Washington for Jobs and Freedom.

In the sea of people they stood and watched.

"I am happy to join with you today on what will go down in history as the greatest demonstration for freedom in the history of our nation..."

"You have a penchant my friend for seeking out revolutionaries."

"I have a penchant for seeking out truth, Rabbi."

"Now is the time to lift our nation from the quicksands of racial injustice to the solid rock of brotherhood. Now is the time..."

"This preacher has tapped into the pulse of his nation. Look at all these people holding signs, singing for freedom. This man's moment is upon him."

"Yes, but will their nation's leaders listen after the sun has set on the day. And on the days after that. Remember us, brother?"

"We were fools."

"We must forever conduct our struggle on the high plain of dignity and discipline..."

"Yes, we were."

The two men stood facing the young preacher, listening shoulder to shoulder with the enthusiastic crowd around them who holding high their signs, shouted their affirmations. In the distant background the stoic figure of President Lincoln presided over his hopeful nation.

Gamaliel nudged his colleague and pointed. "Look."

A few feet away a small girl held up a sign. It read - *John 3:16* in bright blue letters.

"It seems my friend your late night visit has not been forgotten."

He smiled and shook his head. "I am constantly amazed Rabbi at the enduring fortitude of truth. Centuries later... a new world... it is all coming to pass."

"We can never be satisfied as long as our bodies, heavy with the fatigue of travel cannot gain lodging in the motels of the highways and the hotels of the cities..."

"And how little has changed my friend. That is perhaps the most frightening truth of all for this world."

Nicodemus shook his head and smiled sadly. "Remember how he wept for Jerusalem and the temple. To see beyond the horizons of man is a heavy and incomprehensible thing." He surveyed the mass of humanity around them. He wondered what would happen to them all.

"We hold these truths to be self-evident that all men are created equal. I have a dream!..."

"We hold these truths to be self-evident Rabbi."

"Yes indeed.   And long before the constitution gave voice to an unknown land we were witness to these proofs."

"How could we have been so blind?"

"We did not heed the signs, my friend. We studied in the hardness of our masters."

"I have a dream that one day every valley shall be exalted..."

"Ah, the prophet Isaiah speaks even now." The rabbi listened and nodded.

"...every hill and valley will be laid low, the rough places will be made plain and the crooked places will be made straight and the word of the Lord will be revealed and all flesh shall see it together..."

"And all flesh shall see it together. Amen. The man can preach. I'll give him that."

Nicodemus smiled. Yes he can, he thought. Yes he can.

"Well, rabbi," he said taking in the jubilant scene. "Welcome to the 1960s."

FBI agent William Sullivan was bent over his desk, his pen shaking furiously as he wrote. The hour was late and his colleagues' offices had long since emptied.

Finally he threw his pen down and placed the memorandum in the outbox on the corner of his desk. He grabbed his suit jacket and hurried out the door, the words still fresh in his mind...

'In the light of King's powerful demagogic speech yesterday he stands head and shoulders above all other Negro leaders put together when it comes to influencing great masses of Negroes. We must mark him now, if we have not done so before, as the most dangerous Negro of the future in this nation from the standpoint of communism, the Negro and national security.'

CHAPTER 10
FAIRER MINDS

V.22 Some of our women amazed us...

DISTRICT JAIL RAWALPINDI, PAKISTAN, 1979 A.D. - The iron gate clanged shut behind her as she followed the jail superintendent across the dusty compound.

"You are wasting my time again," he said. "I told you last week not to come back until Thursday."

She did not answer. The ugly white washed prison always made her feel sick in the pit of her stomach even though she had been coming here with her family for almost two years now. The superintendent, a tall, rude man with a thick black moustache never failed to disappoint with his curt behaviour and acid tongue.

"I am not at your leisure child. Do you not understand that? You can visit your father as per my orders - and by my schedule."

Again, she did not answer. As long as he kept walking towards her father's prison cell she had nothing to say.

A child? She thought angrily. Would Pakistan ever change now that her father had been removed from power? She was twenty-five -

educated, bright and had seen more of the world than her father's jailer would ever see.

They walked into the building and the smell immediately hit her. It was awful. They passed through two steel doors and down a long corridor. The superintendent unlocked another door and held it open for her. He motioned to a guard standing halfway down another corridor.

"She has twenty minutes," the superintendent barked and slammed the door, locking her in the small corridor. The guard nodded and walked towards her a few feet and stopped in front of a wall of iron bars.

She walked up to the guard and turned to her left. He was sitting on the floor in his tiny jail cell, pencil in hand, writing thoughtfully.

"Hello father."

"Well, Pinkie! I wasn't expecting you today. What a nice surprise." He smiled and pulled himself onto his feet. He clasped her face in his hand and kissed her forehead through the steel bars. She kissed his cheek and sat down on the floor across from him holding his hand. How she hated these iron bars. They were a cold, undignified intrusion. They were everything her country had become under General Zia.

"Are you feeling any better?" She asked, putting her hand to his forehead.

"I'm fine my child. I've told you, don't worry about me. Allah will see to my needs. How is mother?"

"She is coping but misses you terribly." All she speaks of is the courts and a chance for an appeal."

Her father shook his head. "You must tell her that is not possible."

"But the lawyers have told us they can delay the sentencing while they push for a new trial. And we have the press applying more pressure in all the national papers."

Her father sighed. "It is no use. The supreme court has already passed judgement."

"But father." She looked at him and tried to squeeze away the tears that were hanging from her eyelids.

"Benazir, listen to me."

"No father. You are the prime minister, not that devil!"

"My child, look at me. Look at me." She raised her face up to him, angrily wiping away the tears that wouldn't stop.

"You are my eldest child, Benazir. You must be strong for your mother and the others. They will look to you for strength. What happens to me has already been decided."

"What do you mean?"

Her father looked at her. There was a calmness in his eyes.

"They will kill me."

"Father! Please don't say that." The courts will not allow it. Nor will the international community. Support is on our side!"

He held up his hand. "I know what kind of man General Zia is. The trial was a mockery meant to deceive. My fate is sealed but Allah has not failed us."

"Do not speak to me of Allah at a time like this!" She grabbed the bars with both hands. "We must get you out father. Only you can save us - the country, the family..."

He reached through the bars and lifted her chin with his finger. "Do you remember when you came with me to India?"

His voice was calm and made her feel as if there was a solution to all this madness and that reason and gentleness were still prevailing virtues.

"Yes," she said.

"The country was taken with you Benazir. Prime Minister Ghandi took a special interest in you. She saw what your mother and I have tried to cultivate in your mind and soul."

His stern gaze, for a second cut through her fear. "Your time is coming," he said.

Sometimes there is a knowing that permeates the deepest recesses of the soul. It cannot be explained nor can it be denied. Deep down beneath the anguish of her heart, she knew her father was right. There was a calling to be wrestled with amidst the anarchy and pain of a family and nation under attack.

"What is there to be done while Zia holds all of Pakistan under his command?" She asked, sidestepping her father's solemn abdication.

She was not ready to be passed a torch that was the extinguished light of her father who had raised a nation from the ashes of despair. Was this not the man who had ripped up that document at the UN Security Council and marched out in defiance?

"Zia will not last," said her father. "Of this we can be certain. He cannot consolidate power solely from the military. Pakistan is a democracy and the people will not tolerate his deceit for long."

"He needs to be removed immediately," she said, raising her voice in anger.

Her father put his finger to his lips. "Careful. The walls are listening. You must be vigilant my child as I know you have been. Zia will continue to watch the family closely. I fear things will become more difficult for you and mother while you are still in the country. It is imperative that your brothers remain abroad for their own safety."

"I will not leave father. Not on any condition."

"I am not asking you to leave Benazir. I'm asking you to lead. You are the eldest child and responsible for leading the family in my absence."

He smiled and took both of her hands in his. "You are also my daughter. The people of Pakistan are waiting for Benazir Bhutto to restore democracy and unite this great nation of Islam."

෪

CAMELOT, SOUTH WALES, 516 A.D. - The trumpets sounded from the crenelated battlements of the castle's lower wall which ran along the front facade of the castle connecting its two ascending turrets. Below the wall from which three brightly coloured banners swayed in the gentle breeze, three knights on horseback galloped across the drawbridge and into the castle's sprawling courtyard and disappeared down a narrow cobblestone road.

Deep inside the castle King Arthur heard the distant trumpets as he headed to the chamber. The morning's earlier conversation with his wife while rowing together on the river played on his mind. Yes, he felt an old allegiance to Rome but that loyalty was growing tired and irrelevant. He would not put his remaining men at risk any longer for a dying empire that cared little for their years of uncompromising service.

How many times had he let himself be strong-armed by Roman generals and bishops who preyed on his loyalty? He owed his men more. He owed his queen no less. His undying allegiance to the empire was indeed finally dying and there was relief in that.

His loyalty could no longer be split. His kingdom and its people deserved his undivided service.

Guenevere was right. True loyalty was above compromise. The kingdom of Camelot could no longer be both British and Roman. It was time to birth a new beginning. There would be a price to pay. The only question now remained: Could they bear the cost?

The soft glow of the inner chamber spilled out into the narrow passageway as Arthur approached the open doors.

"Are they all present?" He asked one of the royal guards standing at the entrance.

"They are your majesty."

He took a deep breath. He had entered this chamber on hundreds of different occasions. Now everytime he walked through these doors he felt a part of himself disappearing.

Once, there had been a hundred and fifty. Now there were twelve. A piece of him died with each empty seat. Each lonely chair represented a chronicle of stories, a volume of history that had passed away.

The chamber now felt more like a tomb.

The twelve remaining knights stood up and bowed to Arthur as he entered the chamber. He took his seat in the intricately carved tall-backed chair. The others then sat down spread out around the immense round table that filled the chamber. The iconic table's smooth, oiled wood shone in the soft light of the oil lamps which hung from the stone walls.

The table had belonged to Guenevere's father who had gifted the table along with a hundred knights to King Arthur as part of her dowry. The table had been taken apart, carted piece by piece and reassembled in the castle's special meeting chamber.

Only the knights who had served here and a few precious others had ever set foot in the chamber or seen the hallowed table. Most people thought it was merely legend and doubted its very existence.

Arthur looked around at the dozen knights seated at their table and was silently shocked by the emptiness of the room. He remembered when the table was loud and boisterous filled with the men who carried the hope of his kingdom to its furthest boundaries and beyond.

"Gentlemen, I had called you here today to discuss our border concerns with the Saxons." King Arthur paused. "However, it is time to address, indeed to proclaim a new truth."

"A new truth?" asked Sir Lamorak, seated across from the king at the far end of the chamber. "Are you proposing amendments to our code of chivalry?"

"No, Sir Lamorak.   I'm decreeing that we follow them without compromise."

A voice spoke up to Arthur's left. "If the esteemed code has been compromised your majesty, please inform us."

Arthur turned to his left. "Sir Percival, I'm afraid the guilty one is your king."

The men glanced around the table nervously. A few chairs over Sir Bors rose to speak but Arthur raised his hand and the knight quickly deferred and sat down.

King Arthur rose from his chair and placed his sword on the table. "From the time of its inception the code of chivalry has governed this table.   You have heard me say many times its two most coveted precepts are: To fear God and maintain his church and always to flee treason." The dozen knights either nodded or voiced their approval before waiting for Arthur to continue.

"How can we do this and serve Rome any longer? Her empire is crumbling before our eyes. It is essentially dead. We cannot pretend to live in the same world that our fathers fought for and vowed to protect."

Across the table Sir Lancelot spoke up. "Your majesty, many of us have been expressing these views for some time."

"Yes," said Arthur. "And today it was expressed to me in a way that I could no longer ignore. He walked away from the table and opened the door. "Come in your highness."

He led Guenevere into the chamber and immediately the knights rose to their feet and bowed. She smiled at them as Arthur took her hand and led her to the round table where they stood together.

"Your queen has brought me to the end of a revelation which should have manifested its conclusion in me some time ago."

He placed his hands on the great table. "Today is the time for Britain," he pronounced loudly.

"We will not fight against ourselves any longer in a compromised support of an empire that no longer exists. Rome is dead. It is time for a new oath to uphold the old."

Sir Lancelot removed his sword and placed it on the table. The other eleven knights followed suit laying their swords down in front of them in a sign of unity.

King Arthur looked around the chamber at his men. "The knights of the round table have spoken. We are of one mind, of one kingdom, and one nation under God."

He squeezed his wife's hand and turned to her. "Long live Queen Guenevere." He smiled.

"Long live Queen Guenevere!" the knights replied.

Arthur took his sword from the table and motioned the queen to an empty chair. Guenevere took her place and Arthur returned to his seat beside her.

"Please gentlemen, be seated. We have much to discuss and put into action. Our decisions here will not go unopposed. But let it be known to friend and foe - this moment marks the dawning of a new day and the hope of a new age."

CHAPTER 11
IN THE CRADLE OF DEATH

V. 23 They came and told us they had seen a vision of angels, who said he was alive.

Cleopas stood on the roadside talking with Camelot. A warm breeze had brought some relief from the heat of the afternoon and the few lazy puffs of cloud offered an occasional welcome of shade as they travelled. Carolus had crossed the road to buy bread from a local trader.

"His followers will be congregating all across Palestine once they hear the news," said Cleopas. He took the canteen from his shoulder and shook it. He took a long swallow and handed it to Camelot.

"And what are we to tell them?" Said Cleopas as Camelot drank from the canteen. "Many will come to us. We were closest to him, aside from the twelve. They'll want to know every wrenching detail."

Camelot handed the canteen to his traveling companion.

"I am a man of faith my friend," he continued. "But this vision these women spoke of - that he is alive? We all watched him die. There is no mistaking death."

The two stood quietly for a moment.

"There's something else," said Cleopas.

Camelot looked at him but said nothing. He waited for his friend to gather whatever it was he was wrestling with.

"Those women saw something. I recognized it in Maggie's eyes. There is an element of truth somewhere that is missing."

He looked across the road. Carolus was still waiting behind a family to buy food.

"Can I share something with you?" Cleopas asked, staring into the distance.

Camelot nodded.

"A week ago I experienced an inexplicable wonder. That I was witnessing something far beyond my knowledge. I was with a throng of fellow disciples as they laid their coats on the road for him."

He paused, stroking his beard as the memory flooded over him.

"I remember as we headed down the Mount of Olives the joy was uncontainable. It all spilled out of us in praise and thanksgiving. Some of the pharisees covered their ears and yelled at him to rebuke us. I'll never forget what he told them: "I tell you, if these were silent, the very stones would cry out.""

Cleopas was lost in his own thoughts. "The stones would cry out," he whispered. "That's what he said. And I believed him. I believe it now. The moment was too powerful to fully grasp."

Camelot seemed deep in thought as he listened.

"As we approached Jerusalem, some saw him weeping on his mount saying: 'Would that you, even you, had known on this day the things that make for peace! But now they are hidden from your eyes.'"

Cleopas shook his head in amazement. "Nothing was hidden from us that day. Our history from beginning to end was laid bare on that royal road seated on the back of a young colt. We belonged to the King, to serve in the courts of the Almighty."

He looked down the road as it narrowed into the distance obscured by the shimmering heat of the day.

"But where is that kingdom now? Her people have been abandoned to serve again the royal misery of Rome. And even the remnant of hope laid to rest has disappeared."

Carolus paid the merchant and took the bread in his hand. He walked back across the road to the two men who stood waiting for him.

* * *

SAINT PETER'S BASILICA, VATICAN CITY, December 5, 1965 A.D. - The sea of red began to disperse from the immense meeting hall of the basilica, its dazzling columns and archways towering their ornate beauty over the masses below. Small groups of cardinals and archbishops congregated noisily around the expanse of the meeting hall or spilled out into the adjacent atrium.

The Second Vatican Council was in its last days of meetings after nearly four years of scheduled deliberations convened by the late Pope John XXIII back in 1962. The Roman Catholic Church was pushing itself into modernity in an attempt to reconcile its truth and relevance with an ever changing world. Many argued it was an impossible task. Others condemned the task as an exercise of shameless compromise.

The debates and consultations over the proposed final, fourth constitution - *Gaudium et Spes*, the joys and hopes of the world, were proving most difficult of all.

Józef spotted the archbishop across the aisle and began to make his way over to him.

"Józef."

He looked behind him. It was Cardinal Heenan, Archbishop of Westminster.

"This will never pass. Such ambiguities in the language are laughable. Surely your bishops in Krakow would agree?"

"Are you proposing amendments John or just venting?" He could see the cardinal bristle at a junior colleague calling him by his Christian name.

"Well, it's hard to amend claims that are so broad as to obscure their intent."

Józef was young but wise enough to refuse the bait of adversaries circling their opposition in an attempt to win over any dissenting views.

"In respect of your valued contributions to this council Cardinal, I have no doubts as to your sincerity. However your perfunctory objections to these latest statutes are deeply concerning."

"Do not mistake my convictions for lack of thought or consideration for any of these measures," said the cardinal trying to hide his displeasure. "You are still young in this council Józef. The world will not bow to the will of the church upon command as you so eagerly assume."

"Please John. I seek to engage those wills, not dictate them. And any innocence of youth was shed at the hands of the Nazis."

Cardinal Heenan held up his hand. "I didn't mean to imply a brevity of life experience. Only that this is a massive theological shift and the current drafting of many of these statutes in *Gaudium et Spes* lacks any clarity."

"As I stated here yesterday, I don't entirely disagree with that," said Józef. "I'm not against sharpening the text of these statutes under question. But we need to leave some openness in interpretation in offering leadership and guidance without crossing the appropriate bounds of national sovereignty and individual freedoms."

"I'm all for openness," said the cardinal. "But change must be enacted slowly and cautiously."

Józef bit his tongue. There wasn't much point arguing. Cardinal

Heenan would be casting his vote against *Gaudium* when ballots were cast. But Józef would not be swayed.

"We'll see you tomorrow," he said to the cardinal who gave him an unenthused wave and walked away.

One thing was certain, thought Józef. The world neither changed slowly nor cautiously. And the church was still trying to catch up from its debilitating doctrines of the First Vatican Council almost a hundred years earlier.

Cardinal Heenan would have been much more in step with that First Council, thought Józef admonishing himself for even thinking it. But it was true.

The First Vatican Council, convened in 1869 by Pope Pius IX was prorogued a year later as Italian soldiers entered Rome in a bid to bring the Papal States under a united Italy. The council had been attacked by several European powers even before it had officially begun as rumours circulated around a possible enunciation of papal infallibility.

The rumours turned out to be true. Two doctrinal constitutions were passed with the second leading to violent clashes against the church all over Europe. This second constitution enounced the supremacy of papal jurisdiction and its dogma of infallibility.

It read: *'The Roman pontiff when he speaks ex cathedra, that is, when he, in the exercise of his office of his supreme apostolic authority, decides that a doctrine concerning faith or morals is to be held by the entire Church, he possesses, in consequence of the divine aid promised him in St. Peter, that infallibility which the Divine Saviour wished to have His Church furnished for the definition of doctrines concerning faith or morals; and that definitions of the Roman pontiff are of themselves, and not in consequence of the Church's consent, irreformable.'*

It was a denunciation of modern rationalism and liberalism. Józef shuddered inside as he recalled his study of this doctrine years ago. He had been deeply conflicted by its archaic and insular focus. Was it any wonder that so many lost heart and turned to nationalist promises such as French Gallicanism and a host of others throughout Europe, he thought.

Suddenly it seemed sheer nonsense to shelve the reforms of *Gaudium et Spes*. The joys and hopes of the world in the twentieth century and beyond needed to be promulgated by the Church, not tepidly administered through nineteenth century dogma.

The Church was a full century behind! It had become a slow, lumbering institution. The once daring and enduring succession was now tired and lethargic.

He needed to find his trusted ally.

He saw him heading out of the hall. "Raúl," he called and waved his hand.

Archbishop Henriquez turned and smiled when he saw Józef. "I saw you chatting with the Archbishop of Westminster. How did that go?"

"As good as you'd expect. He'll vote against it is my guess."

"Let him. History is on our side. I doubt there'll be more than a hundred who vote against it. You worried?"

Józef thought for a moment. "No, but I do wonder if we're ratifying an incomplete draft which needs to be refined. It is ambiguous and vague in several sections."

"And naively optimistic?" Asked Raúl with a slight smile.

"Perhaps - well, of course it is. But if we don't set the bar and believe in the unfailing hope of the precepts handed down to us, we might as well shut these doors for good."

"We don't need or necessarily want a rigid outline of dogmatic statements," said Raúl. "There's room to stretch in *Gaudium's* current version. It will be palatable for the traditionalists and seized as an opportunity by the reformers. We'll cut a wide swath of support right down the centre. It'll pass."

"Let's hope so. I imagine Heenan and others will lobby hard into the night."

"Don't worry about them. They'll have their book publishers ready to paint their side of history. John's a very bright man. I just wish he could see the world I see every day. London and Santiago are very different places of human existence."

Józef nodded. He liked Raúl, precisely for statements like that. He lived and worked in the harshness of his people's struggles. South America and Eastern Europe had more in common than most realized.

"*Gaudium et Spes* is of deep significance to me. I've been fighting for its precepts my entire life Raúl, much like yourself in Chile. These precepts are the visions of my childhood."

"You gravitate to the political reforms of nations," said the Chilean archbishop, with the hint of a smile.

"Of course, but through encouragement, not coercion."

"Politics does not make such distinctions my friend."

"I think it's quite implicit within the doctrine," said Józef leafing through his draft copy of *Gaudium*. "I specifically like two statements:

'To carry out such a task, the church has always had the duty of scrutinizing the signs of the times and of interpreting them in the light of the Gospel ... We must therefore recognize and understand the world in which we live, its expectations, its longings, its often dramatic characteristics.'

"And this statement," he said, turning the page - 'Any act of war aimed indiscriminately at the destruction of entire cities of extensive areas along with their population is a crime against God and man himself. It merits unequivocal and unhesitating condemnation.'

"The first statement introduces a spirit of sober thought, intent, and interpretation while the second draws the line of the church and humanity in the sand. It sends a clear, practical message to the global *politique*," said Jozef.

The Archbishop of Santiago smiled. "You are an ambitious young man. A product of your country's history wrapped in the church's pursuit of human justice in the world and the rights of God's children."

He paused. "I identify with something different in these doctrines. For me, it's a simple but fundamental shift that can unlock our shared concerns of social justice and human rights."

"What's that?"

Raúl leaned towards Józef. "How we as priests of the succession engage the world out there." He pointed to the windows of the basilica. "And it starts with how we engage its congregations in here."

"I'm not sure I understand you."

"Forget global politics for a moment."

"I'll try," said Józef, smiling.

"Listen, if we are to establish relations with nations we must establish relationships with its peoples. This starts in the church. Finally mass will no longer be celebrated solely in Latin, but in the language of the congregation. Why was this not done in the waning days of empire?"

"I'd keep that question to yourself Raúl - at least until you're off the tarmac and headed home," Józef laughed.

"Dangerously provocative, but true nonetheless," said Raúl who then turned his back to Józef. "Can we discuss the sacraments Archbishop?"

Józef looked confused. "Of course."

"No, we cannot," said Raúl, turning back to Jozef. "Not until I face you!" He said, raising his voice. His voice then became quiet. "The single most important statute of this council is this: Priests and bishops will now *face* the people instead of the altar during mass."

"I'm not sure I agree it's all that significant."

The Archbishop of Santiago raised his hands in frustration. "Stop thinking politics for a moment. Think of the shepherd and the flock."

Józef was quiet in thought. "You're speaking of stewardship," he said.

"Yes, on a brand new scale of shared terms. This is significant for every priest, bishop and deacon who is actively part of the apostolic succession. They must face the people to connect and gather in the flock to lead the people down the road of succession - the path of peace."

Raúl, stoked with the fiery passion of his convictions was just getting started:

"I believe the pews have been screaming at us for centuries: 'Do not hide your face from us!'"

Józef raised his eyebrows and was about to respond but the archbishop was on a roll.

"Genesis: 'The Spirit of God moved upon the *face* of the waters'... Ezekiel - 'I will not hide my *face* from them any longer, for I will have poured out my Spirit on the house of Israel.' Shall I go on?"

"Please," said Józef. He was enjoying this impromptu homily.

"The face of God's own must be recognized and his voice must be listened to in a language that is understood so that the flock of God's people can first recognize and then respond. These are all deep matters of consequence that resound their outcomes in the full span of history as a living requiem to the dead and a light for the living."

Raúl paused but didn't take his eyes off his lone congregant.

"Even the country pastor does not come armed alone with the standing of his own merit. He comes armed and filled with the Spirit and power of the succession and the belief that it will sustain him to his - last - breath." The preacher drew out the last three words for emphasis.

"For those who think a divine life is a road of ease, privilege and quiet existence tell that to the martyrs of centuries passed, tell that to Pope John, tell that to St. Ignatius of Antioch as he was mauled by the lions of Emperor Trajan. Tell that to Cephas and the pride of Tarsus who appointed bishops, St. Ignatius among them, and in death, helped birth the succession so that the whole of humanity might not perish. We must be able to see through the realities of our current circumstances.

Józef nodded, enjoying the moment.

"These are not new truths. They are new revelations of ancient truth - pieces of the sun piercing the deepest mysteries of the divine cosmos."

Raúl gave a satisfactory sigh. "You get all that?"

"Amen," said Józef. He smiled.

The Fourth Constitution of the Second Vatican Council was ratified two days later by a vote of 2,307 to 75.

Cardinal Heenan of Westminster remained bitterly opposed to the doctrine. He claimed, *"Gaudium et Spes* was written by clerics with no knowledge of the world."

* * *

The small café in Cercado de Lima was barely noticeable amid the bustle of tourists and locals in the Peruvian capital's historic downtown district.

A woman sat alone at a table by the window. She held a glass in her slender hand - deep in thought. A long dark veil hung over the chair beside her.

This new wave of revolution. She growled softly. Perhaps it was best to leave them to their own devices?

She raised her glass of port and swirled it in her hand. The oceans washed up the sides, crashing down in rounded dark, thundering waves. Her thoughts screamed at her from inside the glass as she caught her reflection in the flickering candle light.

She set the glass down with eyes closed. The flames subsided and the smashing waves retreated back to their master in the icy depths.

Yes. Each to their own devices, she thought. That would be best.

* * *

CANGALLO PROVINCE, AYACUCHO, PERU, 1981 A.D. - The small pastoral town of Chuschi lay nestled in one of the endless green fertile valleys surrounded by lush rolling hills and beyond them the mountains of Ayacucho region.

On the outskirts of town a group of a half dozen men and women loaded supplies into the back of the rusted white pickup truck backed up to the entrance of a tiny brick house with a whitewashed exterior. The three women were dressed traditionally in their wide brimmed hats and colourful dresses while the men wore faded dress shirts and khaki trousers.

"Let's move out," one of the men said, slamming the tailgate shut. "You and Ernesto get in the back with the women. Watch our tail for policia." He handed the man a shotgun who then jumped in the back of the truck with the others.

"Keep that out of sight."

An hour later the truck pulled off the dusty gravel road that switch-backed up into the hills. They followed a narrow dirt trail deeper into the bush until they were forced to stop in front of some fallen trees that blocked the road.

"You sure it's this way?" Asked one of the men in the passenger seat.

"These were the directions I was given," said the driver.

Suddenly the trees started to move and two men dressed in fatigues stepped through the branches pointing their AK47's at the white truck.

"Everyone out!" One of the soldiers yelled. "All hands in the air. Line up." He pointed to an area away from the truck. The three men and women did as they were told.

"Any weapons?" Asked the other soldier walking to the truck.

"There's a shotgun in the back."

The soldier hopped up and found the gun. "You here to shoot squirrels?" He chided holding up the shotgun.

The other soldier laughed.

"You will not be needing this any longer. If the chairman deems you fit you will all be recruited and trained with new weaponry and supplies."

He turned to the fallen trees on the trail. "Clear the gate!"

Two women in fatigues emerged from the other side of the fallen trees and cleared them to either side of the trail. The man threw the shotgun to one of the women soldiers and motioned the new recruits back onto their truck.

"Everyone in the back. This little jalopy will come in handy for scouting and supply runs," he said as he hopped in behind the wheel.

The other soldier followed the recruits onto the back of the truck keeping his rifle pointed at them. The truck bounded up the trail towards the camp.

As they rounded a bend in the narrow trail they were met by three larger trucks barreling down on them. The lead driver honked his horn and waved his arm out the window motioning them to get off the trail. The soldier veered the small truck to the side but there was still not enough room to pass. The large truck skidded to a stop as did the convoy behind him.

"What's going on?" Shouted the driver of the lead truck as he jumped down from behind the wheel.

"New recruits Commander," said the soldier from the back of the white truck.

He swore. "Terrible timing. We're headed to Maria Parado. There's a push back from the *policia*. They've penetrated the northern boundary of the liberated zone."

The commander looked behind him. "Move off into the bush so we can pass. Hold them until we get back. We may be a few days."

"What's going on here?" A man appeared from the middle truck. He looked to be in his mid-forties with black disheveled hair and dark sunglasses.

"Recruits sir," said the commander.

"Ah, I see. Please, let's interrogate them quickly."

The soldier in the back of the white pickup ordered them out and had them line up for an impromptu inspection.

"Where are you from?" Asked the man in sunglasses.

"Sir, we are from Chuschi."

"Interesting," he muttered under his breath. "Names?"

"I'm Eduardo, this is my brother, Ernesto and our close friend, Juan. These are our wives."

"Were you followed?"

"No sir."

"Can I see your instruction papers and identification?"

Eduardo reached into his shirt pocket and handed the folded papers to the soldier who handed them to the man questioning them.

He looked them over carefully.

"Good. These are legitimate." The man approached the six recruits lined up in front of him. He removed his sunglasses and smiled.

"My name is Chairman Gonzalo. I am the supreme leader of Shining Path. Welcome to the guerrilla movement."

Behind him the commander shifted his weight impatiently, kicking at some underbrush alongside the trail with his foot.

"Patience Commander," said the chairman, not looking back.

He walked up to each recruit and studied them carefully before returning to his spot in front of them. He put his hands on his hips. "There is much teaching and training to be done but we cannot settle you into camp now. We have an urgent field mission to attend to." He put his hand up to his beard, thinking. He looked back to the convoy and then back to the recruits.

"You will all come with us. Consider it a field trip," he said clasping his hands behind his back. "I'll brief you on our way there."

He turned to the soldier standing beside them. "Get them into my truck and have someone from camp retrieve the pickup." He motioned to his top soldier. "Lead the way Commander."

The three trucks kicked up a cloud of dust as they bounced down the road. After an hour of driving the switchbacks the road widened out and straightened as they passed through a large valley before heading back up into the hills.

"We'll be there in about an hour," the chairman said, raising his voice above the incessant revving of the trucks as they traversed the steep terrain. They all sat on crates in the truck bed which was covered over with a tattered green canvas. The opening at the back between the tailgate and the canvas canopy brought light into their cramped quarters revealing the ground they'd covered.

"Listen up recruits." The chairman kept his sunglasses on despite the darkened quarters of the covered truck bed. "We are headed to Maria Parado. You are some of the first wave of guerrilla fighters of Shining Path who will be responsible for establishing and securing a liberation zone in this district. We are currently battling some local resistance for its control. Once we have established a liberated zone we will secure it and then establish another. Through the establishment of these zones we'll control all six districts of Cangallo Province and push out from there."

The villagers smiled and nodded.

Chairman Gonzalo leaned forward so they could all hear him. "There are about thirty thousand people to mobilize in Cangallo Province over an area that covers two thousand square kilometres. We cannot reach everyone obviously. But in each liberated zone we'll actively recruit local policia and local politicians. They'll greatly help us in expanding the movement."

One of the women whispered something to her husband. "My wife says it will spread like wildfire," said Ernesto.

The chairman laughed. "Yes, yes! It will be a ravaging wildfire that will consume all of Peru and then the Americas with the vision of Mao. We'll show the world that his revolution is still alive."

"She was there when Shining Path burned the ballot boxes in Chuschi last year," said Eduardo.

The chairman scowled and shook his head. "Lima chose to ignore our warnings. That government pretends we do not exist. We will show them otherwise. The fires of Shining Path will consume every ballot box in Peru and every dissenting voice that attempts to cast a vote against us."

"We will be armed?" Asked Eduardo.

"Of course."

"When will they be issued?"

"As soon as we get off this truck. You're sitting on them," he said slapping his hand on the crate beneath him.

"Kalashnikovs are secured through our contacts here in Ayacucho at a local university."

"Where do they come from?" Asked Ernesto.

Chairman Gonzalo smiled. "No one knows for sure. But apparently they are shipped from a port on the Baltic Sea."

The truck slowed down and turned off the road into the bush. It stopped a few minutes later and turned off its engine.

The chairman checked his watch. "Ok, everyone out. We'll unload, establish camp, and walk from here. Listen to your commander and remember - you are no longer civilians."

He lit a cigarette. "You are guerrilla fighters."

* * *

The city was awakening to a new day. Much of Jerusalem was still in an uproar over its recent events. Yet, as the rippling circle of distance receded from the epicentre of history on that warm spring day, most of the world remained portentously unaware that earlier that morning history itself had been split in two.

Maggie had stood transfixed in that spot halfway between the tomb and the crest of that scarred hill. Years later, she would share her thoughts about that early Sunday morning.

Though she was by then an old woman, her passion and zeal were just as evident as the morning her and mother stormed in on us with the news that would quite literally breathe new life into the world.

"The vision that we had that morning that he was alive both collapsed and inflamed us with a power beyond the realm of human experience," she said.

"It was undeniable the fire that raged within us. It was an explosion of time's most precious promise in the cradle of death. The rock crying out to release its master.

There is no reasoning what the heart knows to be true. It simply is.

I often think back to what brought us all together in that epoch of time. Why was I chosen to be that close to it? To even share in his brief lifetime on earth?

I never did understand it. After the dispersal of those that were closest to him, I sometimes forgot all that had happened.

Imagine? Even after all of that.

And then it would hit me all over again.

To witness the obliteration of history does not wear well transposed against the dreary hours and minutes of the day. Time and its passing have become an intrusion - a consuming shadow marking only time's lost soul - its master.

Soon these last witnesses of which I am one, will rest in the wholeness of the grace that preceded us. There are always two longings that tug at the human chains of existence. This world is not a resting place for either the righteous or the wicked. We are the dust that is swept into the living grace of the tomb.

I do not despise this life nor do I embrace death. But the preceding chapters are too beautiful not to ponder at length. History has set its course and split the rock of the tomb.

And I have seen it tremble.

* * *

BOISE CITY, OKLAHOMA, 1934 A.D. - This was the eye of the storm. The winds were surprisingly calm as the gray Dodge automobile with its open top pulled out of the dusty barren town at the western edge of Oklahoma's panhandle and headed into the parched farm land.

The country was flat with shallow rolling hills shortening the red darkened horizon in every direction. The hot July sun was trying to peek through the thick haze that hung in the air as far as the eye could see. The remains of withered crops of corn and wheat on either side of the road stood scorched and beaten. Like twigs and scrub protruding from the sands of the Sahara, sparse crop fields dotted the landscape like burial plots in the drought-stricken breadbasket of the nation that now had become a desert wasteland.

The Great Plains and Prairies from Texas straight up into Canada had been ravaged by drought and dust storms that covered everything in a thick blanket of sand and dirt. The relentless winds created huge dunes which covered tractors and implements and sandblasted their way through wood farmhouses. Farm families were leaving in droves all over the country in search of work and a better life elsewhere.

"This is unbelievable," said President Roosevelt as he stared out at the decimated countryside, his arm hanging over the side of the Dodge.

"And this is a calm day," said Senator Gore from the front passenger seat. "Usually traveling in the open air is unthinkable. Still, we'll be covered in dust in no time. The winds are a monster that kicks up red black clouds of rolling dust that balloon to ten thousand feet in the air."

"We got a severe taste of it last month in D.C. New York City was completely black apparently," said the president.

Senator Gore, who was blind, turned to the backseat. "It all started here. You guys wouldn't believe what people witnessed. It looked like armageddon. We lost millions of tons of topsoil in just that one wind storm alone. It was all sucked into the atmosphere and blown two thousand miles away to the Atlantic."

Secretary Perkins who was seated in the back between the president and Senator Russell from Georgia could scarcely believe the devastation.

"How do these dust storms generate such a vortex of power?" She asked.

"It's actually static electricity," said Senator Gore. "It forms between the dry ground and the dust and becomes a staggering force of energy. They say it generates enough electricity to continuously power New York City."

Thomas Gore was in his second stint as a Democratic senator representing his home state of Oklahoma. Much like Senator Russell, he was a reluctant supporter of the president's New Deal programs but had seen enough value in some of the reforms given the precarious state of the country. However, his support was waning in the face of what he saw as economic socialism that paid out the "dole" through federal programs at the expense of state and local input and private enterprise.

When the president accepted his invitation to tour the hardest hit regions of Oklahoma, the senator had invited Senator Russell, a close friend and colleague to join him. Russell, a leading member of the conservative coalition in the senate and strong ally, was increasingly angered by Roosevelt's tight federal grip on economic and social policies.

They along with others were coming to a similar conclusion. The New Deal was dangerous. It was wasteful, arrogant, and some argued, un-American.

"What's the livestock situation around here Tom?" Asked Senator Russell, looking at a small herd of cattle grazing in the sand and red dirt that drifted against one side of a water trough. Aside from a few remaining brown patches of grass, no remnant of grazing land was in sight.

"Cattle are dying every day. They cut them open and their stomachs are full of sand. Never mind the struggle for feed and water."

"And rainfall levels?" Asked Frances.

"Pretty much non-existent. We haven't had a good rainfall in over three years. A tenth of an inch is a soaker these days," said Tom.

He turned to his driver. "Take a left on Temple Road and we'll stop on the hill crest overlooking old Durnin farm."

"I know the place. A real shame," said the driver.

The Dodge slowed down and turned off the lonely highway onto a gravel road. Reddish dunes of topsoil rippled by the wind filled the shallow ditches on either side.

"So Secretary Perkins, Richard tells me you made it down to Georgia last year?"

"I did. Richard and Governor Talmadge gave me a nice Southern welcome."

Frances was lying. She still hadn't forgotten the 'pleasant snub' and warning she had received but had come to accept it as the political wranglings of amassing working capital.

"I stayed at the mansion a few times when Richard was governor. The food was good but they're a crafty bunch," said Tom with a grin.

"Oh, how's that?" Said Richard.

"Well you deep Southerners ply the unsuspecting with food and drink and then go for the jugular. Sound familiar Frances?"

Frances laughed. "Not sure how to answer that in front of my boss."

They laughed.

"I'll answer that for you, Secretary," chuckled the president. "Politics tastes a lot better in the South. I don't mind being taken behind the woodshed if I have a drink in my hand. It's a lot less fun in a cabinet meeting."

"Old Tom's the master of the woodshed," said Richard. You hear about his recent dustup on the senate floor"?

"Oh, come on," said Tom smiling.

"Let's hear it," grinned President Roosevelt.

"So Tom got in a heated argument during a debate with a rival senator whose name I'll not mention. In the heat of exchange this senator muttered under his breath, 'If you weren't blind I'd thrash you to within an inch of your life!' So Tom leaps up and hollers, 'Blindfold the son of a bitch and point him in my direction!'"

The car rang with laughter.

"Bravo Tom."

"Thanks Mr. President," he chuckled.

The Dodge rolled to a stop at the top of a hill. In every direction the scarred countryside wept its red tears of dust leaving its thick ugly coating on all that could be seen.

The driver got out and opened the rear door for the president who slowly pulled himself out of the car, leaned on his cane and rubbed his aching legs.

The other four passengers got out of the car and surveyed the eerie scene around them.

"It's barely four o'clock and it seems like dusk," said Frances.

"I know," said Tom. "It's a strange feeling and when the wind's up it's even darker as the dust clouds blot out the sun. Some farmers have told stories about their chickens going to roost in the middle of the day thinking it's night."

"That's unworldly," said Richard.

Tom pointed to the stretch of farmland to their right. "All this land, about twelve hundred acres was once farmed by a man named John Durnin. He was a typical local farmer with a large family, some cattle and his crops. Then in '32 the rains stopped and the winds came. Like everyone else they figured they could hang on till next year. It only got worse."

"Is that the farmhouse?" Asked Frances, pointing to the remains of a wooden roof poking out of dune of red dirt a quarter mile in front of them.

"It is. Incredible isn't it? It was a family home of eight just four months ago."

Frances felt a lump in her throat. The group stood in silence, visibly moved by the scene in front of them.

Tom continued: "John and his wife lost four of their six children to dust pneumonia - an epidemic that's spiralling out of control. This past spring John loaded up his few belongings onto his truck and headed to California with his wife and remaining two children - didn't even bother to shut the front door behind them. Locals fear the beginning of a huge migration out of the region. Whole towns and communities could be wiped out. Families are starving, malnourished and living in dire poverty with little hope of recovery."

President Roosevelt could scarcely believe what he was looking at. How many prayers for rain had gone unanswered? He thought.

He spotted something moving about fifty feet behind what was left of the farmhouse. Two lonely swings swayed back and forth on a solitary forgotten swing set. It sent a cold chill through him.

As he gazed on the two swings swaying eerily in memorial to Tom's story, he had a vision of two small children laughing and swinging through the warm blue sky of a sunny summer day. Fresh laundry hung from a nearby clothesline in the farmyard that was surrounded by an ocean of gold. The endless wheat fields swayed in the calm breeze shining their glorious provision in the sun's radiance.

The living promise and prosperity of a nation's food stores.

Senator Russell broke the silence. "This is unacceptable. It's a national disaster that's being ignored in the rest of the country. We need action now."

Tom nodded. "Rain or no rain. We can't continue like this. Communities are already losing families, schools, churches, and businesses. It'll only get worse."

The president turned to Tom. "We need to fast track these programs for soil erosion conservation."

Frances noticed Senator Russell roll his eyes.

"Doesn't help us now, Mr. President," said Tom grimly.

"I know, but our drought aid plan will. It provides emergency cash for farm families, livestock feed, equipment, and medical aid to start," said the president.

He slowly reached down and sifted the fine dust in his hands. "Alongside that we desperately need funds for research into better land management practices."

"Better land management?" Said Richard, clearly annoyed. "Now you're gonna tell farmers how to run their business?"

"We're going to help them Richard," said the president. "Take a look around. The land has been beaten by the plow for generations. We can blame the lack of rainfall and send up all the prayers we can muster but we've still got to deal with the problem and fight it wisely."

'Sounds more like the Soviet policies of Stalin," said Russell.

Frances shot the senator a look of disdain. She was about to say something but her boss beat her to it.

"Oh, here we go. Give me a break, Senator. Are you really that ignorant? Look around you?"

The president was mad and the gloves were off. "So we ignore this crisis like Hoover and propose nothing? That's what you'd prefer?"

Richard tried to back down slightly. "I'm not saying do nothing but we can't regulate our way out of every problem." He glanced over at Tom hoping he'd come to his defense.

"Well what do you want to do about all this?" President Roosevelt waved his arm over the desolate breadbasket of America. "We have to fight back."

"What do you mean, fight back?" Said Richard impatiently.

"These are the farmers' battlefields Senator, where the timeless act of sowing and reaping has rewarded a nation's people. But now the land itself is screaming for help."

Richard ignored the president's heightened illustration. "Well to start, give the state more credit and assistance to fund their own programs," he countered.

The president grimaced. "For goodness' sake Senator, we just asked congress to appropriate over fifty million dollars in economic and social assistance for the Great Plains region."

Tom piped in, "Mr. President there's no doubt to the sincerity of your administration - "

"Don't throw backhanded platitudes at me Tom."

Frances had rarely seen the president this angry.

"Fine. All I'm saying is we need more state-level programs and less federal interference."

"Ok, less interference. Got it. So now we have fifty different programs, proposing fifty different solutions. Sounds great Tom. Have at it. How much money do you need for that?"

Tom didn't answer.

Richard tried to jumpstart his argument again.

"We need to be putting more money into helping our industries boost production. We need to be manufacturing tractors and implements, making sure local processors can remain viable and hire more workers as they grow."

"Ah, of course, a corporate bailout." The president threw his hands in the air. "For jobs of course."

"Yes, exactly for jobs. Help industry reinvest in itself and give people sustainable work. These are small to medium-sized businesses, hardly big corporations."

"And give each state a carte blanche and say 'manage all this on your own,'" finished the president. He gave Richard a cold stare. "And how do jobs in industry help farmers like John Durnin stay on their farms?"

No one said anything.

"What good is a new tractor in this state of hellbound conditions? What good is a processing plant if farmers can't grow or harvest a crop?"

"So keep pumping out federally subsidized programs. That's your solution," said Richard sarcastically.

"I want to keep farmers on their farms!" Shouted President Roosevelt.

"Without farms, there is no industry. Without farms, there are no towns or cities to support industry. You two should get that more than anyone - especially me, an old coot from Hyde Park."

Frances casually stepped in between the men.

The men retreated to their corners - Tom and Richard leaning back against the hood of the car and the president at the edge of the road surveying the remnants of Durnin farm.

"As you're well aware, we have a new offshoot of labour unrest from farm migration," said Frances.

Tom nodded. "It's becoming violent. We've had clashes between labour and management all over Oklahoma. They blame the panhandlers as they call em."

It's spreading across the country. These labour clashes are exacting a terrible death toll," said the president.

"Industrial urban areas will see more and more migrants I'm afraid," said Frances. "Locals claim the influx is driving down wages and creating a lot of social unrest in communities and cities."

"All the more reason to promote local industry here," said Richard quietly. National unemployment is almost twenty-two percent." He wasn't interested in another war of words with the president. "With all the campaign focus on the 'forgotten man' these new consumption taxes are a crippling load."

"Blame your friend Hoover for those excise taxes. His Revenue Act came in five months before I did," said Roosevelt. "And national unemployment is down two percent."

"And Hoover's Revenue Act is paying for your new deal policies," grunted Tom.

The president didn't respond.

No one seemed interested in sparking further debate. Spirits were low and patience was thin.

"We need to burn the candle at both ends," said Frances. Market solutions can work hand in hand with government programs. This disaster is unprecedented. It'll require joint action from all sides."

Tom brushed the red dust from his face with his handkerchief. "Let's head in - we don't want to get caught out here. The winds are coming. I can feel it."

The driver got out and opened the back door for the president and then for Tom who got into the front seat. Frances and Richard climbed into the back.

The car started down the road and headed back towards town. No one said a word.

Frances recalled a recent conversation with Ray Moley and what he feared most come midterm elections - "The harvest is past, the summer is ended, and we are not saved."

* * *

Colonel Basbug leaned against the large boulder that had been rolled away decades before.

"This is it," said Kalashnikov standing near the opening. "I came here that evening. I wanted to see him. I had to make sure. But I couldn't move the stone or penetrate the rock."

The moon cast an ugly shadow across the tomb's entrance.

"It must have been guarded."

CHAPTER 12
AT THE ALTAR(ING) OF HISTORY

V. 24 Then some of our companions went to the tomb and found it just as the women had said, but him they did not see.

RURAL MARYLAND, June 8, 1968 A.D. - "When is he coming Mommy?"

"Soon," she said, scooping the toddler up in her arms. The sun was warm as they approached the clearing. She wondered why she had come. His politics had never gripped her the way it had others. Like her father, she didn't believe in the myths of Camelot. But a small part of her had hoped the myth could be true - that his road to the presidency would somehow be realized...

"One change of heart can alter the course of history!"

Robert F. Kennedy stood back from the microphone and waved to the roaring crowd inside the chaotic International Amphitheatre. The convention floor was a sea of screaming Kennedy supporters jubilantly waving their signs and drowning out the frenzied, countering cries of the Humphrey and McCarthy campaigns.

Outside, the city streets of Chicago resembled a war zone.

Mayor Richard Daley had lobbied President Johnson to bring the upcoming Democratic Convention to Illinois to bolster Democrats' support across the country.

He would soon regret it.

Youth from every part of the country protesting the war in Vietnam descended on the city in droves to send a message to a Democratic Party that was covered in the blood of American soldiers. The nation's youth were returning home in body bags at a staggering rate of two hundred lost souls per week.

President Lyndon Johnson's decision not to run again in the upcoming election did little to assuage the anger of a nation. He was still the emboldened and battered face of the Democratic Party.

John Martin, campaign advisor for the Kennedy team pushed his way through the pulsating mob as Kennedy made his way off the stage.

"Bob, Humphrey's guys want to talk to us."

"Forget it," yelled Kennedy who could barely hear above the noise of the convention hall. "We're not cutting any deals. We can win this thing."

"Good, my sentiments exactly," yelled John into his friend's ear. "I'll tell them to forget it. They've already gone to McCarthy."

Kennedy smiled and gave the thumbs up to a nearby television camera. "Sounds desperate."

"They are! I smell an upset here. The whole building is sensing it now."

"Keep our guys on McCarthy supporters right to the end."

"We are. Delegates are moving away from him and finding us. They see the tide is turning."

Bobby flashed a grin and then turned serious. "What's the situation on the streets?"

"It's complete mayhem. Kids are getting beat up by police and arrested. The real story's out there."

"Yeah, and Daley's trying to hide it from the rest of the country. He's got LBJ and Humphrey dancing at his beck and call."

"Bob, look behind you. See that?" His campaign advisor pointed up into the crowd.

"Whatya looking at?"

"Look. Daley's getting an update from the chief of police," said John.

"Unreal. He's calling the shots on the street and right into Johnson's ear in D.C."

"Yep. Humphrey's just a puppet," said John. "We gotta win this now on the next ballot. We lose and the whole country will crush Humphrey in November."

Bobby nodded. "I wonder how Hoffman's doing. I feel bad convincing him not to cancel things."

John waved his hand dismissively. "Abbie knows how to run a protest. Don't worry about him."

"Well I worry. It's a full scale riot out there."

"He's got his job, we've got ours. The worse it is on the streets the more Humphrey looks like another LBJ. Besides, Humphrey's got Daley and the president. We need Hoffman to rally the people on our side."

Kennedy didn't answer. He was worried.

"If we win the nomination on this ballot, you let the press know I'm going to Grant Park to calm things down right away. And I mean right after our victory speech. We're giving two - one here and a second one outside."

"Are you serious? Bad idea. Geez Bobby think. It's not safe."

Kennedy held up his hand. "We're doing it. Make the arrangements to tell the press immediately after - only if we win."

John rubbed his forehead. "Okay. I'll let Rather know and we'll get word out to Hoffman - one way or another."

Over the next hour as they waited for the ballots to come in, the mood in the convention hall only intensified. CBS cameramen jostled with security and police and some in full riot gear, patrolled the exits. Above it all, Mayor Daley scowled over the unfolding scene.

This was not how he had envisioned his rendezvous with history.

Almost ninety million Americans were glued to their television sets watching for the first time in any network's history the chaotic and furious spectacle of a political convention. It had captured a city and now a nation by storm. And for all the wrong reasons. The chaos in the streets had become the story.

On the far side of the convention floor Vice President Humphrey surrounded by secret service held one hand to his ear and a phone to the other.

"It's bedlam in here!" He yelled into the phone.

"No, we're not out of this yet. We're working McCarthy's delegates hard. They want nothing to do with Bobby. They know his apostasy has no bounds."

The vice president was startled by a nearby scream and some shouting as a scuffle broke out in one of the lower rows of seating. Three policemen hauled out a pair of youth who had unfurled a 'stop the war' banner just in time for the cameras to catch it before it was ripped from their hands.

He looked at one of his security agents. The agent shrugged.

He returned to his phone conversation.

"Right,

Yeah, Daley's on it.

Okay, well we'll be here to the bitter end.

 Keep you posted.

Thanks Lyndon."

Some members of Kennedy's team were huddled around a small television set tuned into CBS News. With cringed faces they covered their mouths at the brutal scene that was raging just outside their doors. Amidst the noisy din of the convention hall a familiar voice blared out of the television which had been turned up to full volume. They could still barely hear it...

"Reports out of Chicago continue to come in and the images are cruelly graphic and disturbing. The National Guard has been called in to quell the protesters. Lincoln Park is awash with tear gas, billy clubs and hand-to-hand combat as police in riot gear and gas masks engage students in a battle of ugliness that continues to escalate..."

"Somebody better update Bobby on this," said one of his assistants.

John rushed over to them. "Hey, results are expected shortly!"

"Have you seen this?" Said a campaign assistant to John.

"I have. Bobby knows about it."

The hot, crowded amphitheatre exploded with anticipation at the announcement. "Ballots are in? Ballots are in!" People shouted everywhere and to know one in particular. "Results are coming!"

The campaigns gathered en masse and the whole floor shook to a fevered pitch. Humphrey, Kennedy and McCarthy signs danced above the wild throng of supporters drowning out the cries for order from the convention chair who stood on stage to announce the results. Finally the noise of the crowd abated in a stubborn halting decrescendo.

"I have here the results of the second ballot."

A roar of anticipation reverberated through the crowd.

The votes for McCarthy were read out throwing the crowd into pandemonium.

"I told you!" shouted John shaking a team member in front of him.

McCarthy had finished third. It was down to Humphrey and Kennedy.

"I will read out the results of the top two candidates in alphabetical order."

The chairman placed the results on the podium. The crowd waited tensely, standing and rocking in anticipation.

"Total votes for Vice President Humphrey..."

The results were announced and the crowd was ignited into the throes of a panicked confusion. Was it enough?

"We need thirteen hundred to win!" shouted John. "It's going to be close."

The chairman waited for the piercing volleys of confusion from the crowd to die down. The moment was upon them.

"Total votes for Senator Kennedy..." The convention hall went silent.

"One thousand, three hundred -" The crowd exploded with a deafening roar drowning out the rest of the announcement. It didn't matter. Kennedy had won the nomination.

Bobby stood in amazement and watched as the crowd roared its approval and disapproval at the upset. He grinned as John shook him and his campaign team celebrated around him. He looked up at the sea of Kennedy signs dancing in victory.

This one's for you Jack, he said quietly.

Then the roar intensified as if the entire amphitheatre, the streets outside and the entire nation watching was suddenly aware of what was playing out upon them.

President Johnson had lost. And Vice President Humphrey's campaign had died in his back pocket.

"I accept your nomination," said the senator above the deafening roar of the crowd as he stepped to the podium.

That was all he remembered of the acceptance speech. He had kept it brief - purposefully. He had another promise to keep.

John ushered him towards a side door as people clambered to touch him and offer their congratulations.

"A reporter from the Post found Hoffman and told him about your planned victory speech at Grant Park," yelled John in the senator's ear.

"Good," said Bobby. Is he okay?"

John nodded and grabbed him by the shoulder. "They're waiting there right now - by the thousands."

Suddenly, a group of large men in suits pushed their way through the crowd and confronted Kennedy's small entourage, blocking their exit. Out from the group stepped Mayor Daley. He pushed his nose into Bobby's face.

"I heard about your little side deal with Hoffman." He shook his head. "And after all I did for your brother."

Kennedy didn't respond.

"Get out of my city," snarled the mayor quietly.

He glared at the protesters on a nearby television screen, now celebrating in the park. "And take that commie trash with you."

The woman stood alone at the edge of the overgrown embankment near the clearing in the lush Maryland countryside. She held her toddler on her hip as the marvellous daydream faded from her mind and the roaring triumph of the amphitheatre faded into a low rumbling, that seeped over the gravel and weathered ties of the railroad track in front of her.

There would be no Bobby Kennedy in Chicago to snatch impossible victory from Humphrey at the Democratic nomination in August. She felt foolish for dreaming to the contrary. Were Greek tragedies tragic because of what was lost or because of what was believed in the first place? She wondered.

Instead, Bobby Kennedy would be making his way past her on his way to Washington. That was why she stood by the tracks and waited.

The low rumbling intensified as the train came into view. She had asked her father to come but he had politely declined as she knew he would. "That Bobby is worse than LBJ. At least the president stands for something," he had said more than once. "Those Kennedys complained about J. Edgar Hoover's trampling of civil liberties while Bobby as attorney general authorized more illegal wire tappings than anyone in history."

She hadn't argued. Earlier in the campaign California Governor, Ronald Reagan had mocked Bobby Kennedy's claim to a bevy of conservative policies, saying he sounded increasingly more like Barry Goldwater. Her father was quick to tell her Bobby wanted to be everything to everyone just like Roosevelt some thirty years earlier. A 'sandcastle in the clouds' politician he had called it.

The twenty-one car hearse approached them and the train greeted mother and toddler with a short whistle as it slowly rolled by. She caught a glimpse of the casket in the last train car as it passed. The failed promise of Camelot was gone in an instant as the rolling wake pulled the last car further and further down the distant narrowing track. It was the final procession and last remnant of the Democratic Coalition begun by Roosevelt's New Deal over three decades ago. She watched until the last car disappeared carrying Senator Kennedy to his final resting place near his brother at Arlington Cemetery.

She wondered if anyone else had come to the tracks to pay their last respects. Another lost utopian dream, left forever hanging in the fractured balance of a nation's consciousness. The magnitude of hope in one man, more myth than truth. This isn't real, she thought. None of it is - and probably never was.

* * *

WARSAW, POLAND, 1979 A.D. - The plane touched down on the runway and taxied towards the terminal where a swelling, jubilant crowd stood waiting.

History is a faithful sojourner, he thought as he looked out the tiny plane window - boldly racing towards a collective destination where the vast dimensions of time narrow to its sacred point - the altar place of life itself.

And now the native son was returning home for the first time as its presider.

The lead domino would be Polska.

"A new and dangerous enemy has emerged, Colonel."

"Who is this?"

Kalashnikov leaned back from the huge black chair and tossed the letter on his sprawling desk. "He has taken his place as the two hundred and sixty-fourth in the succession."

"Yes, I've heard."

"He has come in the same year as the man from Qom," said Kalashnikov.

"Sayyid?" Said the colonel.

"Yes. Sayyid must be unleashed as the new face of the Persians. We are destined to do battle."

Three million strong packed into Warsaw's Victory Square exalting their love for their native son who only a year earlier had been chosen to preside in the great line of Cephas.

"Wujek! Wujek!" The crowd cried out to him with great affection and gratitude. Their 'uncle' had not forgotten them.

Wujek adorned in his white cassock and skull cap ascended onto the platform and stretched out his hands to the sea of humanity that overflowed the city square. The whole city shook with a joyful roaring that reverberated across the bleakness of Eastern Europe's Iron Curtain and refused to subside.

In the clenches of Soviet communism, Wujek stood underneath a towering cross radiating its hope in the European heartland of the hammer and sickle.

"Let your Spirit descend!" Wujek implored his people. *"Renew the face of the earth, the face of this land."*

The crowds thundered their approval. He had spoken directly to the forces of hope of a nation and its people. It was a daring and passionate call to action - bring your gifts to the altar and change the story of the world around you.

Wujek continued, boldly raised the white pages of his message to the world: *"Therefore Chrystus cannot be kept out of the history of man in any part of the world."*

The crowd broke out into song. Such words had never been spoken publicly in Poland before.

"Chrystus wygrywa... Chrystus króluge!" They sang. They sang as one voice - freely and unafraid in the shadow of death.

The dome of St. Peter's had become the dome of the free world.

This was just the beginning.

Outside the snow was falling. Red Square was largely empty as the biting chill of winter crystallized the air and the setting sun cast a pale glow over the bitterly cold city.

Kalashnikov retreated from the window and returned to his desk. He had dismissed the colonel for the evening. They had both agreed, the borders of Polska should have been barred shut to this emerging enemy. He was proving a most troublesome and powerful adversary.

Still, a plan was taking shape. They already controlled a great swath of nations to the west. There was no need for reinvasion.

He reached for the letter on his desk and read it again. No, he thought. We will set our sights on a much more strategic target. Once it has been subdued we will unleash the full wrath of our screaming demons in all lands ripe for revolution.

He walked over to the fire. The shadow of an extended hand and long jagged fingers danced in the pale light on the old stone fireplace as he dropped the letter into the flames. With an excited rush they tore across the charred blackened page racing to devour the bold text.

The letter was from the Vatican. It had only four words: *DO NOT ATTACK POLSKA!*

CHAPTER 13
THE TOMBS OF THE ASSASSINS

V. 25 How foolish you are, and how slow of heart to believe all that the prophets have spoken!

PHNOM PENH, CAMBODIA, 1975 A.D. - The army officer came out of the bombed out hotel with an armful of framed artwork and South Asian sculptures. He threw

them in the back of the jeep and climbed behind the wheel.

"Did you get everything?" Asked Lieutenant Kim who was waiting in the jeep.

"Everything that wasn't in pieces. The rats have eaten the rest or used it for their nests. There are still bodies in there."

The lieutenant shrugged. "The Americans did us a favour. The carpet bombing helped us empty the city. Year Zero will empty the rest of it."

General Sar had officially implemented a new calendar immediately after the fall of Phnom Penh to his victorious revolutionary army. It was now officially Year Zero.

Kim had received his orders six weeks ago from his commanding officer.

"The general has ordered that we purge our history and begin again with a new revolutionary culture. The artist, the intellectual - all urban trappings must be destroyed. There must be no link with past traditions and cultural life. Year Zero marks a true beginning."

It made sense to Kim. There was nothing left in the cities anyways. Many neighbourhoods were levelled by the bombing campaign and had been rotting away for nearly two years since the Americans had ended the air attacks.

Now General Sar had captured his jewel. The capital city was theirs. Nol's teetering government would soon collapse much like Sihanouk's five years earlier. Then things would start to improve, thought Kim.

The officer pulled away from the hotel and they raced down the deserted street. Soldiers were everywhere emptying homes and businesses, throwing family belongings, clothes, books, office equipment and furniture in big piles that littered the sidewalks.

"Minh is predicting victory by the fall," said the officer, adjusting his helmet.

Kim nodded. "He may have it even sooner. Hanoi is winning the intelligence war largely through the Viet Cong pushing hard in the south."

"Some say Minh will turn on us next," said the officer swerving around a huge mortar crater in the road.

"Never. When we push Nol out Minh won't have any need to interfere with us."

They headed towards the Southern outskirts of the city to check on the army patrols that were supervising the implementation of Year Zero. The military had commandeered hundreds of civilians to carry out Sar's reforms. Most had silently complied. Those who hadn't were immediately shot.

But now Lieutenant Kim had a growing problem. The bodies were beginning to decay and disease was quickly spreading amongst the razed city's remaining population - as sparse as it was. Rumours were that disease was ravaging the countryside at an alarming rate as the forests and rural villages were overflowing with people who had been marched out of the cities and larger towns.

Several blocks away the smell hit them. They covered their faces with their scarves but it didn't matter. The awful smell of burning human flesh filled their nostrils until their eyes ran. Neither could speak.

Kim looked across the street and for a moment nothing seemed to come into focus. The horror was too much to take in. He felt a wave of nausea sweep over his body. He leaned out the jeep and vomited.

"Lieutenant, are you alright?"

Lieutenant Kim nodded, embarrassed.

They passed a battery of anti-aircraft guns beside the burnt out remains of a primary school. Houses, schools and businesses were razed to the ground at the orders of General Sar to ensure no civilians returned to their homes. Only a few party and military officials occupied the city.

Kim remembered the prophetic pronouncement of General Sar years ago in Ratanakiri Province. Taking Phnom Penh had been seven long years in the making. That military advisor, Kalashnikov had proved he could be trusted. How odd that the general had not spoken of him since.

He had long forgotten his urgent questions of the protracted war that strange man, Kalashnikov had prophesied. Sar had refused to elaborate. It made little sense to Kim.

What made even less sense were the almost daily edicts by General Sar. All food sources were ordered destroyed or confiscated. Now even fishing was banned and planting rice was punishable by death. Communal farms were being established and strictly regulated to meet the country's needs. Private reports from Kim's superiors were all humanitarian aid was being refused.

Kim checked his watch and spit out the taste of vomit in his mouth.

Half a day gone, patrols to check, bodies and a city full of its silent past to burn. Decades and centuries being lost in hours. Year Zero at ground zero, he thought.

He glanced at the destroyed art pieces thrown in the back of the jeep and at the burning piles of people's belongings that dotted the streets. He felt a gnawing panic in his stomach. Phnom Penh in all its former life and beauty had been reduced to an ashtray. And he was in charge of emptying it.

A burst of machine gunfire jolted Lieutenant Kim from his thoughts.

"What the...? Stop the vehicle," yelled Kim.

Two soldiers stood over a group of 'volunteers' who cowered on their knees. They were commandeered civilians. The soldiers had fired their AK-'s over their heads for no apparent reason.

"What's the meaning of this?" shouted the Lieutenant jumping out of the jeep and marching towards them.

The soldiers turned to Lieutenant Kim and saluted smartly. "Lieutenant, the volunteers are slow - very lazy."

"Of course they are. They're starving and no longer fear death. Let them die where they drop."

The Lieutenant pointed his finger at them. "Do not waste your bullets like that ever again or you will join them."

He turned and walked away in a fury. How many times had the order been given? Ammunition was life. It had to be used wisely.

A jeep with half of its hood sheared away from a rocket attack plowed through the mud puddles and stopped abruptly in front of Lieutenant Kim. A soldier that Kim recognized as one of his junior officers jumped out carrying a large field telephone and lumbered towards him.

"Who is it?" Asked Lieutenant Kim.

"It's Sar," said the officer holding the receiver to his chest.

"Yes General," said Kim grabbing the receiver.

The voice on the other end of the field telephone crackled, cutting in and out. A distant voice was barely audible. "We must maintain complete secrecy Lieutenant. Do you understand me?"

"Understood sir."

The phone line crackled again and Kim adjusted the mobile set as the officer held it in front of him. He winced as he brought the receiver to his ear. The receiver smelled of tobacco and weed.

The voice became louder: "I do not exist nor does the party. The CPK must remain invisible. We are only 'Angkar' to the people, nothing more."

The lieutenant scratched his head under his helmet. It was all very confusing and unnerving.

It was almost as if the general had disappeared from the face of the earth. He had not seen him in almost two years. He was rumoured to be in Phnom Penh. At least that was the official story.

The general continued: "You must fully implement the conditions of Year Zero. Complete the purge at all costs."

"We will," said Kim tossing his cigarette butt and lighting another. "General, the people will want to know who their leader is. What should we tell them?"

The voice crackled and became distant again. "Use my codename - Pol Pot."

The phone went dead.

SANTIAGO, CHILE, 1979 A.D. - Archbishop Henriquez heard the confessional door open and close quickly. He slid open the small lattice divider.

"Yes child?"

"Father, forgive me for I have sinned."

"Go on," said the archbishop.

"I bring news from Simon," said the voice of a young woman.

Raúl felt a surge of adrenalin rush through him. He had been waiting for this report. He was about to ask a question and then remembered the code phrase.

"How are his sons and daughters?"

He heard the woman exhale. She was breathing irregularly.

"Do not be frightened child. You are safe here."

"Thank you Father. They have brought two more families to the - to Simon."

"Where do they live?"

The woman began to cry softly. "Just down the road from us. Both families are neighbours. Father has gone to the station to make enquiries."

The archbishop covered his face with his hand. He thought quickly. How did they find out? The dark circle was closing. "Child, you must listen to me. Tell your

father to stop his enquiries. It is too dangerous. The Vicariate will handle this through its established channels. Does he know you're here?"

"Yes, said the young woman stifling her sobs. "He sent me here to tell you."

"Good. That is good child. The committee will investigate these missing families. Tell your father I'll see him before Sunday Mass. He'll know what to do."

"I will tell him Father."

"Now go in peace child. God be with you." He heard the door close quietly and the woman's footsteps faded down the corridor.

§▲

Cuartel Simon Bolivar did not exist. It was hidden from sight. From the road it was just another military facility. Very few entered and even fewer left.

"Where are you coming from?"

"That is none of your business."

"It's in Santiago?"

The man ground his cigar in the ashtray on the table in front of him. "Yes. Just meet us where we discussed and wait."

The voice on the other end of the phone was silent for a moment. "Okay, we'll have our workers parked and waiting on Mexico Avenue as requested."

"Good. That is all." The man hung up the phone on the table.

"Now, where were we? Ms. Riva, why don't you loosen our guest's memory. I have an important call to take in my office."

A middle-aged woman with dark hair picked up the cables from the stained concrete floor. The figure seated in a chair near the wall was slumped over.

Manuel took the stairs two at a time. His dress shoes echoed up the narrow stairwell. He hurriedly looked at his watch — the call would be coming any minute.

He heard the phone ring as he reached the top stair. He hurried through the door and fumbled with his keys, thrusting one into the keyhole of his office door as he reached it. He threw his satchel on the small wooden desk and quickly grabbed the phone.

"Nacional de Inteligencia, General Contreras speaking." He was out of breath.

"Good evening Manuel, am I disturbing you?"

"Certainly not General Ugarte. I was expecting your call." He wiped his brow with the sleeve of his uniform.

"Let me come right to the point." The familiar voice was low and sinister. "The church in Santiago is playing with fire. Its pet project, this Vicariate of Solidarity must be stopped. I've heard enough of this human rights nonsense - providing assistance and even legal services for dissidents and subversives. It's madness."

Manuel leaned against the front of his desk. A tight smile appeared at the corner of his mouth. "I have the intelligence report you requested."

There was silence at the other end.

The man pulled at the cuff of his military uniform and continued. "One of our agents - a rather strange woman posing as a volunteer, infiltrated two families over the past several weeks in Providencia. She was shown boxes of pamphlets and literature stored in their houses detailing the work of the Vicariate."

"They've been taken into custody?"

"Yes. We're interrogating the father downstairs as we speak."

"Anything forthcoming?" Asked the general.

"Not yet, but Ms. Riva is intensifying the conversation."

"Good. Keep me informed. This organization is much more dangerous than its predecessor," said Ugarte in a sombre tone. "At least that so-called peace committee stayed in the shallows of political waters."

"General, we found something interesting."

"Oh?"

"One of the houses belonged to a widow with no children." He held the receiver against his chin and lit a cigarette. "We found a hand-written dossier hidden in the rafters. The Vicariate is working on a manifesto of some kind."

"A manifesto?"

"Yes," said Manuel, shaking out the match and tossing it on the floor. "It outlines the proposed mandate and characteristics of this Vicariate of Solidarity." He opened his satchel and pulled out a small pamphlet. He turned it over and studied what was scrawled on the back.

"In reference to this organization, part of it reads: *'Its condition as a sacrament of communion, a prophetic sign of contradiction, and a voice of the voiceless.'*

"How interesting," said the general.

"And get this," continued Manuel excitedly. "We believe it's written in the archbishop's hand."

"Henriquez." He heard the general whisper. "Who else is involved at the top?" Ugarte demanded aggressively.

"Cardinal Fresno - and others. They've been referring to this organiza-tion as a type of 'frontier ministry.'"

"That sounds like Henriquez," growled Ugarte. "He has grown too big for the simple boundaries of his kingdom. Outside of the cathedral doors he is nothing but a common sympathizer of the communists and agitators. The Vatican should be outraged."

General Ugarte slammed down the phone.

He crossed the balcony and stood looking out at the sea. His boots seemed anchored in place. He tugged at the collar of his military uniform and swirled the port round and round in his glass. He longed for the crashing of the waves.

A plan was beginning to form. This government will show the arch-bishop what happens when the church attempts to wade into the deeper waters of national affairs, he thought.

He clenched the glass tighter. The Holy See had been exporting a dangerous socialist agenda amongst a few of its cardinals. That group of subversive elites would not infect his national agenda.

He raised the glass to his lips and drank. The spicy liquid ignited his senses and renewed his fervour. This new pope was becoming a grave concern. It was time to consult the others, he thought.

The Vatican thinks it can outsmart us by infecting the political jurisdictions of sovereign nations from the inside out. That can never be allowed to happen.

He knew what he had to do. He would consult his lone superior. The one governor who understood the complexities of nations and the true nature required in presiding over them.

The pickup truck slowly circled the city block and turned on to Mexico Avenue. It was still hours before dawn and the streets were empty. The truck pulled over and parked on the street at one end of Santiago General Cemetery. The driver killed the engine and turned off the lights.

"So what now?"

"They said to wait."

"Who?"

"The man I talked to on the phone. A military official I think."

The driver lit a cigarette and tossed the pack to his brother.

"I don't like this. The stories and rumours are getting louder."

"It's good money," said the driver. "We'll be done in a couple hours - get paid and go home."

"They say the army has a biology lab somewhere in the city. Ever hear of Operation Condor?"

"Yeah, yeah," said the driver rolling down his window. "*Los desaparecidos*."

"Yeah, we're burying them."

"You don't know that. They could come from anywhere."

The brother glanced nervously in the passenger side mirror. "They say that lab is a torture and extermination centre. No one leaves alive. You leave as a package."

A white van pulled up behind them and parked.

"Okay, that's enough. Here they are. Grab the shovels and I'll go talk to them."

Three men appeared outside the van. A fourth in military fatigues motioned to the driver.

"Identification?" He asked.

The driver handed over his papers. The man looked them over and handed them back.

"Follow me." The man in fatigues led the driver to the other side of the cemetery.

"I need a hole dug over there at Patio - the common grave site. The dig location is marked out with string," said the man unlocking the main cemetery gate. "I don't want to waste time. There are four deceased. Dig it big enough and at normal depth. You have an hour."

"It may take a little longer to backfill the hole," said the driver.

"No, my men will fill it. Just dig the hole, get paid, and get outa here."

The man held the gate open. "Got it?"

The driver nodded.

"Good. Get to work."

The army officer closed the gate and motioned across the cemetery to his men. They got in the van and headed towards the main gate bringing four of Chile's disappeared.

❧

THE KILLING FIELDS, CAMBODIA, 1979 A.D. - If we had known what Maggie was going to tell us we would have run to *her*. We would have held vigil right there at the tomb.

But all we saw was death. The tomb was only an extension of Golgotha - that place of the skull where darkness reigned.

My lungs were bursting when I reached the place. I saw the stone come into view at a distance and wished I had waited for Cephas. The tomb swallowed me all over again into the darkness of hell's victory.

I wondered how Maggie had felt alone in its ugly shadow before she made it across her ocean of pain and was greeted by light...

It rained harder and harder and still she ran. The tears streamed down her face and the cries had long since left her voice leaving the horror to well up inside of her, strangling her senses.

These were the fears that penetrate the heart until all feeling is lost.

The field had turned to mud and she could barely make out the rise of earth in front of her as the torrential rain washed out everything in its path. She tumbled over the muddy edge and slid down the embankment. As she tried to regain her footing she saw a sea of horrors lying in front of her.

She stopped. It was a muddy ocean of death.

For a time she had run with the rest of them until they had fallen or succumbed. She had run with a man who had hurried by her through the dense forest and then come back for her. He was in rags but had filled the remnants of his pockets with insects, leaves and a small handful of rice that he said he had secretly harvested on the edge of a small swamp.

Then he too was gone.

The forests were filled with walking skeletons and fallen corpses. The bodies were too numerous to bury. Many were piled and burned - their charred remains visible for all to see. Others simply rotted where they fell, picked clean by animals until their white skeletons gleamed their horror in the scorching sun.

Towns and villages were deserted. The cities were all but abandoned having been driven out by the politics of Sar. The death marches had ended here where Maggie now stood in the rented muddy killing fields of the landowner. Kalashnikov gave generously to his tenants who harvested the land in widening swaths of a calculated madness.

If the prefect had washed his hands then, would he have dared to wash them now, she thought?

There was nothing left to run from. She stepped forward slipping on the sea of skulls and human bones washed clean in the rains and half submerged in mud.

The familiar fields of an endless ocean of fear. She was once again in the place of the skull. A thousand Golgothas.

CHAPTER 14
THE SOUL OF KARACHI

V. 26 Did He not have to suffer these things and then enter his glory?

LAHORE, PAKISTAN, 1976 A.D. - The Governor's House came into view as they approached the sprawling white mansion. Long rows of archways and columns stretched across the front expanse of its first and second stories.

The limousine stopped in front of the mansion and two men stepped out the rear door. One carried an attaché case and the other a black leather bound folder. They were greeted by a waiting assistant and disappeared inside the building.

"Welcome to the Punjab, gentlemen. The Prime Minister has been looking forward to your visit."

"We are delighted to be here and grateful that he could meet with us," said the man with the leather folder under his arm. He adjusted his glasses and shook hands with the personal secretary of Zulfikar Ali Bhutto, Pakistan's tenth Prime Minister.

The secretary smiled and bowed his head slightly. "Please, follow me."

They walked up a beautiful marble staircase that wound its way up to the second floor. A wide corridor awaited them awash in sunlight that burst through the rows of windows that ran across the second story. On the white plaster walls, paintings lined the corridor.

"These are all famous Pakistani artists," said the secretary pointing to the walls. "Sadequain, Agha, Pervez - many of their works are displayed here."

They nodded. "Very impressive," said the man with the leather folder. "I'm familiar with some of Agha's modernist paintings back in America."

The secretary stopped in front of a large wood door made from native hemlock. He opened it and ushered them through. A military officer stood guard outside the door. Two women stood up from behind their desks and bowed their heads towards their guests.

From an inner office appeared Prime Minister Bhutto.

He smiled warmly. "Secretary Kissinger, welcome to Pakistan. It is a pleasure to have you here."

"Thank you, Mr. Prime Minister."

The two men shook hands and introductions were made. He invited the Americans into his office.

Tea and some local desserts were set on a round teak coffee table surrounded by four ornately carved wood and leather chairs. The two statesmen and their assistants sat down and helped themselves to tea and the generous assortment of sweets.

The meeting progressed slowly as both sides did their best to set a profitable course and kept the narrative light and predictable.

But the prime minister knew something was coming. President Ford didn't send his top man halfway around the world to make general inquiries. Especially given the precarious state of the president's Republican party. Nixon had seriously handcuffed this administration, Zulfikar had reminded an aide earlier that day.

"Secretary, what brings you to Lahore?"

Mr. Kissinger finished his sip of tea and set it back on the saucer that he held in front of him. "I see we are finished with the formalities."

Zulfikar smiled and waited.

"The president has sent me here to urge you to reconsider your nuclear ambitions. We have some options we hope you will find attractive."

That was no surprise, thought Zulfikar. At least he came right out with it. Kissinger was smart. He didn't push diplomacy past the point of its objectives.

"I have few options in the matter," responded Zulfikar. "India has forced our hand. We have lived under constant threat of their nuclear capabilities for two years now. Pakistan will not live under this shadow undefended."

"We certainly wouldn't ask you to do that," said Kissinger.

He opened his folder and handed the prime minister a set of documents from the US State Department. They were stamped CLASSIFIED across the front page.

"We are willing to supply you with A- Bombers over the course of the next decade."

"Bombers?" Said Zulfikar taking the documents and setting them on the table in front of him. "My dear friend, what good are bombers against nuclear missiles?"

Kissinger placed his cup and saucer on the coffee table. "Mr. Prime Minister, our A-7 Bombers are highly sophisticated and drop their payloads with astonishing accuracy and speed. We used these bombers against the Khmer Rouge in Cambodia."

And look where that got you, thought Zulfikar. This was an insult. He stood up and walked over to his desk. "Mr. Secretary, we do not want your bombers. As you are well aware, we will continue to negotiate with the French. They are willing to supply a nuclear reprocessing plant that will greatly help us in meeting our energy needs."

"You're touting energy needs sir?" Kissinger removed his glasses and began to clean them with his handkerchief.

"Energy is a primary need of ours, yes. That aside, it gives us the nuclear option. I will be very candid about that," said Zulfikar.

"You do realize the delicate nature of our shared political interests?" Said Kissinger holding his glasses up to the light.

Zulfikar shot his guest an impertinent stare. "I realize the delicate nature of your administration. Your president does not expect to win its November elections. And I am unwilling to give any assurances to your government that we will abandon our nuclear program. President Ford is not the only one who seeks re-election."

Kissinger nodded his head and slipped on his glasses. "That is very unfortunate news. The president will undoubtedly be disappointed."

"I am sorry, Mr. Secretary, but I cannot promise to abandon the security of the Pakistani people. We share the intricacies of democracy and as such I am unwilling to commit political suicide."

The room became quiet. It seemed neither man had more to say - neither nation had more to say. Kissinger slowly stood up and offered his hand to Zulfikar. "Thank you for your hospitality."

The men walked to the door. Kissinger turned to leave and stopped.

He looked at the prime minister. "You are a respected friend and colleague so let me make our position very clear. If Pakistan pursues its nuclear agenda..." He paused. "We will make a terrible example out of you."

Kissinger and his assistant disappeared down the corridor.

෨

PUNJAB PROVINCE, PAKISTAN, 1988 A.D. - The smouldering

wreck of the Hercules aircraft lay scattered amongst the rocks and scrub brush, her nose pointing skywards. Flames licked the remains of the charred fuselage as curious civilians and rescue personnel wandered about the crash site.

The President of Pakistan and military dictator was dead along with thirty-one others.

Two men stood on a rocky outcrop near the still-burning Hercules.

"Well, General Zia, you belong to me now," said Kalashnikov surveying the crash scene.

"I am dreaming," muttered the general examining his neatly pressed and unblemished military uniform.

"I'm afraid not," said Kalashnikov. "This is the work of your enemies."

"No. Who would dare defy me?" The former president ran his hand along his lapel and smoothed the military medals that adorned his chest.

Kalashnikov chuckled softly. "Pak One, what is your position?" He said mimicking the last words of the control tower directed to the now destroyed cockpit. He looked at the plane wreckage and then back at the former president.

"You called yourself a humble servant and then seized power in a military takeover greenlit by your new friends in Washington. Then you hung your former master, Zulfikar." He smiled curtly at General Zia.

"You cloaked yourself in American foreign policy, snug in Kissinger's pocket."

Kalashnikov shook his head incredulously.

"You chose to be America's freedom fighter in the war against our Soviet forces in Afghanistan. Another foolish example of the naivety of double mindedness."

Zia tried but he could not bring himself to look the man in the eyes.

Even now he feared a greater danger than the fiery death he had just experienced.

"You imposed martial law and then Sharia law in the land of your fore-fathers. You pursued the secrets of nuclear annihilation and a bloody intelligentsia."

Kalashnikov stepped in between the crash site and the general.

"No one can outwit their master."

He stood and raised himself over his servant.

"And you dare to ask - who would defy you General?"

Zia was silent in the face of his likeness.

"A great many," said Kalashnikov. He stepped aside and motioned to the burning wreckage. "Indeed, a great many."

"Bhutto," whispered General Zia.

"Ah," said Kalashnikov. "The daughter of the east you threw into prison and then allowed to be spared. A shame you chose not to hang democracy a second time."

The general stared at the flames of the wreckage. "The worst mistake of my life was allowing her to live."

KARACHI, PAKISTAN, 1988 A.D. - Three months after the sudden death of President Zia, the Pakistan People's Party returned to power.

"I have avenged my father's death," pronounced the Muslim world's first female Prime Minister, Benazir Bhutto. She stood elegantly behind the podium from where she had just taken the oath of her office dressed in the green and white colours of her beloved Pakistan.

As her father had preached to his children - there was a debt to be paid back to the people of her young nation. Now she stood on the platform of the promise she had kept to him.

She recalled his last hours. On the eve of his execution, he had simply said: "I'd like to bathe. It's a beautiful earth and I want to be clean. Tonight, I'll be free."

Now all of Pakistan could be cleansed and freed from the tyranny of fear. The country would embark on a holy mission to bring democracy and progress to its people, she had promised in her many campaign speeches.

Votes would triumph over bullets.

Her impact was immediate. In the months that followed, a new wave of energy flooded the cities. Towns and villages that had been forgotten dared to hope again. Within a year electricity and clean water were finding their way into these forgotten regions of the country. New schools were built and even polio was swiftly eradicated.

Still, the bullets and the hands of their idle masters waited impatiently. They bided their time and plotted incessantly.

And they were everywhere. In the military, on the street, in the hills and backcountry, even in her own government.

The women crowded around her as close as security would allow. She was used to the lectures from her head of security and had joked he had the hardest job in all of Pakistan. He had not found the joke amusing. Threats poured in daily. The security briefings could scarcely keep up.

She was led outside the classroom and stopped at the doorway. She waved to the roomful of women in training. "Good luck in your studies," she encouraged. "We need all of you serving as proud, capable police officers."

She hoped her speech had made its mark. This was the country she wanted to build. It started with the people stepping up in service to a renewed functioning democracy.

Outside the training barracks the mid-morning sun had burned away the last of the fog. A heavy dew blanketed the grass and shrubs that lined the pathways of the police training academy.

"Prime Minister, I'd like to introduce our district superintendent and station house inspector." The junior officer stepped aside as two senior women police officers greeted their leader.

"We are overwhelmed at all you are doing for us," said the superintendent.

Benazir smiled warmly. "This government and the whole country are grateful to you for your courage and leadership. It is the beginning of great change for our society."

"Do you expect these reforms to continue throughout Pakistan?" Asked the inspector, shyly brushing her dark hair from her face.

"Our government is committed to the rights of women but it will be an uphill battle in many areas, especially in the rural outlying areas of the country. The north remains a battleground on many fronts."

An aide stepped forward. "Prime Minister, the car is ready."

She nodded and turned to the three policewomen. "Please, you're welcome to accompany me to the vehicle." They smiled and continued down the pathway. The junior officer followed behind the prime minister who was flanked on each side by the senior officers.

"My uncle is a district officer in Waziristan," said the superintendent. "He worries the situation is deteriorating in the aftermath of the war."

Benazir adjusted her white headscarf. "Unfortunately these reports are confirmed. The mountains of Waziristan and Kandahar Province are hiding a growing threat. The Afghan war with the Soviets has emboldened waves of freedom fighters armed to the teeth in search of a new enemy."

"Do you see the military as a solution up there?" Asked the junior officer.

"At present, only in a limited capacity," said Benazir turning to the young officer. "We're monitoring the situation as best we can but the social and economic challenges here in Karachi and across the rest of Pakistan remain our first priority."

The inspector looked down. Her voice was low: "I for one don't care what those animals do to each other in the mountains. I had a brother once..." She paused.

The prime minister looked at her curiously. "A brother?"

"Yes." She glanced up the path. "He and a few friends joined the war six years ago against the pleadings of my father. They crossed the border into Afghanistan and started hunting Russians. Then one day a couple years later he showed up back home alone. He was the only one who made it back."

These were the stories she needed to hear, thought Benazir - the struggles of the people. They walked in silence and waited for her to continue.

"Right away my family saw he had changed. He barely spoke and often became violent and belligerent. He terrorized the neighbourhood and would abuse us terribly."

She rolled up her sleeve. The inside of her forearm was scarred with cigarette burns.

"Then one day he was found beaten to death in the street. We never spoke of him again."

The inspector stopped and turned to the prime minister. "That is why I joined the police force. To help bring hope to communities."

Benazir stood deep in thought. Later, she recalled the encounter as a profound moment of her time in office. "I know the pain of losing a brother," she said.

They continued down the path.

"The demons of war will always beckon and at times will need to be confronted. But the progressive policies within a democracy will ensure the insanity of those mountain regions never permeate our soci-ety. This government will not allow it."

They reached the car and shook hands. The superintendent handed the wrapped gift that had been presented after her speech to the prime minister.

"Thank you for coming home," said the inspector smiling.

Benazir laughed. "How could I not?"

"We couldn't stand another day of Sharia law under President Zia," said the inspector. "I'm glad he's gone."

"Me too," said the prime minister, getting into the car. "If I never hear that name again, it will be too soon."

The junior officer closed the car door. She caught her own reflection in the window and scarcely recognized the woman in the sharp blue uniform. A surge of pride filled her as she stood at attention alongside her senior officers.

Finally, she thought. Even in the face of much suffering, a nation could reclaim its dignity.

PART III

CHAPTER 15
THE BLOOD OF PROPHETS

V. 27 And beginning with Moses and all the prophets, he explained to them what was said in all the scriptures concerning himself.

KARACHI, PAKISTAN, 1993 A.D. - Some say the Arabian Sea still harbours a few. They remain as guardians of the ancient mysteries and sing their deep prophecies of all that is to come.

These first and last great beasts of the sea carry with them the secrets of time and their song is a haunting reminder of the blessed simplicity of their vocation. They are the last of the humpback whales plying the ancient waters between the lands of the Persians, Indians and the Horn of Africa.

You remember my fishing stories and father's boat, of course? Back then dreams of greater seas simply did not exist...

The prophetic moanings of the deep sung by these few Arabian Sea monsters proclaim the fullness of beauty to all who search for their song. Much like the prophetic calling and terrorizing beauty that filled my barren existence on that windswept isle of Patmos.

Who can really understand and bear the full weight of such things?

The Port of Karachi on the northern shores of the Arabian Sea was the busiest port in Pakistan. Even with the monotonous traffic of ships loading and unloading their cargo and the constant bustle of workers and port vehicles moving the nation's goods, a brand new energy was in the air.

On the side of a long line of shipping containers a half-ripped campaign poster of former Prime Minister Nawaz Sharif clung in shreds to the orange container. In big green capital letters someone had spray painted *BHUTTO WINS!!* across the face of her opponent.

With her father's widow at her side, the long-suffering daughter of the east was formally sworn in for a second time as Prime Minister, bringing the Pakistan People's Party back into power. She had come to learn many of the hard lessons of leveraging a national agenda.

Now the country was ready to take a giant leap forward under the renewed hope and seasoned confidence of Benazir Bhutto.

"We will provide a mandate for entering the twenty-first century," she had promised at her inauguration speech.

Her words would prove to be a prophetic omen for a world that was sleeping on a mountainous bed of dynamite. The best of political intentions would soon be of little consequence.

It was a month later, early in the evening and Prime Minister Bhutto was settled in one of her parliamentary offices. U.S. Secretary of State, Warren Christopher was on the line. She had been anticipating the call for several days as there was a tinderbox of intelligence and sensitive information to discuss.

"I can't hold the line on this indefinitely, Mr. Secretary," said Benazir trying to contain her frustration.

"We're not asking you to," said the voice on the other end. "If our air force and special operations can have complete access to the requested military bases we can ease the strain on your own deployments."

"Some of that can be arranged but it must be done carefully."

"You fear anti-American sentiment within your military?" The question was posed more as a statement than a genuine inquiry and grated on Benazir's nerves.

"No, not at all," she said emphatically. "I fear the growing sentiment for Islamic extremism in the north and the Afghan border region. And these forces are recruiting in our mosques, schools and street corners at an alarming rate."

"Yes, of course I understand," said Secretary Christopher quickly. "The Iranians are spreading much of this extremism."

Benazir shook her head. "You're not understanding me Mr. Secretary. These regions are full of former Taliban freedom fighters armed to the teeth with American weaponry."

Secretary Christopher interrupted - "Believe me, we're very aware of the situation and working with the Afghan government to ensure some of these fringe groups don't get out of hand."

Fringe groups? Thought Benazir. It was becoming clear to her this young government in the U.S. was in complete denial. "I feel I must warn you that those mountains harbour a different world of existence," she said.

"I realize that. But understand Madame Prime Minister, these soldiers helped defeat the Soviets. We're only looking to contain them at this point. Any major offensives in the region would be extremely damaging."

That was a warning, she thought. They wanted Pakistan to engage passively as usual. That page from the American foreign policy handbook hadn't changed since the day of her country's birth under Khan.

She exhaled and continued: "We're living under an emerging threat that is gravitating southwards into the more populated rural and urban areas. That said, we can discuss access to some of our strategic military bases."

"And in return?" Asked Secretary Christopher.

"In return we need regular intelligence briefings, military resources and above all, strong public assurances that Pakistani sovereignty will not be compromised."

"Okay. Let me brief the president and get to work on this. The Pentagon will need to be consulted as well."

"What about your congress? Time is unfortunately not on our side, Mr. Secretary."

"We're heavily invested in the region - rest assured. We'll move quickly where necessary," he added.

"I'm glad to hear it," she answered. The rise of islamic extremism in Pakistan, intelligence reports in the north and in Kandahar..." Her voice trailed off.

She rotated the globe that hung on its axis beside her. "I fear a Frankenstein's monster is being created in those mountains."

Benazir folded her arm across her side listening impatiently. "Yes, thank you Mr. Secretary. Please keep us informed. Goodbye."

She walked back to her desk and stood over the mountain of work still needing her attention. She thumbed through a primary school textbook the government had ordered out of circulation in all schools. Still, many of the remote villages of northern Pakistan continued to use and study them religiously. She shook her head in disbelief as she read some of the horrifying arithmetic and grammar lessons depicting violent jihad, graphic warfare, and the counting exercises of slain infidels.

She turned the book over and opened the inside page skimming the publishing information. Then something caught her eye that made her skin crawl. Was that even possible, she thought?

She stared for several seconds at what was written trying to make sense of it.

In small letters at the bottom of the page the words leaped out at her:

Printed at the University of Nebraska.

Incredibly, the textbook was stamped with the letter K - for Kalashnikov.

No doubt the collaborative efforts of evil's freedom fighter - Zia, she concluded.

Suddenly she was filled with that old familiar feeling of rage and loathing for the man that had killed her father. The acrid smell of her father's jail and the awful stench of her class C prison cell filled her nostrils. It was a sensation of nausea born out of disgust as if the bile of injustice could never be washed away.

She grabbed the textbook and ripped the pages from its binding and slammed it into the trash bin beside her desk.

She felt the pages taunting her - screaming their destruction at her and all of Pakistan. She closed her eyes and prayed. "Allah," she whispered. "Will this ever end? Restore our hope and bring us to victory."

Benazir stood up and put on her headscarf. There was no turning back, no time left to lament the past, she reminded herself. There was only one way. Forward.

"Get our president on the line," she said pressing a button on the telephone.

If the forces against Pakistan were relentless then her government would match and exceed their zealousness. A storm was coming.

And then it was over as quickly as it had begun.

Amidst a new round of corruption charges her government fell in '97 and Sharif regained power. He quickly jailed Bhutto's husband who would languish in jail for over a decade on charges that would never gain a conviction.

Benazir went into self-exile and moved with her children and mother to Dubai.

The daughter of the east had been erased again from the political map of her father's beloved Pakistan.

⁊⸱

STANTON COUNTY, KANSAS, 1935 A.D. - "Get'em loaded up." The supervising foreman was determined to keep his schedule and he was growing impatient. This was their fifth cattle farm of the day.

The truck driver opened his back doors and tied them to the sides of the loading ramp.

"What's the highway like headed east?" He asked.

"There's a convoy of cattle trucks headed to the stock yards from every corner of the state," said the foreman checking his papers for the head count.

"We may send you across the state line into Okie. Might save you some time."

"Who's doing the paperwork for that?" Asked the driver, frowning.

"Don't worry about it. It's all federally regulated by the Agricultural Adjustment Administration."

"The what?"

"Roosevelt's program," said the foreman. "This cattle slaughter is part of the Fed's Drought Relief Service."

The truck driver spat tobacco on the ground and wiped his cheek with his sleeve. "Seems like a terrible waste to me."

"Of cattle or money?"

"Both. These sorry beasts ain't worth ten a head, never mind twenty."

The foreman glanced over at the figure in overalls by the barn moving the small herd towards the truck. "You want him going bankrupt?"

"Don't much care to be honest," shrugged the driver. "Roosevelt gonna bail me out too when I need it? Not a chance."

"This is your bailout. You throw that farmer under like thousands of others and whole communities and businesses will keep disappearing. Then what are ya gonna haul?"

A stream of tobacco juice landed near the foreman's boot. "It's throwin' good money after bad. That's all I'm sayin'. People starving and all this meat being destroyed to prop up prices?"

"Not entirely. Meat from healthy cattle will be distributed to poor families."

"Ah I see," said the driver sarcastically. "All in the name of drought relief."

"Feds have to do something. Hoover proved waiting and doing nothing was not a solution the market could fix on its own."

The driver waved him off. "This is the devil's economy and nothing's gonna stop it till it's run its course."

"Well I'm sure you'll be cashing your cheque regardless," muttered the foreman walking away.

He approached the cattle farmer who was herding a few of the starving beasts out of the corral and into the curved narrow race leading to the truck's loading ramp. The farmer was young but the recent years of hard toil had aged him with an exhausted and slightly emaciated look.

The foreman tipped his cap. "Afternoon."

He shook the farmer's lean bony hand. "I just need a couple signatures. What are your plans?" Asked the foreman.

"We'll probably follow the caravan out west. Never been to California but walking away while we can may be better than staying here."

The foreman pulled off his cap. Every story seemed to be the same - people were leaving every day not knowing where they would end up. Farms were being deserted.

"You want some cheap advice?"

The farmer shrugged and smiled wearily.

"I've been loading cattle for this government purchase program all over Kansas. Most farmers are older than you and staring bankruptcy in the eye. Some of 'em too old for second chances. Take the money for your cattle and get outa here."

He looked the man over. He was barely twenty-five, he thought.

"You have a family?"

"Wife and I have a boy. He's three."

"Listen. You're young enough to come back when times improve, if ever. Your house and land are near worthless. Don't sink another penny into it as much as it hurts."

The young farmer looked ashamedly at the ground. "I'm glad my papa died before he could see what I was doing - selling his cattle and walking away from his life's work. He was always so proud to be a landowner. Most of his friends and mine now were tenant farmers. This Agricultural Act cut back farm production and put them out of work. I'm all that's left."

"Boy, look at me." He put his hand on the young black man's shoulder.

"You've been stuck on this island of pain long enough. Every farmer's battling for his life and his family. The family farm legacy is now a scene of death and devastation.

"The rains have gotta come sometime," said the young farmer.

The foreman looked over the young man's shoulder at the long weary span of dusty, battered horizon blackened from east to west by a devouring sky.

"I've visited too many of these barren islands. These farms that used to shine like beacons on an endless sea of gold withered into blackness and disappeared into dust."

He looked at the last of the beaten Angus cattle disappear from the corral as they headed down the race and up the ramp. The driver followed them cursing their every step.

"I've seen these emaciated animals packed into the stockyards of Kansas City. Their hides stretched over ribs you swore were about to bust through making sounds no man should have to hear. In the end man and beast stare death in the eye." Some see through it - most don't how.

He handed the papers to the farmer and held out a pen.

"Sometimes there's life in every direction 'cept the place you're standin'. Go west young man."

𐫱𐫱

WASHINGTON D.C., APRIL 14th, 1935 A.D. - The day would forever come to be known as America's Black Sunday.

St. Thomas Episcopal Church was a thousand miles from the darkness but a blackened fury was descending on her in a rolling tide of staggering devastation.

The black wave yearned to crash again. This time in an overland tsunami of destruction.

Who controls the forces that can swallow light? When the sun scorches land and the rains are hoarded greedily over oceans. When dust returns to dust and hastens the collapsed blackness of the heavens.

My scribe shook with fear as I cried out the vision. That island prison revealed nothing happens that has not been foretold. And still the warnings go unheeded.

The evening service at St. Thomas had ended and its parishioners slowly spilled out its front doors congregating in small groups outside to visit and chat.

A few looked curiously up at the sky. The setting sun in the west was oddly coloured by a thin veil of haze that tinted the daylight and obscured the long shadows of the late afternoon sun.

At the far corner of the church yard, four men chatted amicably in a circle stopping to shake hands occasionally with parishioners passing by.

Rex Tugwell tipped his hat at a passing couple who smiled at the group.

"You survived the service Jim," said President Roosevelt patting his shoulder as he stood beside him.

Jim smiled. "Sure. Liturgy is pretty much the same in the Catholic church. Poor Harry. He was lost after the opening prayer."

Harry chuckled. "I was waiting for the altar call but I guess everyone here is saved."

The President grunted. Touché Harry. So we'd all like to think."

"So Mr. Director, where's the money coming from?" Asked Harry glancing at the sky.

Rex laughed. "You're starting in on me already?"

He had been appointed Director of the Agricultural Adjustment Administration earlier in the year and had overseen the government controlled slaughter of livestock to stabilize meat and dairy prices. It was a hugely controversial move.

"The Commodities Purchase Section," said Rex. "Most of the payouts have already been processed."

James Farley gave a pronounced thumbs up. "Those farmers deserve it. Forget the urban cries of dissent. Livestock and dairy producers are part of the backbone of the heartland. We need ranchers and farmers with cash in hand. If they don't survive, neither do we."

"That's exactly right Jim," said President Roosevelt, standing beside him.

Rex nodded in agreement. "The purchase and removal of surplus cattle and calves from drought-stricken areas is moving along well. We've also been moving stock feed into drought areas to save as many cattle as possible."

"What's your take on the implementation of supports from our Drought Relief Service? Asked Harry.

"I've got a few complaints but nothing worth bending your ear to," said Rex.

"Excellent," said Harry smiling. "I won't ask for details."

"Best you don't. Lots of pushback from local politics trying to curry favour to community supporters."

The president rolled his eyes. "Bashing Washington is always the easy way to raise campaign dollars from local dissenters."

Jim shrugged his shoulders dismissively. "Promise a golden calf to the local butcher and he'll parrot your agenda all over the county."

"How'd you guys escape so quickly?" Muttered Raymond as he approached his colleagues. "A couple parishioners had me cornered the second I left my pew."

"Gotta stick close to security detail," said Jim with a chuckle. "Nice to be recognized isn't it?"

Ray grunted. "Hard to challenge an argument you don't necessarily disagree with."

The President shifted his weight on the forgiving grass numb to the pain that was a constant companion. "How so?" He asked.

Harry and Jim glanced at each other, both wanting to avoid an impromptu policy debate.

"The church wardens were at my throat over taxes funding the New Deal," he said with a shrug. "Called it a shell game."

"Ah, all of them economics majors of course," said President Roosevelt dryly. "No mention of all the good done by our spending programs?"

It was the trigger point Ray had been fighting off like the flu for some time. An anguish that was growing inside of him and had to come out. Political truths were extolled in good times and excreted in bad. As the nation's quarterly numbers trickled in, Ray had become increasingly alarmed.

Their New Deal policies weren't producing. Early on the hope of the New Deal shone in its beauty. Now two years later the truths they'd campaigned and banked on were tried, tired and turning ugly - the stagnant numbers turning foul. The men beside him disagreed. For them there was no turning back. They'd staked their political lives on the New Deal.

"Mr. President," he said, sucking in his breath. "Our spending isn't increasing jobs in the economy. The money spent on our programs largely comes from taxpayers who now have less money to spend on themselves. We need people buying food, cars, houses, gifts for wives and children to stimulate the economy."

"That'll come Ray. We're climbing a mountain here," said the President patiently.

"I fear we're sliding down it," said Ray. It's a classic case of 'the seen versus the unseen.'

"What's that mean?" Asked Rex indignantly.

"It means we can see the jobs created by our spending programs but we can't see the jobs destroyed by New Deal taxing. This could be turning into a massive shell game."

"Dammit Moley! Are you with us or against us?" Snapped Rex.

"Be careful, Tugwell," said Raymond coolly. "According to Kieran at the Times, you could be the first brain trust bounced from cabinet if things don't change." He knew how Rex hated the label.

The President shot Ray a nasty look that Rex took notice of and decided to bite his tongue. The group went silent. Jim took a long puff on his cigar. Harry, embarrassed by the exchange stared down at his shoes.

The president checked his watch. "I should get moving gentlemen. I need to prepare for my meeting this afternoon with Joe Kennedy."

"Another good Irish Catholic lad," said Jim, happy to change the subject. I hear he's doing good work at the Securities and Exchange Commission."

"He is," said Harry. Wall Street's learning he won't be bullied. He's putting an end to this insider trading business among other questionable practices.

Rex took out a fresh cigar and waved it towards Harry. "Just keep him focused on straightening out Wall Street and keep him out of any political rancouring."

Jim frowned but said nothing.

"Before you leave sir, I have something to show you guys," said Harry reaching into his coat pocket. "Mr. President, you received the briefing earlier today on the dust storm rolling across the midwest?"

"I did at two o'clock this afternoon. Reports were skies were black and visibility was near zero. Another report is most likely waiting on my desk."

Harry took a deep breath. "It's bad sir - worse than any report could've forecast. It's actually worse than anything I've ever seen."

"What are you talking about?" Said Rex. "You've seen it?"

"I brought the pictures with me. These were taken around noon in Oklahoma." He handed the photographs to the president.

"Good God," whispered President Roosevelt as he studied the pictures. "How is this even possible?"

He handed them to Jim who held them up for Rex to see as well. Neither man could speak.

"I know there's a lot of pushback from locals on soil conservation but how much more do you need to see?" said Rex, still immersed in the horror of the photos.

Harry looked up towards the west. "It's headed this way. Millions of tons of rich topsoil from farmers' fields blown straight out to sea."

"Listen gentlemen," said President Roosevelt. I think we need to push ahead with our resettlement agenda. Rex, you're in charge of this new administration. We need an implementation plan immediately - in the next few days."

Rex nodded vigorously. He looked at Raymond defiantly. "We're on it."

He handed the pictures back to Harry. The president took one of the photos out of Harry's hand. He stared in disbelief at the story playing out in America's breadbasket.

"It's almost apocalyptic." said Jim. "I've never seen rolling clouds of dust like that swallowing the horizon and everything in its path."

"People across the midwest are calling it a black blizzard," said Harry.

The president handed the photo back to Harry. He shook his head slowly. "For decades a few wise dissenting voices - most of 'em farmers themselves have been warning everyone about protecting the soil and its rich nutrients. They were laughed at and ridiculed."

He looked sternly at his trusted advisors. "New ways, new programs, new deals are subjected to the lashings of their critics. No doubt we're bloodied but we'll soldier through these blackest of storms in search of truths that have always been there to guide us on.

They stood quietly for a moment.

"Well, we best be on our way. Our wives are waiting for us as usual," said Ray glancing across the church yard. He now regretted the timing of his outburst. The President was swamped by a barrage of national tragedies on a daily basis and he was a part of this administration. He would have to dig with the rest of them or turn in his shovel and go home - an option he utterly detested.

Harry handed the photos back to President Roosevelt. "You can keep these. Apparently the press is referring to the midwest as a dust bowl."

"Judging by the pictures, an apt description," said Rex.

"There were some families who thought the world was ending," said Harry.

The president looked at one of the photos and then skyward at the impending darkness.

"And who could blame them?" He said uneasily. "Who could blame them?"

LUCANAMARCA, PERU, 1983 A.D. - I do love being in the field. There weren't many of us that day nor did the demons scream passionately like in Sar's Cambodia or Basbug's Chechnya. This was not a battle. It was a massacre meant to teach Lima a lesson. Most of us were not discharged. Machetes and axes did most of the killing.

The long night of that dirty war had begun.

I never invested more time than necessary in Chairman Gonzalo. He was sloppy and delusional, lacking the precision of Sar or the subversive cunning of Ugarte. He had not the skills to be a head of state. We supplied his needs and left him to his own devices. Our warnings of patience especially in avoiding the cities, in the end went unheeded as Professor Morote suspected they would. Lima was eventually his own undoing.

Even the reckless General Zia calculated risk with more sense than

Gonzalo ever did with his Shining Path movement. Still he remained unrelenting and unrepentant to the end. A loyal disciple of mine, he was.

His response years later to the massacre only reinforced his discipleship:

"In the face of reactionary military actions and the use of mesnadas against our Shining Path liberators, we responded with a devastating action: Lucanamarca.

Neither they nor we have forgotten it, to be sure, because they got an answer that they didn't imagine possible. More than 80 were annihilated, that is the truth. And we say openly that there were excesses, as was analyzed in 1983.

But everything in life has two aspects. Our task was to deal a devastating blow in order to put them in check, to make them understand that it was not going to be so easy.

If we were to give the masses a lot of restrictions, requirements and prohibitions, it would mean that deep down we didn't want the waters to overflow. And what we needed was for the waters to overflow, to let the flood rage, because we know that when a river floods its banks it causes devastation, but then it returns to its riverbed.

I repeat, this was explained clearly by Lenin, and this is how we understand those excesses. But I insist, the main point was to make them understand that we were a hard nut to crack, and that we were ready for anything - anything."

He was an attentive pupil, thought Kalashnikov. He looked down on the small village of Lucanamarca from his perch on a rocky outcrop of the mountain side. He closed his eyes again and recalled Gonzalo's shocking deposition - longing again for the crashing of the waves.

Yes, the waters must overflow their banks to let the flood rage. The waves must crash and assail unleashed from the sea and the riverbeds and only then, after the devastation, swiftly return to the icy depths of its master.

Kalashnikov tossed a stone over the edge. Perhaps I have underestimated the man? He thought.

From a distance one could barely make out the tiny silhouette standing on the rocky outcrop far up in the mountains. But the shadow was unmistakable as a thin figure of twisted blackness stretched across the valley as if to outdistance the sun.

❧

"Did you not retrieve the body?" Screamed Chairman Gonzalo as the masked men entered the tent.

It had been raining for two weeks and everyone's patience was spent. Even the veteran recruits were growing weary of guerrilla warfare tactics up in the hills where few of the government's military ventured. It seemed more of a standoff.

That had suddenly changed.

"There was barely anything to retrieve Mr. Chairman," shouted a soldier looking down.

"What do you mean?" The chairman's eyes were wide as he shook the soldier with both arms.

"They set Commander Olegario on fire after they stoned him," whispered the soldier.

Gonzalo stepped back in shock.

"They burnt him?"

No one dared to answer.

"Did you see the body? Answer me boy!"

The soldier took off the black bandana that covered his face. He could not have been more than fifteen. "I saw his charred remains from a distance. It wasn't the military. It was the *ronderos*."

"*Ronderos*!" Gasped the chairman.

The *ronderos* were local peasants turned militia fighters and recently employed by the national military to fight Shining Path in the jungles and villages of the countryside.

"Our scouts were correct then. These traitors have been recruited in Ayacucho."

Chairman Gonzalo sat down on one of the crates near a folding table covered in topographical maps.

"Lucanamarca will pay for the transgressions of their own," Gonzalo said quietly.

"How many kills have you in the field, boy?"

"Twenty-seven," the young boy said confidently.

"And you know the exact spot where the execution took place?"

"I do."

"Good. You will help lead the charge in avenging our lost commander. Shining Path will not be denied its revolution. They have cast the first stone."

They marched in silence and in singing. They marched down the hill-sides that wound their way down the road carved through the mountain pass and down the path that cut through lush green jungle. Some of the villagers sang passionately, some with tears streaming down their faces. Some walked in stoic silence. Some shook with anger. Others sang softly, resigned in their grief.

The marching convoy of white coffins snaked its way down to the burial grounds. There were sixty-nine coffins in all. Each of them carrying innocent villagers, the youngest of them six months old. Some carried young mothers and their unborn children.

The shiny white coffins were carried on the shoulders of loved ones while others carried flowers and walked in front or followed behind.

Others remained missing. Some would be found years later piled together in mass graves on the outskirts of town.

The waves had crashed over Lucanamarca and flooded the village with devastation and death. Now the dark waters had retreated back to their icy depths.

Who stopped to pay honour to this lonely funeral procession in the hills and mountains near the bottom of the world? Where was Lima and a civilized order when the fires of death danced on the waves that crashed and flooded its banks?

When does rest come to those who march in pain? To those who carry the coffins?

It whispers to those who remember. The agony in the garden of Gethsemane long forgotten, crying out to the tired shoulders of Lucanamarca.

KARACHI, PAKISTAN, 2007 A.D. - Even in the hardness of his military stranglehold on the country, he had feared the whisperings... The daughter of the east was contemplating the unthinkable. She was coming home.

Much of Pakistan secretly dreamed of a return to civilian government. President Musharraf's grip on military rule was weakening Pakistan politically and badly straining relations with her increasingly frustrated allies.

The native daughter's homecoming was both inconceivable and inevitable. It was also dangerous. But the day finally came in October.

The airport was a wild scene of chaotic ecstasy and celebration for the return of their own. A mass of humanity was everywhere; the tension masked by the jubilant crowds.

"We begged her not to go back." Her husband would sadly reflect afterwards.

But Benazir clung to her people and the dream of a holy place beyond. A democratic Islamic republic was possible again. The dream of Zulfikar Bhutto was alive once more in the awaited return and promise of his own bloodline.

Kalashnikov felt the adrenaline surge through his cold blood. "That's when we knew we had her," he had told Sayyid. The trap had been baited and set. She could have fought and lived in the arms of my calling but she chose to die instead.

Democracies and Kalashnikovs are not so incompatible as one may think, he thought, opening his eyes. Strategic alliances are the soul bearers of one's history. Any shame is soon lost in its footnotes.

Our young recruit had done well under the tutelage of Colonel Basbug and had successfully completed his assignment in Chechnya. We dispatched him to Karachi when we heard the news of her planned return.

True, the ghost of Zia was alive and well in the fervour of his follow-ers. To disrupt and to tear down is the struggle of the conqueror. New territory is not ceded any other way. Death is the martyr's lantern.

The young recruit reached into his jacket...

I waited patiently when John the Baptist dared to point the way to a new altar place of life.

Did you hear the relentless cries of Isaiah as he prophesied to the ages? I was there. Is Mohammed the enemy of Moses? And Moses the enemy of Mohammed? I watched them both. The earthly scribes record my rule also.

Have I not had a hand in all of these? And so it continues.

The explosion rocked the planet. The amassed tidal roll of waves roared over the bank and smashed into the street-filled procession. For several seconds the entire scene was sucked into a silent oblivion as the force of impact resonated its demonic screams and all senses were obscured, weightless, even serene. Then the full weight of the force slammed into being and the chaos and terror ripped through the panic of the masses. Senses regained trying to process pain and horror simultaneously.

"Get her out of here!"

"She's alive?"

"Drive! Drive!"

Zia cursed every fragment of the young recruit whose death had failed to avenge his own. It was a failed mission. Bhutto had survived - for now.

Before dawn the next day, General Musharraf stirred his coffee slowly as he gripped the morning paper tightly in his right hand. "Now what am I to do?" He muttered to himself. He dropped the paper on his desk and took a sip of coffee. She had survived her homecoming and her people would not rest until she was crowned once more.

General Zia and Colonel Basbug had words the following evening back on ship. I was unconcerned.

Another chance would come.

§.

And it did. Kalashnikov was right. This time in Rawalpindi, the twin city of Islamabad.

"Bhutto! Bhutto!" The jubilant crowds shouted and sang, their hands in the air pressing in around her vehicle that slowly made its way through the throng of supporters.

"Benazir! A woman shouted as she ran, throwing flowers to her as she stood waving from the opening in the sunroof. "Do not leave us! The woman needn't have worried. Pakistan's native daughter was home to stay.

"She was never interested in the moment," her husband would recall. "She was interested in life at the end of the tunnel and history itself."

Perhaps this is the difference between those who look to the past for life and those who look forward? Those fleeting 'brief shining moments' that never last, cycling in the shadow of a perpetual 'repeat'. Only a few see beyond to the shining that illuminates a greater meaning. The beginning and the end of history itself.

As dusk set in the crowds continued to parade with their returned promise in a mass of joyful celebration. The street lights strangely flickered and then turned off casting darkness over the procession.

Seconds later the assassin's bullet found its mark before detonating a suicide vest.

Another bomb ripped through the crowded street scattering a sea of blood and humanity in every direction. The explosions rocked the heart of the free world leaving a nation orphaned once again.

That evening the street was cleaned and any evidence was quickly washed away. Simple forensics would not be allowed to record the truth surrounding the assassination of the beloved daughter of the east.

I remember waiting that night in the Garden of Gethsemane. The weight of unfolding history was spared our dimmed thoughts. Sleep does not come to a discerning mind. In the aftermath of our shameful slumber we had been given mercy.

All truth remembers its history. Pakistan's daughter of the east, a prophetess in her own time became an emblem of historical truths. Everything else eventually falls away. History is a remembering. The faint call of a deeper reckoning - a yoke we carry as our own until we collapse at the rail.

Our collective destination and all dimensions of time lead to the altar place of life itself where all history is raised up in a reckoning of the ages. Where the prophet's blood runs deep and wide for all who read the work of their scribes.

"Do this in remembrance of me."

"Oh Jerusalem, If only you could see the things that make for peace."

Cleopas suddenly realized the road beneath his feet had disappeared.

He had been fixated on the words of Camelot as he spoke of the prophets and all they had promised. He looked at Carolus. He too was transfixed even in the silence the three of them now shared as they walked the road.

Carolus looked at Cleopas and shook his head in amazement. Cleopas nodded, keenly aware of the surging deluge within. It was a longing for impenetrable depths and unscalable heights in a unison of time and place that shook the boundaries of human dimension. They were awash in the flood of a new understanding of mysteries that minutes earlier had been locked in the neglected and forgotten writings of the ancient scribes.

The road was the hope of Camelot himself carrying them to an outer frontier that revealed itself through the lone ray of a strange familiar calling that beckoned them onwards. His words passed over the ancient messengers of the Arabian Sea, through the dream destroying dust storms of the Midwest and beyond the warring mountains of northern Pakistan towards an awaited holy inferno.

The fires of hidden truth burned within leading them to the next village in that place beyond that has always been - nestled just outside the dimensions of time.

Off in the distance, Emmaus drew nearer.

CHAPTER 16
GUENEVERE OF NEW GOLGOTHA

V. 28 As they approached the village to which they were going, he acted as if he were going farther.

BRITAIN, 519 A.D. - Queen Guenevere slumped to the cold floor of her bed chambers. The fragile peace with the Saxons had come to a crashing end. Sir Lamorak had come to deliver the terrible news to her himself.

Arthur had been captured and taken prisoner.

The Saxons had skillfully planned their attack and cut off Arthur and a few of his men from their reinforcements. Refusing to retreat they chose to fight valiantly until the enemy's swords finally cut away their own. Camelot had fallen to the enemy. Her king led away in chains and the mocking curses of men.

Almost immediately the road to that one brief shining moment enshrined in Camelot became a treacherous journey. A dangerous road that once embarked upon refused to yield easy passage to its travelers.

Much like that early morning when Camelot walked the shoreline with Cephas.

I followed at a distance not wanting to yield even the few feet of sand that separated us as the sun rose and bathed its glory on that quiet beach. It was our dawning of a new road, a new journey that would bring much pain and suffering before we were ready to fully receive the beauty and splendour of its promise.

In earthly memoriam, once each year - Maggie can still be found praying at the tomb. Neither noticed nor recognized she keeps her vigil. She was a comfort to Guenevere amidst the tyranny of the Saxons some fifty decades later.

In the days following the king's capture, Camelot's mourning queen would turn the pages of Maggie's story and ponder their meaning. Who was she to believe in Camelot? The promises of a broken kingdom gone and the bitterness of a forbidden fruit passed down through the generations, still zealously devoured in greedy mouthfuls.

The Kingdom of Camelot that had promised to take them all farther, had taken Guenevere to the edge of despair.

The passing of history and its generations would inherit the ponderings of Guenevere during those broken days in the tumultuous succession of apostles and kingship. A perilous royalty had not yet discarded her purple robes as new worlds of Romans and Saxons eager to pay tribute to the demons of Golgotha, gnashed their teeth at the throne of Camelot.

The siege would come as it always did - in waves.

* * *

"Ms. Petrov, there is a letter for you." The secretary handed the small envelope to the school teacher and hurried out the classroom.

"Children, carry on with your writing assignments." The teacher sat down at her desk and opened the letter. It had no return address. The first thing she saw was the red letters stamped: *Confidential - 'A memorandum for employees of the Soviet school system'*

The first sentence sent a chill up her spine: *The pope is our enemy.*

What could that possibly mean? She thought. Was this really true?
She read on...

*Due to his uncommon skills and great sense of humour he is dangerous because he
charms everyone, especially journalists. Besides, he goes for cheap gestures in his
relations with the crowd, for instance, he puts on a highlander's hat, shakes all
hands, kisses children, etc... It is modeled on American presidential campaigns.
Because of the activities of the church in Poland our activities designed to
atheize the youth not only cannot diminish but must intensely develop. In this
respect all means are allowed and we cannot afford sentiments.*

Comrade Y. Andropov

Komitet Gosudarstvennoy Bezopasnosti

She had not heard of this man or the subversive activities of the Polish
church. Was not all of Europe atheist? She wondered. How good it
was that General Secretary Brezhnev was keeping them safe from the
plottings of the West.

She felt a surge of pride. She carefully folded the letter and placed it
back into the envelope.

"Ilya," she said, handing the envelope to one of the younger boys not
yet able to read.

"Throw this in the fire and return to class." The boy took the State's
directive in his hand and left the classroom.

Despite the efforts of West Germany and the Vatican for a new
eastern policy, I ensured Colonel Basbug and his Grey Wolves would
not stand for any form of detente. A thawing of tensions between the
Eastern Bloc and the former bloodlands of Central Europe could not
be allowed.

It was I that authored the fall of Ostpolitik. We had in fact been planning it for centuries.

* * *

ST. PETER'S SQUARE, VATICAN CITY, 1981 A.D. - It was late afternoon and a few clouds slowly drifted over the square bringing shade to tourists and congregants who gathered in the warm spring afternoon to welcome home Wujek. He was scheduled to be returning from Milan.

Across the square people began to filter in and find a spot along the procession route. Many posed for photos or admired the beauty of the surrounding architecture. On a bench near the procession route two men sat leisurely writing postcards.

Cleopas later recalled the uncertainty he had felt for Carolus as they walked the road.

"I felt the same way about Tarsus," said Gamaliel when he heard of Cleopas' dark omen. "He was a master pupil but somehow I knew he was marked for something else. Damascus should have shocked me but it didn't. Our God had his man and the tables in the temple had been upturned again."

Kalashnikov watched from a distance behind one of the many columns of St. Peter's Basilica careful to stay out of the sunlight lest his shadow be revealed.

Well, Basbug, he thought. Now it's up to your Grey Wolves. They had planned so very carefully. Each detail of the operation had been examined and cross-examined multiple times. Mock operations had been executed and evaluated.

Nothing had been left to chance.

He rested his long hand on the pillar. The waiting in its final moments was a dreg's longest hour, he knew all too well. A steady hand in the seconds before was vital in executing that one pivotal moment. The mind of the dreg had to be completely emptied and deadened to conflicting thoughts and emotions.

Kalashnikov glanced up at the sun and noted the time. "Do not keep your flock waiting son of Cephas," he growled softly, looking out over the growing crowd. They were minutes away...

"No, the threat is definitely Bulgarian."

"Bulgaria?" The Vatican police official shook his head as he held the phone. "But this Turkish man has been implicated before."

"Yes," said the woman on the other end. "And he remains a considerable threat but he's a hired gun possibly working for Bulgarian intelligence or the East Germans."

"So it's a Russian operation."

"We haven't been able to penetrate our Soviet contacts yet. It's not likely we'll get far."

"Why on earth not?"

"I've been working the Special Investigations Division of Interpol for six years now and I'll be honest with you Inspector, their counter intelligence corps is a massive network that can shut down an operative in minutes."

The inspector looked out the window at the amassed crowd in the square. "So where does that leave us?"

"We're trying to locate this young Turk to keep tabs on him. He has a few aliases we're tracking and a European alert has been issued to police forces in every major city."

"Yes, the alert came in here at one-thirty pm local time."

"Good," said the woman. "There's also another Turkish national that may be involved in this threat to the Vatican. "We're working on it and will keep in touch with you over the next few days as information comes in. Have you heard of the Grey Wolves?"

The inspector was puzzled. "Indeed I have. A dangerous fascist sect. Mostly ultranationalist thugs. They've been known to recruit into Bulgaria as well."

He paused. "I'm not sure I understand the connection?"

The woman sighed. "It's complicated. We were able to intercept some communiques from Bulgarian intelligence but they're heavily redacted and unverifiable."

"What was gleaned?"

She hesitated. "Their leader - a former colonel in the Turkish Army is head of the Nationalist Movement Party - a eurosceptic."

"Yes, I've heard of him."

"Well it seems he's gone underground again. He'll often disappear for long stretches at a time. He was spotted by one of our agents recently in the Baltic states."

"The Baltic? That's odd. What's he doing up there?" Asked the inspector.

"We're not sure. His movements are difficult to track. Anyways, we'll keep you updated. Thanks for your time Inspector."

"Thank you."

This was unnerving he thought, still holding the receiver in his hand. The threat seemed to extend from one end of Europe to the other; from Istanbul to the far northern reaches of the Baltic and emanated from behind the iron curtain.

The dial tone interrupted the disturbing thought. This he knew was what Wujek was ultimately battling - a void was taking its ugly shape to shade the rest of the world under a spreading cloak of darkness.

He exhaled slowly and hung up the phone.

Outside the peals of bells could be heard signalling the arrival of the Bishop of Rome.

One of the two men seated on the bench nearby stood up, put his pen in his shirt pocket and dropped his postcard in a trash bin as he walked past towards the oncoming white Jeep carrying Wujek...

Guards had been posted inside the castle at every corridor and entrance of the living quarters much to the objections of Queen Guenevere. However the knights had insisted and given their orders after she had finally given her assent.

The hallowed table had reminded its few remaining knights their kingdom without Camelot was at the mercy of the world around it - separated from the protection of its king.

Maggie had waited till nightfall and then crossed the drawbridge. The horses had become restless sensing a presence but she slipped past the king's soldiers standing guard and continued down the cobblestone road. It was a moonless night and the outline of the castle loomed over her as she made her way past the main entrance and found the narrow passageway that led to the servants' quarters.

In the forest beyond the sleeping castle the low call of an owl announced the arrival of a haunting wisdom.

Once inside she had quickly found the carving on the door transom of our nets draped over father's boat. Waves playfully lapped at its sides. Maggie slowly pushed open the wooden door as guards stood at each side unaware of their intruder.

The fire was burning its last embers in the darkened bedchamber and the shallow breaths of sleep could be heard beneath the warmth of the animal furs that covered the large bed.

Maggie sat on the edge of the bed and closed her eyes. The night was still and quiet. Yet the peace of Camelot was not upon them in the chamber. She looked at Guenevere asleep in the weariness of her turmoil and despair.

"Guenevere," said Maggie softly. "Hear what I've come to tell you."

The wind rustled the trees outside as the forest slept. The breeze danced through the drawn curtains of the open window. Guenevere stirred in her sleep.

"Find your king who has pledged to unite all of Britain under one banner. Do this under the one who will unite all nations under the Kingdom of Camelot."

Maggie leaned over Guenevere and whispered: "Implore him: Do not leave! Stay with us! For the day is almost over and we are without a shepherd to lead us farther."

She closed the door quietly behind her and made her way outside the castle in the way that she had come. Maggie crossed the drawbridge and walked down the road that disappeared into the forest. Before the castle was out of view she turned around and looked up at the window of the royal chamber.

"Do not despair," she said. "On his road there is safe passage."

Wujek appeared growing closer as the Jeep approached. He was smiling and waving at the adoring crowd. His white cassock gleamed in the sun. Several meters behind him a thin shadow slowly retreated back into the shade of the columns.

The young Turk pushed his way through the crowd getting himself into position a few meters back from the procession route.

Guenevere opened her eyes. It was still dark. She arose from her pillow and sat up with a start. The encounter tumbled through her mind in pieces. How could this be? She wondered.

Her thoughts found their order and she gasped. Guenevere threw off the covers and rushed out of the bedchamber. She hurried down the stone staircase and called one of the commanding guards. "Go quickly and summon Sir Lancelot."

The mother's face beamed as Wujek took her child in his arms briefly and blessed the young boy. He gave the child back and smiled at the mother. A small girl was hoisted up and Wujek reached down and put his hand of blessing on the girl's head.

Ease into place boy. Keep moving.

Thirty meters ahead the white Jeep slowly made its turn and headed straight towards the young man. He felt for the cold steel jammed against his back. He looked over a family with several children laughing and waving in excitement, they held blue and yellow balloons blocking his sightlines.

"Get away," he muttered. It was no good here. He needed to reposition closer.

The Jeep was now fifteen meters away.

The man hurriedly sidestepped the family briefly putting his hand on the father to move by him.

Hold your position. Settle in boy, hissed Kalashnikov gripping the column as he peered around it at the impending victory. He felt the demons within raging in anticipation.

Five meters...

Suddenly the man realized he had overshot his angle and struggled against the crowded bodies to regain position.

Now! Now boy!

It was too late. He had missed it.

What are you doing? Kalashnikov screamed to himself. The piercing screech of demons thundered down the abyss beneath the violent thrashing of the waves. We've only got one chance at this!

The young Turk scrambled to catch up but steadily lost ground in the crowd as the Jeep moved farther ahead down the procession route.

Take it over, he mouthed at the second assassin across from him on the other side of the route. He motioned with his head but couldn't seem to get the young man's attention.

He looked up. The Jeep was nearing the end of the procession and about to leave the square. Months of training wasted, he screamed at himself in a panic. Then a rush of adrenaline surged through him. The white Jeep had turned left and was making another round.

Okay, okay. Regroup boy! Mark your spot and wait.

Wujek held the roll bar of the Jeep with his right hand nodding and waving as they made their way to the far side of the square at the farthest point from the Basilica. He smiled at a white banner with a simple greeting: '*PAPA.*'

Across the crowded square a thin sliver of shadow peered out from the columns. Darkness would soon tower over St. Peter's... The shadow lengthened its form eager to devour the crowd in the impending madness. There would soon be no need to stay hidden in a kingdom he called his own.

Kalashnikov quickly found the young Turk in his sights. He had staked his place and was waiting.

As Wujek doffed his skullcap to the crowd another child was thrust into his arms. The blonde haired girl carried her blue balloon almost oblivious to the smiling man in white who blessed her and returned her to the hands outstretched in the crowd.

I won't abandon my position this time, the man vowed silently. He reached behind his back and wrapped his hand around it finding the trigger.

The Jeep inched its way closer until it was right in front of the outstretched hand that held the death knell of Ostpolitik. Wujek turned towards him.

Three shots rang out in succession...

"You summoned Your Highness." Lancelot bowed his head and remained on one knee. He held his shield in front of him. The candle light colourfully played against the ornate coat of arms that was embossed across the dazzling shield.

Queen Guenevere crossed the marble floor of the throne room and stood in front of him. She had placed the Queen's crown of Camelot on her own head.

"Rise Lancelot and hear what you must do."

Lancelot rose to his feet and faced his queen.

"The time of Britain versus Britain is over." We will rouse our subjects to voluntarily join your few men to fight for Camelot and the return of our king. I will go with you."

She walked to the window and stared out in the direction of Saxony.

"Sometimes I despair, oh God. We are caught up in a history we did not write. Yet the anguish is our own."

Guenvere reached out and clasped the cool bricks of the turret and leaned out through the open window.

"Out of this pain something new will be born!" She whispered to the darkness.

Guenevere had crossed the battle line for her king and his kingdom. She dismissed Lancelot after giving him her orders and returned to the royal chamber and fell into a deep sleep.

The shots echoed through the square. They resonated deep into the backlog of time thundering against the succession of the saints and across the Kingdom of Camelot.

"No!" Shouted Maggie as she heard the deafening gunfire that reverberated in shock waves through the forest. She stopped on the road and fell to her knees. This time there was nowhere to run.

"The killing fields have found us again," she cried. She covered her ears with her hands but the cracking of the sonic booms would not dissipate as it echoed back through the ages to its intended origin.

The place of Golgotha screamed again and then went silent as the bullets found their mark.

Then all went deathly quiet.

She saw the blood in St. Peter's Square. She saw death scurry through the columns.

"Stop him!" She cried out into the night.

Maggie shuddered. He was always there - lurking in the shadows.

I will make my way back, she thought. I will keep vigil and make my way back to Cephas.

She brought herself to her feet and continued down the road. The night drew in around her daring not to make a sound. It was as if all life in the forest and the skies above it had bowed in a still silence. Like a tamed animal that knows its master, the wild things of the forest paid homage to theirs.

Wujek slumped back into his seat. The blood began to seep through his white cassock. He knew he was badly wounded. He felt himself pulled backwards into the clutches of one of his aides as the Jeep quickly accelerated.

Guards ran behind the Jeep as it raced through the crowd and out of the square leaving the panicked masses in a state of terror and confusion.

Why the second agent failed to execute his duties, I'll never understand. He froze without firing his revolver or detonating the bomb. He killed us all that day. The two hundred and sixty fourth in the succession was there for the taking.

And we missed. We would have to wait again - possibly generations; possibly longer than that.

* * *

It was nearing midday and Maggie sat on the grassy bank of the ditch. Her knee length white dress though stained by the dust and tall grasses of the fields gave her an organic look of purity and elegance.

She stared across the ditch at the other side. Here lay the remnants of history's forgotten kingdoms. To this day it is referred to as the devil's dyke. Few really knew why even all of these centuries later.

But Maggie remembered. It was during the time of King Arthur and Queen Guenevere when the epic battles of Britain and Saxony raged here at the defended border carved out of the earth. This was the last frontier of two warring worlds. The last place Rome could not defend.

The earthen grass covered ditch ran a straight line for seven miles in Cambridgeshire, England. It marked a shallow depression in the countryside leaving little trace of the horrors it entombed.

Beneath the grass and the layers of earth that time had buried lay the bones of men cut down by the sword. The border ditch was the first and last line of defence that separated Britons and Saxons.

This was the place where Camelot came to die. The place where something new was born as Guenevere had foretold in the hour of her greatest pain.

Maggie stared across the unmarked graves of devil's dyke setting her gaze on the horizon - that holy distant harbour where the heavens descended into blue sky touching the farthest reaches of earth with the ancient invitation of new life and new promises.

* * *

The small convent was hidden away in the forest near the village of Amesbury.

For many weeks Guenevere had known she was dying. Arthur had been dead many years. That one brief shining moment they thought would last forever had disappeared in the setting of a few precious suns.

It was the promise of a greater Camelot that had brought her to the tiny convent. Out of the bones and ashes of that border ditch she had pitched her final camp - a last battle of wills - surrendered.

The small group of nuns and a handful of villagers who recalled those brief shining moments gathered around the day strength left her and she found herself at the crossing.

Guenevere looked at the kind faces that returned her solemn gaze. She had once been a queen who was now the subject of a new King, one greater than the legend of Arthur and one more ancient than the storied annals of his indentured service to Rome.

Kinship had deserted her at the convent's door. Friends and memories had faded away. But her will and remembrance of a greater history and its sacrifices had not.

"We must always return to the place of the skulls for here entombs the end of division and carnage and marks a new beginning for all," she reminded them.

With that she closed her eyes and took her last breath.

CHAPTER 17
A WORLD OF DEMONS

V. 29 But they urged him strongly, "Stay with us, for it is nearly evening; the day is almost over."

THE BALTIC SEA, 2001 A.D. - The waves crashed against the hull as the storm raged. A bolt of lightning lit up the black waves followed by rolling claps of thunder. The fishing trawler bounced violently on the angry sea, its nets hanging like the crooked legs of a giant spider on either side of the ship's rusted steel belly.

The swells were unrelenting, swallowing the swamped fishing vessel and holding it in its deep foaming valleys before spitting it back up on the roaring waves only to be pulled down again into its frigid grasp.

On the trawler's starboard side a flicker of light could be seen in a small window of the cabin amidst the fierce spray of salt-watery foam.

"Tell the helmsman to leave her be now," growled Kalashnikov to one of the deckhands.

"Aye, Cap'n." The bony man's dark face could hardly be seen as his rain hat was pulled down over sunken eyes. He retreated up the narrow steel stairs to the bridge.

"She'll steer herself tonight as the waves drive her," muttered Kalashnikov. He smiled as he looked out one of the small windows. "Home again."

He closed his eyes as the waves crashed against the hull and hurled its spray over the bulwarks. Reaching into his coat he took a swallow from his flask and returned to the galley where his guests were finishing a late supper.

Supper had been a tense affair. The presence of Sayyid did not help matters. He dined in open disdain of the others whom he considered his acolytes. He deferred only to Kalashnikov though at times reluctantly. Even Colonel Basbug was cautious in the presence of Sayyid.

Two hooded ship mates cleared the dishes from the large oak table and returned with brandy and cigars. All but Sayyid accepted.

Sar and Zia were engaged in an animated discussion on South Asian politics and military incursions in the Southeast.

"Your supply lines could be re-established through Laos," declared General Zia lighting his cigar.

Sar shrugged. "What does it matter now? Much of Ho Chi Minh Trail was bombed into the stone age. Only fringe political groups operate through its backchannels."

"And why are they not being re-mobilized?" Asked Zia.

"The region has been largely pacified. Would you prefer we ship them to North Asia?"

"If only it were that easy," grunted Zia throwing back his brandy. "You must have mobilizers on the ground in eastern Cambodia General?"

Sar shook his head. "No. The last of the Khmer Rouge elite died with one of my best field advisors. Lieutenant Kim was killed in an ambush on the Ho Chi Minh Trail years after the Americans fled Saigon."

"A shame," said Zia refilling his glass. "Good military personnel are bought at a premium."

General Ugarte sat back from the table and nodded in brooding silence largely disinterested in the conversation.

Kalashnikov stood up from the head of the table and raised his glass. "Gentlemen, it is good of you to join me on this beautiful evening. I trust the meal was to your satisfaction."

Basbug and the generals nodded and raised their glasses. Sayyid remained expressionless and waited for Kalashnikov to continue.

"The Persians are preparing the region nicely in the wake of the coming fall of Nebuchadnezzar," he said waving affirmatively in Sayyid's direction. Pakistan, thanks to General Zia's successor and Afghanistan have now entered the fold."

Zia held his familiar expression of crazed delight, his hands folded neatly on the table in front of him.

Kalashnikov continued: "Tonight we stand on the cusp of a new global order as we enter a fresh millennium. We are everywhere, strapped on the backs of the world's freedom fighters."

He looked out at the waves as they slammed into their starboard. "Many moons have been spent on this ship in discussions around the fall of the succession. It may be we can operate parallel to it at times while countering it heavily at others."

He turned to General Sar.

"We have turned the page into a new century and the next thousand years. General Sar, we have a new Year Zero."

"Excellent sir. Much work begins," said the general excitedly.

Kalashnikov set his glass down on the table and leaned forward. He seemed to rise above them. "We will render the succession into a state of complete indifference. The masses are well on their way already."

"And the two hundred and sixty fourth?" Asked Ugarte.

"We will try for Wujek again and the ones who may come after," said

Kalashnikov. "But our focus must be on scattering the remaining flock."

Kalashnikov motioned to his right. "I have asked Sayyid to join us this evening to brief us further. The floor is yours sir."

Sayyid held the front of his dark robe as he rose from his chair and stood over them casting a suspicious eye on his reluctant colleagues. "We must regain a footing in the southern kingdoms."

"The southern kingdoms?" Asked Ugarte confused.

"Yes," said Sayyid, staring straight ahead. "South Asia, North Africa and South America."

"What are you proposing?" said Colonel Basbug, not hiding his contempt.

"The most effective form of nationalism is a theocracy," Sayyid pronounced loudly.

Colonel Basbug scowled at his brandy but said nothing.

Sayyid shot him a brackish glare and continued. "When your flag is the face of God then all other dissidents become the great evil. Our flocks wait eagerly to be given permission to hate. I have ordered an escalation of our military exercises in the Strait of Hormuz."

Kalashnikov smiled to himself. He could always count on Khomeinism, he thought deviously. The God of humankind could be stretched like a thin canvas to cover all ambitions of the transgressor. This was the nectar of Sayyid's hold on his people.

"You're speaking of an Islamic radicalism rooted in jihad," shouted Ugarte. "Chile and the rest of the Americas will not allow it!"

Basbug nodded in agreement.

Sayyid remained unmoved. "Your Christian conservatism follows different methods? Your friend, Henriquez and his Vicariate of Solidarity would testify to your employment of these methods General."

"Do not speak that name in my presence," Ugarte seethed menacingly.

Sayyid ignored him. "And your Grey Wolves, Colonel?" He asked accusingly.

Basbug shot him a glare but said nothing.

"Hear me well." Sayyid raised his fist in the air. "We disdain liberalism in equal measure and believe in the same God. Our means are shared and justified in their intent."

"I am not you, nor share in your kind," growled Ugarte slowly.

"Nor do I appreciate your uneducated attacks on the truths of socialism," barked General Sar.

Kalashnikov stood behind them beaming. A ravenous look pierced his eyes.

"Your petty ideologies are of little concern to me," Sayyid hissed. "Either way, we shall regain a footing in the south." He fixed an icy stare on Ugarte.

"I believe a compromise can be negotiated," offered General Zia smiling. He took a long puff from his cigar and exhaled slowly. "Terms can always be satisfied in the balance of time."

Sayyid could not bring himself to look at Zia. He resembled everything that he had despised in the Persian monarchy - everything the revolution had sought to destroy.

"Truth can never be compromised," snapped Sayyid. "Much like the last Persian infidel who called himself king and rid Persepolis of snakes and scorpions for his own lavish purposes, we will rid the south of its crawling vermin to establish a great kingdom of purity."

"You speak of a mongrel purity!" Shouted the colonel, leaping up from the table, no longer able to contain his outrage.

Sayyid glared across at him but did not raise his voice. "You mean to challenge my authority Colonel?"

"Your authority is delusional and self-appointed," said the colonel quietly. He was acutely aware a line had been crossed.

"Now gentlemen, please," Kalashnikov intervened chuckling. "We must channel our aggressions wisely."

He motioned for Sayyid to sit down.

"Do not forget the legions who remain dependent on us to supply their needs."

"Yes Commander," said Zia. I urge us to put away ideology and focus on our strategic requirements. Supply lines must be filled and kept operational."

Kalashnikov nodded. "Agreed, General."

He pointed below them. "Down in the hold are fresh crates of our screaming demons recently loaded. How wonderful it is to convert a fishing boat into a supply ship. Our weaponry undetected under a few pounds of Baltic herring.

"Where are you proposing we dock, Commander?" Asked Sar.

"We'll head into the Gulf of Riga and moor on the east side of Saaremaa if necessary. We can unload through Estonia for the time being. The port of Gdansk would be preferable but that meddlesome trade unionist, Walesa created problems for us that still complicate our shipments."

"What about other ports of entry?" Asked Zia.

"We may have to unload in Kaliningrad," said Kalashnikov pointing a long finger to its location on the map that hung from the grimy wall.

"Anymore questions?" He asked.

The table was silent.

"Then that is all. I'll retire to my quarters gentlemen. Your berths have been prepared."

The galley emptied quickly.

Kalashnikov found Sayyid on the bridge staring out over the bow. The storm had abated but the waves still frothed and dashed themselves against the hull.

 "Well, Sayyid?" Kalashnikov offered him a glass of brandy. "Do we have much more use for them?"

"Perhaps. Perhaps not," said Sayyid, declining the drink with a wave. "There are new recruits proving their mettle. Time has passed these by and our world is changing. We must sharpen our swords. No kingdom governs itself."

Kalashnikov nodded in agreement. "Then it is settled. We'll send them to the depths before we reach the Gulf."

* * *

LIMA, PERU, 1992 A.D. - What happened on Tarata Street was the beginning of the end. The chairman and his Maoist revolution had descended from the mountains and jungles to fight an urban war that would soon put an end to them.

A fatally-wounded guerrilla fighter who had passed the threshold of fear had asked the question his fellow comrades dared not yet ask: "When did Shining Path ever illuminate the road best traveled?"

Revolutions are native creatures to their own time and place. Exporting such movements is a foolish business. Just ask Che.

A delivery truck pulled up alongside the curb. There was a knock on the side window.

"Sorry, sir, you can't park here."

The driver was startled and nodded quickly. He pulled away and circled the block finally deciding to park just off the intersection on Tarata Street. He turned off the engine and opened his thermos of coffee. The steam poured out of the cup as he filled it with the hot black liquid. He took a sip and yawned as he stared out the windshield.

The narrow residential street in downtown Lima was bustling with evening activity. It was a mix of shops and high rise apartment blocks offering the best of modern Peru.

So this was how the bourgeoisie lived, he thought. He wondered what the chairman worried about? These people seemed harmless. They were happy, laughing as they walked leisurely about. And not an AK-47 to be seen anywhere.

He took another sip of coffee. He'd been a member of Shining Path for eleven years now, recruited in his home province of Cangallo. His family and friends had heard of Chairman Gonzalo and his mounting stories became legendary throughout the Andes. He and his brothers and their wives had volunteered their services with great anticipation.

He was beginning to think it was a terrible mistake.

In the field they were referred to as freedom fighters. Behind their backs, they were called dregs and made to feel like it. They attacked local police, burned villages and recruited what was left. Long ago the movement had been exhilarating. Revolution had meant something.

He checked his watch. Ten minutes.

Then the chairman had ordered him back to base camp in Ayacucho.

"A special operation is being planned, Eduardo. Your commander and I want you as our lead operative."

The chairman brought his face close to Eduardo's and whispered: "We're going to Lima."

He had been shocked. For years the movement had carefully avoided the cities. Now they were crossing a dangerous threshold.

Before returning to his training post he had stopped by his local church to visit the priest. He was an old family friend having baptized him and his siblings.

The priest was an elderly man. He had smiled upon seeing him and led him to a small room at the back of the sanctuary. After enquiring about his wife and brothers he had stared at him for what seemed an eternity.

"Eduardo, listen to me." He closed the door.

The young man had expected a lecture. Perhaps that's why he had come.

The priest had grabbed him gently by the shoulders.

"Do not huddle in your cramped trenches jostling with others for a warmth that can never be had. It will consume you and your fellow band of wanderers. For it is a dance of death. But push forward in the truth of *his* fires and all the furnaces of Babylon will not harm you or singe a single hair on your head."

The priest had offered a prayer and then led him outside.

"Choose *your* path Eduardo. It waits for you and will guide you home."

He took a last sip of coffee and closed his thermos. He started the truck and pulled out into the middle of the intersection. In the distance he heard music coming from one of the busy shops.

He slipped the gear shift into neutral, got out of the truck and walked away in the opposite direction.

The truck rolled silently down the street carrying five hundred pounds of diesel and ammonium nitrate towards its unsuspecting target.

Oh foolish pride - the fear of its own undressing. Open the floodgates to an ocean of repentance that began as a trickle in the river Jordan.

* * *

The four long wooden boxes slid off the gangplank splashing violently into the black foaming waters. The fierce struggles and muffled screams could scarcely be heard as the waves swallowed their captives and the gun crates slipped beneath the surface and descended to the icy depths.

The two thin black figures stood on deck and stared out at the feasting waves that rushed and swirled over the entombed. The sea roared its delight.

CHAPTER 18
THE BREAKING OF THE BREAD

V. 30 When he was at table with them, he took bread, gave thanks, broke it and began to give it to them.

CAPITOL HILL, WASHINGTON D.C., 1934 A.D. - Senator Thomas Gore rose from his polished wooden desk in the historic north wing of the Capitol Building.

"Now Secretary," he mocked. "Is this not just a teeny weeny bit of socialism?"

Secretary Perkins smiled as she sat perfectly-postured across from her longtime antagonist from Oklahoma. She had been called to testify at the Senate hearings on the proposed Social Security Act. She knew what was coming.

"Senator Gore, you of all people should understand the complexities of hardship and compassion in sculpting a balanced response to the nation-wide struggle of hard working Americans."

She poured herself a glass of water from the pitcher on the table in front of her.

"No man or woman, no family should live in fear of being unable to perform this simple act - pouring a cup of water or putting bread on the table."

"Ms. Perkins, no one is denying bread to the weary of this nation but there must be limits to what government can provide."

"What government can provide?" Asked Frances rhetorically. "Senator, this nation is dealing with a crisis of means, not idleness as you're suggesting."

Senator Gore dismissed her with a wave of his hands. "I'm suggesting no such thing Ms. Perkins."

"Then we must define a national policy to strengthen the means for abundance that extends compassion alongside market incentives. You speak of setting limits, Senator."

She looked out at the members of the chamber. "This government speaks of removing them for the greater freedoms of all."

"Well ,Socialism has many paths of origin," said Senator Gore. "Even the American Bar Association and the U.S. Chamber of Commerce -"

"Oh yes," Frances interjected with a note of sarcasm. "They've accused Social Security as an attempt to Sovietize the country. How utterly ridiculous." She pushed her half glass of water away from her.

"Opponents of this bill would like to see hard working Americans' daily nourishment remain just out of their reach while the Soviets would like to see us waste this nourishment in the name of a bullish pride that erases all compassion."

Ripples of murmuring could be heard throughout the chamber. She placed her hand on the pitcher of water.

"Now you tell me, Senator. Is giving refreshment and hope to our elderly and unemployed a Soviet virtue or an American one?"

More murmurs reverberated across the chamber.

"Communism has no virtues!" Someone shouted from the back row of desks.

"Here here!" Another senator yelled.

"Order please." The Chair nodded to his right. "Senator Gore, you have the floor."

"Thank you Mr. Chairman." He smiled across his desk in the direction of the small table where the Secretary of Labor sat patiently.

"Secretary Perkins, you have spoken repeatedly about the provision of economic security for our most vulnerable." He motioned to his fellow senators.

"I don't believe anyone in this chamber who collectively represent the people of this nation want to deny the basics of life to its own. But the means of security do not rest solely or primarily in the hands of government." Perhaps you disagree with this statement?"

Frances ignored the bait. "I completely agree with your statement, Senator, as does this administration. The backbone of America's economic security is its people. Families, farms, industry and private enterprise fuel her engines of growth and prosperity."

The chamber became quiet. Frances sensed the mood was changing and decided to shift gears.

"These are the values and principles that must be fiercely protected for they are now under severe strain if not, a direct attack."

She glanced at Senator Gore who waited for her to continue. The questioner was now listening. She had the chamber.

"Traditional sources of economic security have always been tied to labor, family, assets and charity. The threats to economic security - old age, unemployment, illness, disability and death are unchanging facts of life. They are as true and real today as they were in the time of Abraham."

Secretary Perkins surveyed the semi-circle of desks that faced her. For a moment she allowed herself to enjoy her job. These moments were few and fleeting in the deluge of partisan noise that obscured them.

"Land is our foundational asset - the cornerstone of our nation's bless-ings." She paused for emphasis. "And it is under direct attack, affecting all other means of economic security across the country to one degree or another."

In a middle row of desks Senator Russell scribbled a note and summoned a page. He watched as the note was delivered to Senator Gore's desk.

"I would like to take you back to the president's message to congress this past June," said Frances, opening her folder on the table.

"It was delivered upon creation of the Committee on Economic Secu-rity by Executive Order. It reads:

"Therefore, we are compelled to employ the active interest of the Nation as a whole through government in order to encourage a greater security for each individual who composes it. This seeking for a greater measure of welfare and happiness does not indicate a change in values. It is rather a return to values lost in the course of our economic development and expansion."

Senator Gore opened the note on his desk. He read it and smiled, glancing quickly at his impatient ally across the chamber.

If you're not gonna go for the jugular, let me have a go at her. - R. Russell

Just down Pennsylvania Avenue, President Roosevelt sat in the oval office hunched over a stack of letters. He exhaled deeply and sank back into his chair. His hand dropped to his side still holding the neatly folded handwritten letter. He looked at it again -

Dear Mr. President,

I'm a 60 year-old widow greatly in need of medical aid, food and fuel, I pray that you would have pity on me.

He reached for the next letter from the stack on his desk. It was from Virginia. He opened it. It simply read:

I'm 72 years old and have no one to take care of me.

He stared back at the pile of opened letters and the stack still waiting to be read. Against every impulse of pent up frustration, the president gently placed the letter on his desk as if not to shatter whatever hope remained for a lonely and forgotten elderly woman who was afraid.

The old order had run its course, he thought. He'd stewed all day over an early morning phone call with Raymond Moley who had implored him to readjust their taxation policies. Many at the Treasury Department were up in arms. He claimed that a 'soak the rich' tax structure would be the death knell of any hope for economic growth. The president had argued increasing social unrest and a deepening sense of unfairness required a wider distribution of wealth.

President Roosevelt looked again at the gut-wrenching pile of letters on his desk - the work table of the nation. No, he thought. He would not abandon his position, nor jump ship only to flail rudderless in the cold waters of public opinion. There was no decision to be made. It was being rendered in the moment. A new course - a new way was being thrust upon them.

* * *

Carolus handed the water and the basin to Camelot. The shouts and laughter of passing children could be heard as the sun cast its long peaceful shadows into the small home. The day's last vestiges of sunlight danced slowly on the whitewashed walls gently receding into evening.

Cleopas had greeted his family and disappeared out back to start the fire and prepare for the evening meal with their guests.

The day had been uniquely strange and overwhelming, thought Carolus. The horror and confusion of the morning and preceding days weighed heavily. But there was something else that was equally confounding. He felt at peace. As though a consonance had been found amidst the storm of a raging dissonance that had not yet been resolved.

He tossed the towel he was holding to Camelot comforted by the assurance of these thoughts.

Cleopas appeared holding a young girl who playfully clambered onto his back.

"Preparations are underway."

The child squealed as she slid down into her father's arms.

He smiled. "The meal will be served shortly."

* * *

ROUTE 66, OKLAHOMA, 1935 A.D. - It was the beginning of the largest migration in American history.

Over two million people would leave the mid and southwest states over the next five years. The dust bowl had claimed its territory and was devouring farms and communities at a staggering pace. America's breadbasket was being starved into a barren wasteland.

Oklahoma was battered with the winds of death that would sweep four hundred thousand people out of the state. Most of them were poverty-stricken and destitute.

A rough looking man in his fifties thanked the family for the ride as they pulled into town. He was an Okie like them looking for work and a new life. A woman and three children were in the back seat.

"I've been here four months now. California ain't what a lot of people thought it'd be."

The man nodded slowly behind the wheel. "There a church in town?"

"You a preacher?" He asked.

"No, just a regular attender."

The man nodded. "Church in town here is empty most Sundays. No matter really," he said. "Three or four is all you need."

He touched the brim of his hat. "Again, much obliged for the ride."

He turned and disappeared into the mess of tents of yet another American shanty town.

Carolus stood several yards off the road in an adjacent drought-stricken corn field separated by a shallow ditch. He was lost - mired in the wonder of the prophecies Camelot had unravelled for he and Cleopas as they walked.

He looked down, surprised to see he still held the towel and the basin in his hands.

Carolus looked around him. It was a land foreign to him in a time he did not recognize. He shook the strange red dust from his sandals.

Suddenly Carolus recoiled in horror.

A long pointed shadow cast its known reflection across the basin and towel. A cold chill gripped his senses as he followed the length of shadow as it moved across the field.

The shadow ran into the ditch and up the far side onto the road and finally found its source at the feet of a young man. He was tall and lean. He wore the clothes of a working man. He walked slowly but with purpose, his shadow casting its ugly darkness on the dusty ground in the midst of the traveling caravan of people, overloaded farm trucks and broken down automobiles.

"You!" Whispered Carolus in shocked disbelief.

"I know you."

Somewhere - that terribly familiar fear. "The desert... Yes, the desert."

The columns! He thought.

I've always known you.

Yet this time, he saw he was walking with another that Carolus didn't recognize.

Then they disappeared in the crowd of migrants slowly making their way down the dusty gravel road. Still, the long shadow fragmented by the crowd greedily lashed out its peculiar jagged scar across the ditch running parallel to the road.

"I watched as you said goodbye to your mother," said Kalashnikov. He adjusted his fedora to shield his eyes from the dust that obscured the sun's light but not its relentless heat.

"Do you not think I feel compassion? That only you are capable of empathy?"

Camelot did not answer.

"I remember our time in the desert," Kalashnikov mused. "You refused to make bread from the stones."

He paused looking at the tired parade of refugees scattered along the road as far as the eye could see.

"And here we are again," he said. "People are hungry. Will you refuse them too?"

Kalashnikov watched as two sons and an aging father tried to push a Ford Model 48 out of the ditch. A few men dropped their belongings and walked over to help.

"You speak of hope. Where is your father's guiding hand in all of this?"

"Follow me," said Camelot nodding to the road ahead.

He saw his traveling companion. In his right hand Carolus held the basin and the towel that had been offered to him moments earlier.

"Of course," said Kalashnikov grinning wildly. "Another exodus to a promised land that will not welcome them."

He chuckled. "I shall wait for your weary wanderers in the wilderness."

Kalashnikov stared at a young girl with face drawn and head resting against her mother's side.

"And then I shall feed them the riches of this world."

* * *

The water and the blood - living and dying.

The outstretched hand of the cosmos and the holy groanings of the saints - resurrecting life amid the dying and cultivating the narrow path into fields of abundant splendour that span the horizon of holy skies.

On that lonely isle I ached for distant horizons.

And I saw them.

Billions upon billions of skies that exist to this day in undiscovered places that we have never seen nor will eyes ever gaze upon. In all of these strange, unknown virgin skies beyond their vast horizons, lies the altar place. The journey's end where the Feast awaits.

One cannot talk about the eucharist without talking about the broken body and the blood.

It is impossible.

The cosmos thunder every time the bread is broken at the altar place. How could it not?

The Risen One is celebrated with the same joy and assuredness that Maggie and mother poured into our dim minds that blessed morning.

His proclamation among the waving palms that sang his promise. *'Even the stones would cry out,'* he had said.

Would not then even more the vast powerful spaces of the universe cry out?

O to witness such things with the human eye and hear the sounds of cosmic glory that reverberate across the galaxies of His Dominion.

Perhaps there are places amongst the cosmos where we can see God? And perhaps that is why for now, those places are spared our pitiful intrusion.

The sacraments are crowned with the Eucharist. He seals his covenant with the blood, having completed his journey so that we may complete ours.

That blessed river Jordan did not spill its banks to avenge the blood on the hands of the prefect. Its sacred waters knew the blood would cleanse what it could not.

Carolus stared at the jagged scar of shadow that receded into the distance. It pulled his most troubling memories through the dried out corn stalks. He felt a nausea of panic seize him and he wanted to chase after them. He saw his own fear.

The receding image of his childhood as Ginka faded from sight on the train station platform, her face creased and distorted in the jagged corn leaves.

Krakow... the spider of evil scurried through the stalks.

A furious thundering crack ripped across the field and razed what was left to the ground. Carolus clutched his abdomen and fell back. He saw the basilica towering over St. Peter's Square and still the jagged shadow seemed to be dragging him through the field as if caught in the nets of a trawling terror.

Carolus saw the waves and the lightning. The field was being swallowed in a tsunami of staggering destruction.

"The road!" Screamed Carolus. He turned to look behind him but the waves hit and plunged him deeper into the roaring sea.

He saw the abyss as it flooded with the terrible waters that engulfed him in wild screams of fury.

He gasped and fought for the surface. The water was icy cold. He ripped away the few corn stalks that clung to his face. Carolus broke the surface and was startled by the blackness of night. The nets still dragged him to where he did not want to go.

He had seen it for an agonizing moment before the thunderous waves had swept over him.

The ugly fishing vessel with its drooping sweeping arms loomed ever closer as the nets returned to their master.

He closed his eyes.

"Carolus."

The net cut into his side as the angry waves lashed their fury at the night's catch.

"Carolus. Remember!"

He opened his eyes amidst the raging storm. He heard a voice faintly call his name.

"Help me!" He cried.

The ugly fishing trawler towered over him now and he heard her engines groan and hiss as they gathered in the heavy nets.

"Remember Capernaum!"

Capernaum? Carolus's mind reeled, madly trying to push through the fear.

'And will you also go?' The cliff's edge... The ring of the fisherman!

"Cephas!" Cried Carolus as the nets closed around him. He saw the tall silhouette standing on the deck as the waves pounded the vessel.

"Save me!"

The voice was calm above the roaring waves.

"You are not mine to save. We are the bookends of the succession."

The inky black waves howled above in a frenzied madness.

"Look to Emmaus."

Emmaus! Suddenly Carolus remembered his traveling companions.

"Cleopas! The prophecies!"

"Yes Carolus. The Feast of Life."

"*Quia corpus Christi fractum*," whispered Carolus.

He braced for the watery fangs of death. Then he heard the fishing trawler's retreating engines.

The waves bowed low and went calm. The waters receded into the abyss. Everything stopped and went utterly quiet.

He felt himself being pushed up to the surface. The waves dissipated and the water receded. He felt roots and dirt against his face. Then he was back in the corn field. He pulled himself up on his side. In front of him a glistening drop of water fell from a husk of corn and splashed onto the red ground by his face. He watched as water seeped back into the soil and disappeared into the dust.

Kalashnikov rose from his black throne of ice. He took a few steps towards Camelot and thrust a long pointed finger up at the swirling rim of the abyss that rushed in a circular towering madness around them.

"We will try for him again. The succession will be undone. For I am the Prince of this world."

Camelot stared at Kalashnikov in the belly of fear he had mastered long ago. A full descent to the icy depths.

Kalashnikov hissed: "Remember, I am the opiate of the disenfranchised, the downtrodden, the revolutionary."

He tapped the long crate at the foot of his throne and held an open hand above it in mock blessing.

"My soldiers are everywhere and it is I alone who have armed them in the cold steel of my precision."

Kalashnikov walked to the swirling wall of foaming waves that rushed in a demonic fury around the icy depths of the abyss. He watched as he spoke, his back turned to Camelot.

"You may elude me but the world remains mine to conquer."

He turned and faced his former master, his dark eyes - gleaming sapphires. "I will find every corner of Camelot and extinguish your ill-guiding light. I will shine darkness!"

The waves rushed up to the surface in a crushing roar of unleashed ferocity, hissing in long tongues of destruction. All the oceans' depths combined could not reach beyond the first league of the abyss.

Kalashnikov watched them rise towards the surface of his entombed world and returned to his throne.

"Now leave me."

He heard the sound of children and felt the soft cool air of the evening. Red hues of light from the last offerings of the sun's setting still hung on the wall.

Carolus stood alone with Camelot. He looked down and found the towel and basin in his hand.

Behind him Cleopas had set the bread Carolus had bought on the roadside on the table.

The presider of the elements of the depths would continue to wage war with all presiders of the elements of bread and cup.

 From the altar place of the Feast back to the killing fields of Golgotha. The feasting of body and blood. The place where Maggie ran through the rain, slipping over that muddy field of skulls.

* * *

It wasn't until they took the bread from Camelot broken for them, that death's long dark veil was lifted.

Camelot before Calvary, was the promise.

Now he was the promise fulfilled.

It is done. "It is finished," he cried out as he drowned in a sea of hells at the place of the skull.

Camelot had gone down into the abyss. The quiet of the tomb was only of a resurrected nature.

The battle had been fought leagues below in depths and places unfathomable to the created order. It had been consummated in the basin of the prefect and its waters of deceit that could not wash away history's guilt-ridden pages.

And it was to this first post-resurrection eucharist that he had cried out to in death.

The return from the icy depths.

Cleopas and Carolus received the body back for the first time in the breaking of the bread that was offered to them by Camelot.

The war of the ages is finished. Victory has been secured.

All of history, all of politics is not fought for its own end. It is fought for the cure of souls.

No political ideology or single act of history is exempt from passing before the altar place where the body and the blood await.

Carolus once confided in the physician - "What if we had not implored him to stay?" He was startled by the revelation.

Indeed, that is the moment of our own history; our own personal politik. No mind's eye can avert itself from the holy destination of the Eucharistic Feast.

The encounter awaits.

It is inescapable.

CHAPTER 19
ECLIPSE OF THE SON

V. 31 Then their eyes were opened and they recognized him, and he disappeared from their sight.

What do we do with the time when Camelot is obscured from our mind's eye?

* * *

SANTIAGO, CHILE, 1987 A.D. - Tear gas wafted over the altar obscuring Wujek who undeterred, presided over it. The amassed crowd of congregants that overfilled the square refused to yield to the armouries of Kalashnikov. General Ugarte had refused to meet with Wujek who had openly condemned his government as dictatorial and inhuman - an accusation he had directed at both his fascist and marxist enemies.

A crowd of over one million people stood in growing agitation during the Mass as anti-government protesters hurled rocks and projectiles at police and military units who dispersed water cannons and tear gas on the angriest mobs in the emboldened crowd.

Guenevere and Arthur stood packed into the middle of the crowd.

The opera music cascaded out over the amassed assembly as the altar was prepared for the holy meal.

A few yards behind, Maggie watched them in agony.

It was a pain unlike few others where one watches another slowly slip away. The infinite unassuredness of the damned.

Maggie screamed at Arthur - "What on earth are you looking for? It's right in front of you!"

He said nothing. He seemed confused and unsure, unable to move grasping the hand of his queen he had loved since childhood.

The altar was only a few hundred feet away. But neither Guenevere nor Arthur could see Wujek presiding through the crowd and the thin veil of smoke that still hung above the blessed chaos.

"Go!" Maggie yelled frantically. "Damn you Arthur! Go!"

He turned and stared at her. His expression was vacant and stubbornly calm. He held Guenevere's hand in his as the tear gas and smoke thickened. The King and Queen of Camelot faded from view.

Then they were gone.

* * *

Cleopas looked around for Carolus but couldn't find him as the smoke filled the square.

He pushed through the crowd assembled for mass, making his way blindly up towards the altar. His knees smashed into the railing and he fell forward onto them grasping at the smoky air in front of him that engulfed his lungs. He coughed uncontrollably and held onto the rail with both hands daring not to let go, lest he lose his way completely.

Guenevere reached the altar brushing against his shoulder as she knelt at the railing. She had been separated from Arthur in the chaotic procession to the holy feast. He had seemed lost and hesitant as if trapped by dueling allegiances. Her struggling panicked grip of his hand had been severed by the crowded processing of the masses. She had frantically looked back searching for her suddenly lost king of Camelot. Finally she had no choice but to turn and face the altar and approach the rail alone.

"*Quia corpus Christi fractum.*" She heard the words in front of her and felt the bread in the palm of her outstretched hands. She bowed her head, brought the body to her lips and began to cry.

A hand appeared through the stinging smoke of tear gas. Cleopas took the bread.

Then for a moment the fog in front of him was lifted.

He saw him.

He saw past a lifetime of 'brief shining moments' as he held the bread and its promise in his hand.

"Rabbi!" He shouted.

* * *

Few can bring themselves to kneel at an empty altar unpresided and see beyond their fury at a God in love with the dark side of the moon. An absent creator 'busy with other things.' The tiresome needs of a lonely planet's inhabitants - neglected yet again.

The physician wrote of Camelot's words as he taught in the Court of the Women: "*There will be signs in the sun, the moon, and the stars, and on the earth distress among nations confused by the roaring of the sea and the waves.*"

For it is these celestial bodies - foreign and distant that taunt us with their friendly skies while a cold alien moon plays with the waves, churning oceans from wrathful dissonance into serene consonance and back again. There is no safety in her manic relentless beauty.

She is the cliff's edge - the magical point of no return where the ring of the fisherman was thrown from her heights. This is the battered railing where the weary collapse with hands outstretched towards the altar to receive the crumbs of bread and the bottomless chalice.

Somewhere in an unknown universe, the purple skies of a small planet splash its euphoric painting on a strange horizon. As the stones longed to cry out at the feet of a young colt, the whole of created order celebrates in an other-worldly fascinating beauty.

They cry out in recognition at the eclipse of the Son and that brilliant shadow of light as he passes through the ancient dimensions to kiss the outer boundaries of his Holy Kingdom.

How the great poet, Vaughn was blessed to observe: *'There is in God a deep but dazzling darkness... O for that night where I in him might live invisible and dim.'*

CHAPTER 20
HEARTS AFIRE

V. 32 Were not our hearts burning within us while he talked with us on the road?

He was a career minor-league infielder with no business in major league baseball.

That is until Billy Beane called. "The last place I imagined myself was in an Oakland A's uniform," he said.

"Somehow I managed to stick around through spring and in that glorious summer of 2002 found myself in the middle of the streak.

It was our one brief shining moment.

We won three in a row, then four, then five. The team felt good. We won our next five and felt even better.

Then something happened. We caught fire. The city of Oakland followed and after that the entire country. It was a magical run. We won twenty ball games in a row. In a hundred and three years of American League baseball no one had done what we did and haven't come close since.

Then it was over.

That team didn't last long. We were traded, demoted, some of us retired. As quickly as we'd arrived, we were all gone. But every once in awhile I think about it. That motley crew of castoffs that became a band of brothers. I get a tinge of that feeling.

After we'd won something like seventeen or eighteen in a row I looked into the stands as the crowd was celebrating in pure delirium - absolute joy. A woman held up a sign that captured it all. It was that feeling that everyone celebrated together that beautiful night in Oakland Coliseum.

It simply read: 'We may never lose again!'"

The woman saw Winchester Castle in the distance and unwrapped the long dark veil around her. It had been many centuries since she had approached its Great Hall. Now it was all that remained of the once prominent castle. Centuries before it had served as one of the great ruling places of the Norman Kings.

She turned off the road and cut through the shallow ditch that ran alongside, clearing its far bank with an agile leap and bounded into the dense thicket that led in behind the castle ruins.

Once inside the pale darkness of the Great Hall she saw it. Her back rose like a wild timber wolf of the far north rising to its feet. Her limbs lengthened and she glided to the huge round table that sat timelessly, partially hidden under the dust and darkness of the centuries.

Kalashnikov extended a long bony finger and traced the names of Sir Lamorak and Lancelot that were carved at their places on King Arthur's mystical table.

"All of history is mine," said Kalashnikov quietly. "From me, this world and all that has happened in it - is inseparable."

Kalashnikov adjusted his long black vestments and stood at the legendary round table. He leaned forward, his grotesquely long hands resting on the table of truth - the wheel of life. He felt the ancient wood and shifted his weight forward, grasping at its ancient structure the way a preacher embraces his pulpit.

"I am the Vestment of Fear and will stoke the real passions of the world," he growled softly.

Sayyid understood best how to harness the sacred fury of passion. He ruled with an iron fist cloaked in the vestments of fear as only the fabled Prince from Qom could.

Now Sayyid, there was a man worthy of knighthood. If only King Arthur had listened to such counsel. Instead he worshipped at a 'table of truth' that betrayed him into the hands of Saxons. Forever remembered as the last vassal of Rome.

He stretched out his long jagged fingers across the ancient table and closed his piercing, wild eyes that shone like arctic sapphires, feeling the cold history of the world under the weight of his hands.

CHRISTMAS DAY, VATICAN CITY, 1991 A.D. - "Are you sure?" The young aide nervously pulled at his collar and loosened his tie as he held the phone to his ear. "I've been ordered to brief our secretary of state immediately."

He stood over the end table with his left hand leaning against the burgundy leather couch that was set in the middle of the extravagant ministerial office.

"And these events have been confirmed on the ground?"

He stared at the floor as he listened, scarcely able to believe what it was telling him.

The Soviet Union was dead.

He slammed down the phone and rushed out of the room. He ran down the length of the corridor and shoved open a doorway, leaping down the steps of the stairwell two at a time as fast as his dress shoes could navigate the winding wooden treads. Three floors later he burst into the crowded meeting room.

"It's true!" He shouted.

"We know!" An aide said, pointing at the crowd of people huddled around a small television. "It's all over CNN."

"What did you find out, Michael?"

A figure in a black suit and clerical collar turned to him. It was Cardinal Sodano, Secretary of State for The Vatican. He was a calm and patient man who conducted himself and his staff with purpose and due diligence. He was a seasoned emissary having served in the diplomatic corps of the Holy See since the 1950's.

The young aide bowed his head quickly. "Your Eminence, I was told the Soviet flag was lowered from the Kremlin an hour ago."

Cardinal Sodano shook his head in disbelief. "The hammer and sickle are no more..."

A staff member handed the cardinal a folder. "These communiques just came in."

"Ah, thank you." He put the folder under his arm.

"Anything else, Michael?"

"Yes, your Eminence. Our contact also told me the Soviet missile launch codes have been handed over to Mr. Yeltsin."

The secretary of state nodded. He took hold of the Cross that hung on a long silver chain from his neck. A smile burst forth. "In that case, I think we ought to brief Papa."

Wujek was alone in his study. A stack of newspapers and beside it, a worn bible written in Polish lay on the hearthstone of the fireplace that warmed the small upper room. Of the many ancient and secret hideaways of the Apostolic Palace, this modest enclave was his favourite refuge.

As the years drew on he felt a distance from the world around him he had not felt since his childhood in Wadowice. So much had changed and the dawning of a new millennium resigned his thoughts towards a sweeping obscurity.

Heads of state had risen and fallen during his long tenure. For the first time he had begun to question his own fleeting relevance as the aging Bishop of Rome. No heads of state were ever immune from the passage of time he had often reminded himself.

It had been over seven years since the fall of the Soviet empire. The fall of communism had ushered in a new era for Europe and unshackled much of the world's tormented from the red scourge of Lenin.

Still, the chains of men were patient and cunning.

Now there would be new enemies - new threats to church and state and the people who gave them life. Indeed, they were already hard at work. These forces were ambitious, intelligent and inexhaustible.

Wujek tossed his newspaper upon the others on the hearth and slowly pulled himself out of his chair. He walked over to his desk and caught himself in the small mirror hanging on the far wall. He flexed his right arm, feeling the scar where one of the four bullets had pierced him years earlier.

I'm an old man, he thought. Time which had once carefully moulded him and built him up was now methodically stripping him down. He longed for the vigor he possessed on the football pitches of his youth.

Many days he felt exhausted. He tired of past accomplishments which his aides and visiting dignitaries generously lavished upon him. How many armies does the pope have? They would remind him of the famous Soviet query and the historic end of Lenin's failed utopian nightmare. He knew they meant well but realized they couldn't understand where he now was and what he next envisioned.

He was giving himself over to what lay ahead in a new time and an old place. It was one that belonged to an ancient dimension and brought refreshment to those who felt that familiar longing.

The aging cleric sat down at his desk. He reached for his pen and tended to the stack of papers in front of him, haunted by the distant memory of an old friend.

CAPITOL HILL, WASHINGTON D.C., JANUARY, 1936 A.D. - Frances sat a few rows up from Raymond Moley who was seated beside James Farley. She was curious to see his reaction to the president's State of the Union address as he had crafted most of it. Halfway through she had considered it one of his finest speeches.

"We have earned the hatred of entrenched greed," boasted President Roosevelt, as he gripped the lectern.

A few feet away in the first row Raymond chuckled, in spite of himself. It was another swipe at the unscrupulous money changers. The president had chided him on his moxie as they went through the first draft. "Moley, you've finally found my sweet spot."

Ray knew there was more to come. Yet for the first time, he questioned the words he had so carefully crafted.

"They engage in vast propaganda to spread fear and discord among the people. They would gang up against the people's liberties. The principle that they would institute in government if they succeeded in seizing power is well shown by the principles which many of them have instilled in their own affairs. Autocracy towards labour, towards stockholders, towards consumers, towards public sentiment. Autocrats in smaller things, they seek autocracy in bigger things. By their fruits ye shall know."

Frances clapped her hands together as the applause cascaded through

the chamber. She laughed out loud as she watched James elbow
Raymond. James scrambled to his feet to enunciate his approval.
Behind them a few junior members followed suit and rose to their feet.
But Ray could not bring himself to do so.

"Shall we abandon the reasonable support and regulation of banking?"

"Nay!" Someone shouted.

The president adjusted his glasses and continued. *"Shall we say to the
farmer - the prices for your products are, in part restored. Now go and hoe your
own row."*

"Never!" A voice bellowed.

*"Shall we say to the several millions of unemployed citizens who face the very
problem of existence - yes, of getting enough to eat: We will withdraw from
getting you work. We will turn you back to the charity of your communities.*

*Shall we say to the needy and unemployed: Your problem is a local one. Shall we
say to the child in the factory. Child labour is a local issue. And so are your star-
vation wages - something to be solved or left unsolved by the jurisdiction of
forty-eight states."*

James Farley looked back and smiled as he caught Frances' glance.
They knew these moments were rare. Tomorrow's politics would soon
overtake the evening's victory.

*"Shall we say to the aging and the needy: 'social security lies not with the provi-
dence of the federal government. You must seek relief elsewhere."*

Raymond exhaled. The speech was good and the delivery was a gem.
Still, there was a tinge of nervous anguish that tore at his gut. He
feared most, that which he wanted to believe but now felt he could
not. Even so, he'd put pen to paper for his commander-in-chief
extolling a New Deal that now troubled him greatly.

He had always believed it was the duty of government to devise, with
business, the means of social and individual adaptation to the realities
of the industrial age that were the heart and soul of the New Deal.

But the administration's methodology was failing. For three years they had deliberately rammed 'all too severe' bills through one House for bartering purposes in the other. The mantra had become - *When you want one loaf of bread, you've got to ask for two.* Congress was losing confidence in a White House that continually cried wolf.

"But in the hands of political puppets of an economic autocracy such power would provide shackles for the liberties of the people. Give them their way and they will take the course of every autocracy of the past - power for themselves and enslavement for the masses."

More applause broke out in the House.

As the address unfolded Frances began to feel a growing restlessness settle over her. Would he even mention it? She wondered. The president had beat the drums of a foreign policy that railed against the growing crisis of autocracy in Europe. But she was hoping for more.

She knew Raymond was fixated on the nation's domestic well-being and used this argument as a front-line defence for his own isolationist sentiment. He'd aired his concerns in caucus that the New Deal was overplaying its hand and turning the economy into an 'economy of maintenance' which could do no more than redistribute the wealth that already existed. "Frances, he's playing nine-pin bowling with the skulls and thigh bones of economic orthodoxy!" He'd once vented in frustration to her in a Baltimore cab.

Still nothing. Move on, she implored.

Frances looked across. Raymond remained in his seat while James stood, applauding heartily. She began to shake her head and then caught herself. Come on Ray, she admonished silently - where was the call to action in Europe? Why pander to the isolationists?

"I repeat my words of March 4, 1933 - We face the arduous days that lie before us in the warm courage of national unity with a clear conscience of seeking old and precious moral values with a clean satisfaction that comes from the stern performance of duty by old and young alike. We aim at the assurance of a rounded and permanent national life. We do not distrust the future of essential democracy.

I cannot better end this message on the state of the union than by repeating the words of a wise philosopher, at whose feet I sat many years ago:

What does great crisis teach all men? From the example and counsel of the brave it inspires this lesson: Fear not. View all the tasks of life as sacred. Have faith in the triumph of the ideal. Give daily all that you have to give. Be loyal and rejoice whenever you find yourselves part of a great ideal enterprise."

He removed his glasses and motioned to the House. *"You at this moment have the honour to belong to a generation whose lips are touched by fire. You live in a land that now enjoys the blessings of peace. But let nothing human be fully alien from you. The human race now passes through one of its great crises. New ideas, new issues - a new call for men to carry on the work of righteousness, of charity, of courage, of patience, and of loyalty."*

President Roosevelt paused and looked out over the assembled chamber.

"However memory brings back the moment to your minds, let it be able to say to you: That was a great moment. It was the beginning of a new era. This world in its crisis called for volunteers, for men of faith in life, of patience in service, of charity, and of insight. I responded to the call however I could. I volunteered to give myself to my master..."

And there it was, thought Frances. Finally.

The House rose to its feet and applauded. For several minutes they cheered mightily and clapped their hands. A nation acknowledged its leader.

Not even the president could have fully understood the prophetic urgency of his own words. It was the first notes of an impassioned plea to stand and meet an impending hell.

There are moments that seem to consume time itself.

Their chestnut coats gleamed in the afternoon sun as they hurtled down the mile and a half track, their muscles rippling with every powerful stride.

No greater rivalry existed between either man or beast that unforgettable spring than the battle between Affirmed and Alydar. They were the best. No one else was even close. The most intriguing part was that each seemed to know it.

They battled each other over the course of ten miles spread over a few short years. Running for the roses in Kentucky; for the brown-eyed susans in Maryland; and finally the crown at Belmont.

In the end the distance that separated them over those ten miles was less than sixteen feet.

At Belmont the distance was mere inches.

They owned the last half mile of the showdown. It was just the two of them side by side doing what they did best - running for the finish and inflaming the passions of the world who cheered their every stride.

President Roosevelt was in no hurry to leave the chamber Frances observed as she stood in the aisle a few rows up.

He was holding court with his protégé, Harry - gallantly touting the latest data from the Works Progress Administration program no doubt, she thought. Even Senator Thurmond from South Carolina, no friend of the president and a few other Southern Democrats huddled around them laughing loudly and slapping backs of passing friends and colleagues.

She felt a hand on her shoulder. "Looks like Hopkins is enjoying himself for once," said James with a grin.

Frances laughed. "He's always enjoyed an attentive audience."

"And the data to back up his program deliverables."

"He has you to thank for that?" Asked Frances rhetorically.

"Of course," said James with a sly wink. "We'll see you tomorrow. I have to run - some follow up meetings with the Holy See and our boss wants an update."

"Good luck. That's important work," said Frances.

James waved and headed down the aisle.

Across the chamber she saw Raymond and Rex head out towards the rotunda. Rex was beaming as he should be, thought Frances. Ray was more stoic.

She had become increasingly cautious with Ray. His disagreements with the president and the administration were growing. She didn't think he would last much longer. A few members of cabinet had expressed similar concerns.

James had managed another stellar election campaign but the real force was the president. His vision had been unswerving and well-articulated.

The new deal was finding its foothold, albeit a precarious one in the fabric of American life.

And for every criticism, there were thousands upon thousands of families who were a bit better off today than they were in the crushing despair of 1933. Of this, Frances had no doubt. Hope had kindled a flame. It was no longer an ideal linked to the past but a refined hope that dared to look forward.

Frances took in the scene around her. The room was full of a bustling energy that was positive and healthy. The House of Representatives at that moment felt like the dreams of the nation, she thought. There was a spirit at work that was ambitious, compassionate and whole.

Politics in these moments were the noblest of endeavours.

Suddenly she was acutely aware of the gift of the moment and the scarcity of the scene.

Politics doesn't colour one's life as much as it convicts it, thought

Frances. The same could be said of history and its truths. She remembered being awestruck by the dome of the Capitol the first time she saw it. The gratitude of that moment now struck her again and took her to a different place.

A much deeper and significant place. The altar place of life itself.

Frances blushed at the thought. Her cabinet position, the oval office, even the flag that hung behind the speaker seemed suddenly futile. Who has the authority to author new deals? Who dares to be the architect of hope? Emperors, presidents, even prophets are judged in the end. For there is no middle ground of exempted territory.

Perhaps the trick to finding truth is knowing what part of us is fiction and what part of us is real, she wondered. Many believed in the New Deal. Others thought the New Deal was failing. Frances wasn't sure herself.

She sat down again in her seat recalling her meeting a few short years ago with Senator Russell and Governor Talmadge in Georgia. The truth back then seemed much more distant and daunting. It was a lobbying maze of kaleidoscopes and chameleons all chasing and leading to one's own end. Nothing breathed the purity of a greater revelation in seeking a wholeness of truth.

Yet it was all there to discover if one wanted.

She remembered her drive with Senator Gore and the resident in Oklahoma in the heart of the dust bowl.

Every neighbourhood, every town, every family and individual were deeply connected through an alignment of truths that resonated a rich human scale of harmonics across the soul of the nation.

These were the orchestrated chords of truth that the New Deal sought to play. It had been a noble gamble by a noble president. But Frances feared the brush strokes of the New Deal were scaled too broadly to sufficiently detail a portrait of recovery on the canvas of the American people.

Frances rose from her seat, unsure what to do next. A line of people waited to congratulate the president. She caught Ray's eye as he rose from his seat and left by a side door. He didn't have to say a word. Frances knew he was done. She felt neither relieved nor disappointed - only conflicted. That tortured feeling had become her constant companion. She headed down the aisle and stopped at the side door. Would history kindly redeem the price of loyalty?

Frances thought for a long moment - then finally turned to join the line of her colleagues waiting to congratulate the president.

CHAPTER 21
A NEW DEAL

V. 34 *"It is true!"*

CAPITOL HILL, WASHINGTON D.C.,   March 23, 1937 A.D. ‐
Frances, one of a few invitees watched with a reluctant appreciation as
Raymond Moley addressed the Senate judiciary committee.   It had
been less than a year since he'd finally resigned from Roosevelt's inner
circle and left the Democratic party. It had been a bitter breakup. Old
friends had disappeared and his once beloved New Deal no longer
resonated the truths he still so fervently believed in.

 Ray removed his glasses and set them on the lectern as he moved into
his closing remarks. All ears in the chamber listened intently:

*We who honestly believe in the purposes of the President but oppose his reorgani-
zation of the Court, cannot help but see in his course the perpetuation of a basic
wrong. Does the President mean that we shall have no more amendments to the
Constitution? Does he mean that in the future there will be change to meet the
changing times only through interpretation?*

*Does he mean that the Constitution must always be what the judges say it is? Is
our constitutional destiny, from generation to generation, to be vested in a long
succession of reinvigorated Courts?"*

The ends which Mr. Roosevelt has so courageously made his own can be achieved within the grand mosaic of the American constitutional tradition. But to seek to achieve them through the destruction of the American tradition is to open the way to the death of the ideals that gave them birth.

Frances had heard this accusation of hypocrisy before. Opponents argued this was the Achilles heel and a fundamental flaw of the New Deal - the legislation of policy cannot trump the ideals and values it seeks to implement. She had struggled with the issue herself and often feuded with Raymond as his loyalties drew him away from the New Deal policies he had once espoused.

But as in similar fashion with the president, Raymond Moley was a man to be listened to. He was shrewd and patient. A thinker - always fair and unrelenting.

I should like, in concluding, to stress once more a point which I have made in the course of this statement. The time is ripe for a basic and fundamental restatement of the law to make possible the attainment of the humane objectives of progressive thought. I deeply regret to see that golden moment pass. We have, as the President pointed out, a rendezvous with destiny. There are generations ahead whose welfare and aspirations and hopes can be realized if we, at this moment, avoid the easy path of expediency and spend our labors and our energy in facilitating the future evolution of our society and our nation on a democratic basis. The institutions of democracy grow and strengthen only through their use. When they are neglected in the interest of quick and easy material gains, atrophy sets in and death ultimately results. Let us make democracy work by working through the instruments of democracy.

Surely the New Deal was a democratic instrument of the People? Thought Frances. Only the harshest critics of the President had questioned his intentions. Most believed them to be noble, even if not entirely effective and the administration was only four years into their mandate.

Frances had always known President Roosevelt to be 'of the people.' The rich man's friend, the poor man's brother, the stern puritan conscience, the easygoing, indulgent and forgiving friend of the irregulars.

Raymond folded his glasses and tucked them into his breast pocket, aware that his time was up and the moment was upon him.

Mr. Chairman, Members of the Judiciary Committee: In presenting the reasons for my opposition to the proposal of the President to provide for new appointments to the Supreme Court, I should like to pass over the original arguments advanced for this plan the idea that the Court is inefficient, the notion that age is related to efficiency and even the contention that age and conservatism inevitably go hand in hand.

This proposal does not offer a permanent solution. It does not prevent the recurrence of exactly the same evil it is designed to remedy.

I believe in the purposes of this New Deal. But I am not for this New Deal alone. I am for future New Deals as well, unhampered by the dead hand of the past; even if that past be our resplendent present. I am not just against the dead hand represented by the majority of this Court. I am against all dead hands through which the past seeks to control the future. Our New Deal will be an Old Deal sometime. All of us who believe in the reforms of the past four years and who had some part in bringing about those reforms, will become old. Even the six justices that the President now wants to appoint will become old, and, as the President says, will wear glasses fitted to the needs of another generation.

I would think the physician would have especially enjoyed this speech. The argument held a timeless quality. Indeed the dead hand of the past continues to haunt whenever we break rank with the ideals of Camelot. The New Deal of the tomb cannot be broken by the gnarled dead hand of Kalashnikov. Death's hand hath no power over life even amidst the scurrying shadows of an earthly hell. Only Camelot had the power bestowed from the highest authority of the universal court to resurrect a new deal from the old.

For empires and nation states - new deals will become old deals. There is no renewal of flesh and bone in a passing world order - that is until the New Deal of Camelot, fitted to the needs of all generations.

Kingdoms of earth throughout their abominable glorious history could not offer what Camelot could on that golden distant road to Emmaus.

A New Deal that would conquer all dead hands, serve all nations and outlive history herself.

⸙

He leaned against one of the pillars outside of St. Peter's Basilica. Kalashnikov stared at the stone tablet inset into the square where so many people had begun to congregate to pay their last respects.

Wujek was dead.

"Goodbye Carolus Józef," he said.

Kalashnikov placed a long hand on the pillar. "I am stronger than ever. My unwitting disciples, more numerous by the day." He closed his dark eyes. He was aware of a gathering history that played on the seams of victory and defeat.

"There will be no shipwrecks on the Baltic tonight," he growled softly. "Our supply lines will remain open and secured." New ports of entry would inevitably emerge, he thought. He longed for the crashing fury of the icy waves and the trawling safety of his den.

Across the waters of the great ancient sea nestled in the ancient world, the old city slept. Out of the darkness of a moonless night a figure appeared and then disappeared along a narrow street that wound its way past the sleeping homes scattered about.

The figure arrived at the church. Removing her veil, she looked up at the Church of the Holy Sepulchre. Her eyes drew in the image, peeling back the layers of history.

Maggie closed her eyes. Time slowed. She gazed at the spot.

"Sometimes I come back here," she said standing beside me.

I smiled, recalling how Cephas and I had run with lungs bursting, to the place.

Maggie approached the spot and knelt on the ground outside the church walls. She had come to pray for Cephas - the next in the succession to succeed Carolus, and for all those who remained.

"This earth was precious," she said. "Dangerous and fleeting - but precious."

She remembered Carolus's words.

"For all who are lost," she shouted into the black night.

"Do not despair! We are the Easter people and hallelujah is our song."

ॐ

SKOPJE, REPUBLIC OF MACEDONIA, 2005 A.D. - It all happened as Camelot said it would.

"Yes, I'm sure he will be made aware if he isn't already," said one of the men as the river came into view. "After all, they were travelling companions."

Nicodemus and Gamaliel walked through the Old Bazaar Quarter and onto Stone Bridge. Its ancient archways stretched across the Vardar River. They stopped on the middle of the bridge and looked out over the peaceful waters.

"Wujek's passing has gripped much of the world," said Gamaliel.

Nicodemus nodded gazing upriver. "He has served the succession well. His work will be honoured by his contemporaries and those that come after."

Gamaliel nudged his friend's arm. "Ah, here he comes now." He motioned to the south end of the bridge.

A man appeared, walking towards them. He smiled broadly when he saw them.

"Well, Father," said Gamaliel. "We've been waiting for you."

"Rabbis!" said the man excitedly.

The three men embraced.

Nicodemus placed a hand on Carolus's cheek. "How wonderful it is. You've carried your load well."

Carolus smiled.

"Your old friend sends his greetings," said Gamaliel.

Carolus nodded and waited. Ancient memories tumbled through his thoughts. "Cleopas... Of course... Emmaus," he said. "I spent a lifetime trying to remember." He shook his head in amazement. "The long road to my master."

They watched the boats lazily pass beneath them as they drifted silently down river.

"Kalashnikov will continue his attacks. The opposing forces of the sacraments become more emboldened by the hour," said Carolus, watching the people as they walked along the shore. He wondered what would happen to them.

Gamaliel nodded towards them. "Their road continues."

"Victory endures," said Nicodemus. "And the journey's end calls each by name."

"Come," said Gamaliel, resting a hand on Carolus's shoulder. He led him to the other side of the bridge.

"Look," he said pointing out to the east.

Carolus felt the winds hit his face and the smell of sea water filled his senses. He stepped forward and felt uneven ground under his feet. He glanced down and saw the pavement had disappeared.

He was standing on the rocky sea cliffs looking down on the Greek waters of the Aegean Sea.

Then he saw what Gamaliel was pointing to. He didn't recognize them right away for they were still a hundred yards from shore.

But I did.

It was father's boat.

The fishing boat was approaching the shore far below them with Cephas and the others. Father was among them still preparing his nets.

Cephas waved.

Carolus felt another hand on his shoulder. "Time for you to return your key," said Nicodemus. "You don't need it anymore."

The gales of wind blew strongly around them invigorating Carolus. He suddenly realized why he had always been drawn to the water.

He laughed out loud.

"What happens now?" He shouted over the wind and the roar of the sea.

Gamaliel smiled. "Need you ask? You're going fishing of course."

Carolus laughed again. He stared out into the same foaming sea as I had centuries before, a free man no longer a prisoner of prophecy.

The promise had arrived.

"Are you a fisherman or not?" He heard Nicodemus shout.

Carolus instinctively reached for his ring. Yes... Yes I am, he thought.

He slipped the ring from his finger, held it tightly in his left hand and headed down towards the boat.

Nicodemus and Gamaliel watched from the windswept cliffs as the boat reached the rocky shore. Carolus waded into the warm sea. Around him the waves smashed into the rocks and cliffs with a rolling thunderous roar as the sun shone brightly overhead glittering across the waters.

An arm reached out over the bow. Carolus looked up and saw the extended hand of the fisherman.

Nicodemus smiled as Cephas pulled his man into the boat.

EPILOGUE

A NEW BEGINNING

The world is contracting again into old alliances and enemies. Nationalism is on the rise in the West, much of Eastern Europe and the Balkan Peninsula is once again feeling the weight of its former master.

The holy land and its middle eastern neighbours live in its infinitely precarious state - exorcising the demons of a new cruelty amidst the shattered remnants of a collective uprising. It has become a distant fallen promise, largely unrealized for most and for some - a horrific nightmare that won't go away.

And somewhere nearby, that forgotten road from Jerusalem to Emmaus remains buried under a history of time and travel.

The seven mile journey has become for many a life-long journey, a pilgrimage to a destiny that is ever ancient and ever new. The road of promises fulfilled.

We search for truth.

We search frantically, all of us in our own crazy ways because we know it waits to be found and we are a part of it.

So we search for ourselves. The clues are scattered across the continuum of history. And because history has all the time in the world, she will surely give us a piece of ourselves bound together in a labyrinth of secrets screaming to be discovered.

No road is linear. We are suspended in passing layers of being. Discovering ourselves is the search for new dimensions recorded in the remote places beyond and within.

These are the roads less travelled. Much like that dusty road to Emmaus that is just as real today as it was all those years ago.

Perhaps that is why Tarsus said it best in his request of his then young disciple - "Bring my cloak, my books, and above all... the parchments."

- *John*

Present day

www.ingramcontent.com/pod-product-compliance
Lightning Source LLC
Chambersburg PA
CBHW072235190626
46809CB00018B/2104